The Bad Decision Legacy

The Men of Machismo

by
Morgan Kay

THE MEN OF MACHISMO
Morgan Kay
Copyright © 2016
Print Edition

All characters in this book are fictional and figments of the author's imagination.

Chapter One

THE BOLD FONT stood out, catching her eye as she scrolled down her work email. SURPRISE, it announced, stopping her in the action of deleting it. It wasn't the subject heading, but more the sender name—Clint Fairweather, her ex—that made her pause. At one time, his name signaled a desirable man in her mind. That was before she knew him and some of his bizarre tendencies.

The blinking cursor hovered over the delete button. Most of the time she trashed his messages, never reading them. Technically, the message shouldn't have even made it into her mailbox due to being blocked. Then again, her misfortune lay in having a mean-spirited ex-boyfriend who also was a computer genius. *Yay me, I sure know how to pick them.*

Tonya's shoulders hunched forward. God, she didn't need this now. Her company was looking at personnel to cut since they'd failed to make projected goals this year. It didn't matter that she worked harder than almost anyone did in the department. No company wanted an employee with a stalker ex. News stories illustrated that they tended to come with guns blazing, taking out not only the object of their obsession, but half a dozen innocent people in the process.

Her first instinct was to send the email to the cyber dumpsite with the many dozens he'd sent the past year. Something stopped her. This one was different. It felt as if ice-cold water splashed down her back.

Wincing, she opened the document that was tying her insides in knots. An impressively long list of things to do left her with no time to dither about a whiny letter from her ex. Besides, then she'd know what it said. Wrinkling her nose, she glanced around the room, noticing her workmate's failure to arrive.

Michelle lived in a different time zone, a much later one. Oh well. She rolled her eyes. This time she didn't mind her co-worker's tardiness. An overabundance of fruity fragrance wafted around Michelle, similar to her personal atmosphere. A quick glance at the open door assured her she'd smell or hear Michelle before she arrived. Tonya opened a file, ready to switch the screen when her co-worker finally arrived. With jobs on the line, she trusted no one.

The open document mocked her with one sentence. *I bet your boss would enjoy seeing this, as would everyone else in your company.* That was it. Where were the platitudes about her letting go of the best thing she ever had, and how she'd never find a man as wonderful as him? Wait. See what?

Michelle's voice floated down the hallway as she stopped to talk to the custodian. Tonya's eyes flicked down the email to notice it had an attachment. *Damn.* Her heart jumped up into her throat. She had to know what bomb Clint was going to drop on her. Her co-worker's cheerful chatter showed no sign of winding down. *Click.*

An image of her, looking beautiful and festive, wrapped in holiday greenery and Christmas lights filled the screen. It was from more than two Christmases ago, back when she wanted to do something special to celebrate the holidays. An ad for boudoir photography sounded like a perfect gift. Who knew it would come back to haunt her?

Listening to her co-worker's grating laugh, she studied the photo. Technically, everything was covered, but she still looked nude. This wasn't good. Her boss would fire her for sure. One of the accountants had to remove a calendar with an attractive model attired in a hockey jersey due to the fact another employee claimed it was sexual harassment.

The lack of laughter had her closing the email, deleting it, and emptying the trash can. A creeping sense of horror had her erasing her history. It would remain on the company server for about forty-eight hours before it disappeared with the rest of the trashed messages.

Richard, the IT manager, informed her he could recover anything for up to forty-eight hours after she deleted it. After that, no luck, he'd explained, since they didn't back up all data, only the essential. Emails didn't figure into that, thank goodness. The email was gone. Would Richard search the files?

Tonya twisted in her chair, crossing and uncrossing her legs. *Be rational, think logically*, she reminded herself as she tried to slow her rapid breathing. Pushing up out of her chair, she walked to the file cabinet and began to rifle through the files as if she were looking for something. Michelle breezed into the room.

Her co-worker's purse landed on her already crowded desk, as Michelle searched for an empty place to set her oversized soda. Her rain slicker fell onto a brightly colored plastic chair. Michelle pivoted on her stiletto boot heels to greet Tonya.

"Hey, girl. Sorry, I'm late, but my youngest had…" Her voice drifted off.

Her co-worker's excuses were endless as to why she was late. Her children figured prominently in them. It was hard to say if she was making them up, because kids do get sick, and are difficult, or might even lose the car keys as her eldest did yesterday. It was odd for her to stop in the middle of a sentence.

"Hello, trouble with the kids?" Tonya pushed out the words, hoping her voice sounded ordinary, not showing the strain.

"Yeah, something like that," Michelle responded, not elaborating like she normally would. A furrowed brow and a tilted down chin indicated something else might be troubling her. "Tonya, you're as a white as a sheet. I mean, I know you're white and all, but…"

Normally, she might find Michelle's discomfort amusing, but not today. Especially since she wasn't hiding her stress. Oh, she knew Clint's plan very well. It wasn't as if he hadn't explained it in those first letters. In them, he detailed how he'd ruin her if she didn't come back to him. Funny, she'd laughed at the time, thinking how ridiculous his whole scheme was.

Seriously, why would a woman go back to a man who ruined her career? She'd told him after their split, when he contacted her a year later, that she'd go to live with her widowed mother in her cramped home rather than go back to him. It wasn't as if they'd ever lived together. Despite his offer to move her into his luxurious home, she'd refused. At the time, despite the good thoughts she had about the two of them having a possible future together, something stopped her from agreeing. She'd rationalized that she needed time to herself, which was true, but maybe part of her knew something wasn't kosher.

Too bad she couldn't tap into that part. Apparently, it was smarter than the rest of her. Forcing a short laugh, she attempted to smile at Michelle. "Oh, you're right. I probably could do with a visit to the tanning salon."

"Yeah, if that's what you like." Her co-worker sat, scooted her chair up to the desk, using only her feet. The moment of inquiry had passed.

The woman spent part of her day texting or conversing with relatives on the phone. Of course, Tonya pretended not to notice. Her goal was to protect her job, but she may have inadvertently secured Michelle's for her, too.

Great. Something else she didn't need to consider. Lynne, her best friend, wandered into the room. Cradling a large coffee mug, she walked over to Tonya's desk, resting one hip on the clean surface. "Hey, chickee, got some news you might like."

Maybe Lynne had the lowdown on whose jobs stayed. If Michelle's didn't make the cut, there was no reason for her to hear about it via office gossip. Tonya slid into her desk chair.

"All right, Lynne, spill it." She kept her voice low, hoping Lynne would do the same.

Her friend looked thoughtful and placed her cup down near the small printer on her desk. Leaning forward, she softened her voice, but not much. "You still dating that lame-o boyfriend?"

"Which one?" The words popped out of her mouth before she could reconsider them. It earned her a laugh from Michelle, who immediately looked down at her phone as if not listening.

Lynne raised her arm to do a bicep and patted it. "You know, old Hercules, all muscle, but not much brains."

Oh him, she'd almost forgotten the man. His most attractive feature was his brawn, especially with Clint's threats. Brian, his name was Brian, she remembered. Not a bad guy, but not great either. She'd hoped he'd develop this great passion for her and beat up Clint or at least intimidate him. He did neither.

Instead, he'd become more of a growth on her couch, rather like an extra-large throw pillow due to her cable package's several sports channels. Cable would be the first thing to go if she lost her job.

"Oh him, I quit dating him a couple of months ago." Her lips pulled down in a grimace, remembering the painful breakup scene. Awkward for her, she couldn't quite make him understand that she didn't want him coming by to watch her television while she prepared food. It was probably more like he didn't want to understand.

Lynne clapped her hands together in delight. "Glad to hear it."

Her gaze fixed on Lynne's happy expression. "You didn't even know Brian. What do you have against him?" As a happily married woman, her friend showed, at best, a cursory interest in her dating life. Not like some of her unhappily married friends, who imagined a much more exciting love life than she actually had.

"Well..." Lynne hesitated, wiggling on her precarious desk perch.

Nervous antics in her collected friend seldom happened. "You're acting peculiar. What's up?"

"Um, yeah." Lynne agreed, shaking back her waterfall of caramel-colored curls. "Marc, my husband—"

Nodding her head, she interrupted. "I know who Marc is." Circling her hand, she gestured for her friend to continue.

Lynne stuck out her tongue before continuing. "Marc invited his friend, Will, the lawyer, over for dinner."

This conversation wasn't making a whole lot of sense, but that might be because too many other things crowded her brain. "This concerns me how?"

"Um, yeah, that part." Lynne slipped off the desk and came around to grab Tonya's hands. "I'm begging you to help me out. I will owe you forever and then some."

Her earnest tone indicated this was no joke. Did Tonya need one more complication? Still, Lynne was her only real friend at the company. "What's the favor?" She crossed her ankles, hoping that counted the same as crossing her fingers.

Lynne leaned forward to hug her. She allowed the hug, but said, with her face smashed against her friend's hair, "I haven't agreed, and you haven't explained."

Dropping her arms, her friend threw her a strained smile. With both hands out in a beseeching manner, she explained, "It's like this. I knew Will was coming for dinner tonight. Marc's worried about him because he's been down ever since his fiancée dumped him."

"He should be rejoicing. It's cheaper than a divorce." She'd bet good money that Will wasn't threatening the woman who'd dumped him. Then again, she didn't know.

Lynne nodded. "Yes, that's what Marc told him. Anyhow, Will is sure he's dating poison. He hasn't been out on a date since the break-up. Dinner is supposed to cheer him up. I'm in charge of providing the single woman who will find Will fascinating to help him get his mojo back." She dropped her hands, brought both palms together in a prayer-like pose, and cast a begging glance.

Tonya tapped her own chest with three fingers. "I'm supposed to find Will fascinating?" She definitely didn't need to add this to an already crazy day. The man was probably a power freak or just plain boring. There had to be a reason his fiancée dumped him.

"Not you, really. I had Lila lined up."

Lynne's words conjured up the image of her friend's little sister,

Lila, who currently sported lavender hair and insisted on everyone calling her Lilac. "No offense, Lynne, but your sister's crazy."

Her friend wrinkled her nose and smiled. "True. Same thing Marc said. She'd love Will."

There wasn't a man Lila didn't like. Only ones she didn't know. "What's the deal with Lila? Is she a no-show?"

"Something like that. She got a better offer. An old boyfriend offered to fly her to Vegas." Lynne reached for her cup. Tasting the coffee, she frowned and put it back down. "Cold."

"Vegas does sound like a better deal, especially considering the wet weather here." It was all starting to come together. Not exactly what she wanted to do, but on the bright side, she'd score a free meal.

"You have no idea. He whisked her off in his private jet. Can I count on you arriving around seven? Act surprised that Will is there as if you didn't know. Marc doesn't want him to suspect a fix-up." She picked up her coffee cup again, ready to leave.

"Okay, I can do surprised, especially since this was sprung on me. By the way, why did his fiancée leave him?" If the reason was too horrendous, she reserved the right to bail.

Lynne stood in the doorway. "Oh, that. She decided she wanted to be a man. In fact, I heard she's already started the process. Instead of being Erika, she's now a short, slight man going by Eric."

Tonya watched her friend leave, wondering if a natural disaster might get her out of the date. Michelle's voice cut into her reverie.

"Woo-whee, sounds like a real winner. A man that causes a woman to rethink her options enough to become a man is no prize."

Even though Michelle's words mirrored her own thoughts, she felt the need to defend the unknown man. "Oh, it could be she always felt that way. It wasn't until it came down to getting married that she actually evaluated her feelings about wanting to be a man." Her explanation sounded feeble in her own ears.

Her co-worker snorted, looked up, waggled her eyebrows, and then added, "I'm sure you'll find him fascinating."

Yeah, right, and you weren't eavesdropping, either. "Who knows, he might be a charmer." She doubted it. "Besides, Marc is a chef."

Lynne's husband was an executive chef at one of the trendier restaurants in town. Of course, her friend complained that he seldom cooked at home because he was tired of work, as he put it. The result was they ate out a lot, sometimes he brought food home from work, but Lynne almost never cooked. Early on in their relationship, she confessed to her sweetie that she couldn't.

While he didn't drop her on hearing such surprising news, he never taught her how to cook, either. It made the idea of a free meal not as great as she pretended it was. *Yay, me, the great exaggerator.* It could be the source of her problems.

TONYA CONTEMPLATED THE outfits on the bed. She tried to evaluate them as a man might see them. The red dress would work for speed dating. The black wrapped top leaned toward the fancy side. No one got that dressed up for dinner with friends, unless there was an intention to impress.

Nothing on the bed was suitable. She didn't want to give the poor man even a suggestion of interest. Kicking off her heels, she stripped off her suit. While she might be doing Lynne a favor, there was no reason to dress up. Might as well wear something comfortable and make one person happy. It would certainly be a more realistic pretense that she didn't know Will was there.

Twenty minutes later, attired in worn jeans that hugged her curves and a peachy V-neck sweater that warmed her skin tone, she was almost ready. Her old cowboy boots gave her confidence that she didn't feel. A woman in boots always had attitude. Taking her hairbrush, she pulled it through her long mink-colored hair. What should she do with her hair?

Women used their hair to flirt. If she left it down, it would be an indication of a flirtatious mood. There was a reason why in all the parodies of librarians, the women always had their hair tightly pulled back. She tried to scrape her hair back into a bun. Tendrils kept escaping, ruining the severe look she wanted to affect. Besides, she never wore her hair in a bun. Lynne would probably tease her about it in front of everyone.

A ponytail ended up being her hairstyle of choice. Unfortunately, it made her look about sixteen. Oh well, it might discourage Mr. Lonely Heart. Tonya considered that Will might not like her. It could happen, especially if Will turned out to be a decent person.

The abandoned outfits on the bed drew her attention. *No, it's too late to change.* Besides, why was she worried about attracting a man she formerly worried about avoiding? *No female liked to be undesirable.* In this case, she did. Well, not actually undesirable, but uninteresting would be a better description.

A slight whimper reminded her that Sebastian, her rescued puggle, watched her with accusing eyes. He knew the routine when she was going out. They would not spend the evening snuggled on the couch catching up on their favorite shows. Well, make that her favorites. However, she was convinced he did have a fondness for some of the reality-based animal shows.

Picking up the chubby pup, she rubbed her nose in his fur, smelling the familiar mix of canine gaminess, bacon-flavored jerky treats, and the familiar aroma of Old Spice. She liberally doused Sebastian with it in between baths. The scent reminded her of her deceased grandfather. Better smelling dog and a sense of comfort made it a win-win situation.

The alarm on her phone chimed, reminding her she'd spent as long as possible glamming up to still arrive on time. As she passed a mirror, she smirked at herself. Yeah, very glamorous. She looked more as if she was ready to head out for a trail ride. A rawhide treat distracted Sebastian enough for her to slip out into the garage. He'd figure it out after he gnawed the bone into a soggy, disgusting lump that she'd later step on in the dark.

A twinge of guilt nagged at her. Sebastian waited all day for her to get home, and she was hardly home for an hour before she left again. She weaved through the boxes to get to the exterior door and her car. Inside her car, she second-guessed her reasons for even showing up. The car coughed into life. Tonya allowed it a few minutes to shake out the roughness before reversing down her drive.

Her phone chimed. The tone indicated it was a text, not a call. Oh well, it would have to wait. She wasn't going to chance reading it and get a ticket in the process. If life were good, Marc would cook. Otherwise, they'd be eating something Lynne scraped out of a restaurant carryout container.

Her friend's house came into view. An unfamiliar high-end sports car sat in the driveway. The metallic-silver car concocted images of a man with graying hair and dead eyes.

Stall, what could she do to slow the inevitable awkward meeting? Her phone. She needed to check it. Deep in her purse, she located the blinking cell. Good chance the message was from Lynne, giving her last-minute tips on what to wear or even double-checking to make sure she hadn't chickened out. The thought had crossed her mind. An evening spent in her pajamas with her favorite puggle looked like a better option.

The unfamiliar number puzzled her. It must be the wrong number. Just in case, she'd read the text.

No answer to my email. Makes me think you want to share our photos.

God, it was Clint. He must have gotten a different number. He could be using someone else's phone since she'd blocked his previous number. Her teeth chewed on her index fingernail. Now would not be a good time to lose her job.

Her fingers posed over the tiny keyboard. She'd read somewhere you weren't supposed to reply to stalkers. Still, she needed to buy time. Hating the fact she was replying, her fingers flew over the keyboard.

What email? I didn't get any email.

If she could convince him she hadn't received anything, it might buy her some time. She sent the text, wondering if Clint was sitting somewhere waiting for her reply, probably surrounded by a half-dozen cronies while he gave instructions on how to make a woman crawl back.

Nope, it wasn't going to happen. She'd do whatever she needed to do. The tap on her window startled her, causing her to drop her phone.

Lynne stood outside the car, wrapped in an oversized *Kiss the Cook* apron. Tonya lowered the window and threw her a forced smile. "Do you have any real right wearing that apron?"

"None," her friend admitted with a shrug. "Marc brought dinner home from work as a favor, since I scared up the single female."

"'Yippee,' said the single female," Tonya teased, before powering up the window and grabbing her phone, regarding it the way one would a poisonous snake.

Her friend backed up, allowing her room to exit. Tonya slammed the car door ready to follow her friend, but Lynne wasn't moving. Instead, her friend pursed her lips as she perused her outfit. "You wore that?" Using her tongue to make a clicking noise, she announced her disapproval as if her face hadn't already.

Balling up her fists, Tonya placed them on her hips. Pushing her chin out at a belligerent angle, she asked, "What's wrong with what I have on? I happen to like it."

Before Lynne could reply, a mellow baritone interjected. "Looks good on you."

The surprised expression on her friend's face announced she was just as stunned that their dinner guest had overheard their conversation.

Might as well make polite, they'd have to meet sometime. Placing one boot behind the other, she pivoted, expecting to meet some senior partner or steel-jawed legal tiger. The smiling brown-haired man standing next to the sports car clutching a wine bottle looked ordinary, even pleasant.

A quick scan revealed he was in his business attire, minus the suit jacket. His loosened tie and undone top button announced he was ready to leave work behind for the day. He held out his empty hand. "Hi, I'm Will, Will Robinson."

Tonya gave his hand a vigorous shake, remembering from her business training that a weak handshake always decreased the client's confidence in your ability. "Hi, Will Robinson. Wasn't your family trying to get to Alpha Centauri?" The quip may have been ill advised, but his name brought up memories of an old science fiction show sometimes featured in black-and-white reruns. It also helped cover her surprise that a simple touch jumpstarted a chemical reaction, one she'd considered out of commission.

Will kept her hand a tad longer than needed, while he smiled with his eyes. "Ah, we weren't that Robinson family. Mine was the one that hadn't seen the show and didn't understand why naming me Will was not a kindness."

Tonya found herself grinning back at the witty male. "Did the other kids pick on you?"

"Not too much, but there was this one female who gave me a hard time, and I didn't even know her name." He nodded toward the front door where Lynne stood waiting.

She almost asked him what grade that was until she realized he was referring to her. "Oh, her. The name's Tonya Smiley."

Her last name embarrassed her. It was such a cute name. Why couldn't she have an ordinary name like Tyler or Brooks? To push past the inevitable remarks about her being smiley or having a beautiful smile or even her name suiting her, she went defensive. "Why were you sneaking around eavesdropping on our girl talk?"

Her abrupt question triggered Lynne's coughing. In between coughs, she managed to mutter, "Watch it."

Will threw his hands up over his head, one still wrapped around the neck of the wine bottle. "You got me. I'm guilty. I snuck out the side door that Marc showed me to retrieve the wine I forgot. The two of you were deep into conversation. I didn't think it was my place to interrupt, but when I felt your outfit was being criticized, I had to say something."

His excuse made sense. "Put your hands down. It sounds reasonable to me."

Lynne merely lifted an eyebrow as she opened the front door. Her friend waited for them both to pass, before speaking.

Their hostess babbled as they entered. "Ah well, we got the awkward introductions out of the way. I forgot to mention to Tonya that Marc invited you." Lynne managed to deliver the words with a straight face, but winked in Tonya's direction.

Tonya sucked in her lips, controlling her laughter. Unfortunately, her friend would never be a great actress. Her words sounded as stiff as any business owner who attempted to make his own cut-rate commercial.

Tonya excused herself by pointing in the direction of the bathroom, not trusting herself to resist laughing. Lynne acknowledged her signal while guiding Will to the family room, where mellow jazz music and glassware tinkling emanated. Marc must already be making his special martinis. The memory of various drinks in brilliant colors, with exotic names, made her regret her detour to the bathroom. After shutting the door with a little more energy than needed, she turned on the faucet full blast, covering her laughter.

Seriously, did Lynne think she was fooling anyone? Did Will think she showed up on her own, with no hint a single man might be the lure? A quick glance in the mirror revealed a flushed face. It was hard to tell if it was from laughing or playing her part in this farce. Dampening a washcloth, she patted her face. Thank goodness she hadn't bothered with full makeup. Her goal was to look like she hadn't expected to encounter an eligible male. Well, she accomplished that all right with her ponytail and jeans.

Nothing she could do about it now. She stuck her tongue out at her mirrored image. Her goal was not to encourage the man, but to score a free meal. A small sigh escaped as she turned the doorknob. Remembering the spark that zipped up her arm when he touched her hand, the man had potential. *Try not to think about it.* The last thing she needed was the emotional roller coaster that came with dating. She never managed to exit the horror ride called Clint. It was still going, whether she wanted to be on it or not. That would be a hard thing to explain in a budding relationship.

God, listen to me. Budding relationship. Get a grip, chick. Michelle pointed out the man must be a mess if his own fiancée abandoned him to become a man. On the other hand, Will would be smart to avoid me, because I'm a train wreck in the making, with a full-time stalker and the possibility of unemployment in the near future.

Chapter Two

THE SOUND OF voices forced her to plaster a smile on her face before she entered the room.

"Hey, Marc, hope you made me one of your special drinks." She grinned in her host's direction, hoping her smile didn't look too manic.

Marc winked. "Got something new. You're going to like it. All the women at the restaurant do. It's called The Milky Way Martini."

"Sounds good." She tried to put the right amount of enthusiasm in her voice while trying not to stare at Will. "What's in it?"

Marc lined up his shot glasses. Tonya remembered Lynne remarking that he measured out all his ingredients before combining them in the shaker. It would make him a very slow bartender. Marc looked up briefly. Had she spoken her observation aloud? His reply indicated she hadn't.

"It has vanilla vodka, chocolate liqueur, and Irish cream." He poured the contents of the shot glasses into the shaker with a flourish.

"Whoa." Will's remark forced her to look in his direction. To refuse to look at him would be strange.

Marc offered her the brimming martini glass with an eyebrow wiggle. She took it gratefully and took a sip of the sweet, potent drink. Fortified, she directed a cool stare at her almost date. "Whoa, what?"

The man shrugged. "That's pure alcohol. Despite the name, it's not a girly drink."

Was he trying to say she couldn't hold her alcohol? "Don't let the ponytail fool you. I'm plenty old enough." She leaned toward Will, enunciating her words, similar to a belligerent drunk determined to prove sobriety. The man's face reddened as he threw up his hands to protest.

"That's not what I meant. Really, it was just a random comment." He put out his hands as if pleading. "About the drink, I mean, not you."

Tonya watched the man flounder, knowing his comment wasn't half as bad as hers was. She sipped her cocktail, feeling the burn through the sweetness. It was probably her turn to say something, but she had nothing. Damn. Somehow, she'd ruined the evening, and they hadn't even gotten to eat yet. Could it get any worse?

Lynne came up behind her and plucked the empty glass from her hand, placing it on the counter. "Oh, you have to excuse my friend. Tensions are high at work with looming budget cuts."

Good thing she never mentioned her problems with Clint to her friend. She retrieved her glass, edged it toward Marc. The first drink just took the edge off. Besides, she could use a second after the day she'd endured. Work, normally demanding, was more so when she did the work of two, in tension so thick she could wrap it around her and use it for a blanket.

Marc nodded and poured the ingredients into the shaker. He slid the finished product across the bar without looking up at his wife.

Lynne would probably be pantomiming behind her back. Staggering around or holding her arms in front of her like a mummy to indicate Tonya didn't need a second drink. In the end, it would make Will think Lynne had drinking issues.

The man in question moved closer and sat on the next bar stool, which put him at eye level as she tilted her second martini up. "I realize job security can be tricky. I never meant you can't hold your liquor."

"No problem." She waved her hand in the air dismissing the matter. His tendency to keep apologizing struck her as odd. Most men she'd encountered never apologized, even if they were rude or wrong. A glass platter appeared in front of her.

"Crab Puff?" Lynne inquired with a raised eyebrow.

Tonya took two before her friend could say something about her bellyful of booze. "I love it when Marc brings work home." The giggle that followed invalidated her claims about holding her liquor. Normally, she stayed with one cocktail, considering it a type of luxury. She never drank alone, afraid she'd become one of those women always finishing a bottle of wine every evening. It seemed so sad, right up there with women who knitted outfits for their cats.

The oven buzzer had the effect of relocating them around the dining room table while Marc went off to retrieve dinner. Lynne took her usual chair while Tonya sat across from her, which was her regular spot. No matter where Will decided to sit, he'd be next to her at the small table. Nodding to the end chair, he waited for Lynne's acknowledgment before pulling the chair out and sitting.

A heavenly aroma, redolent with pastry, butter, and salmon floated into the room. Taking a deep breath, she savored it. Salmon Wellington was one of Marc's specialties and one of her former favorite meals until she discovered the pastry wrapped seafood had about a gazillion calories.

She'd have to eat it because it would be rude not to. Yep, she'd have to eat it all, including the flaky calorie rich crust. The group looked up as Marc entered the room with the entrée resting on a bed of kale leaves, with roses created out of radishes to add color.

"Tonight, we'll dine like kings on Salmon Wellington, roasted red potatoes, sautéed asparagus tips, and shiitake mushrooms."

There was the sound of clapping. Tonya noticed the other two diner's hands remained flat on the table. Her eyes focused downward on her hands in the prayer position. Ooh, it was her. Salmon Wellington was worth clapping about. It beat nuking a frozen entrée.

Marc smiled in her direction and continued his recitation. "I have a nice Sauvignon Blanc to go with the fish—a lovely, unpretentious wine

I discovered on my last trip to France." Lynne caught her eye and mouthed the words *none for you*.

That might be best, especially considering she needed to drive home. She didn't want to be obvious about forgoing the wine. "It sounds wonderful, Marc, but none for me. I am boycotting all things French."

His eyebrows shot up at her comment. "What?" Before Marc could ask for a more detailed explanation, his wife shook her head, stopping the conversation.

Lynne jumped in to cover the lull. "Tell us what is for dessert. I bet it's grand."

Marc worked his way around the table, delicately centering a serving of salmon on each plate. "It is, my sweet. For you, I brought home Henri's renown Baked Alaska."

Her friend gushed, a little more than Tonya thought necessary for a rather traditional dessert.

"Oh, Marc, how wonderful."

Will's eyes went back and forth between the two, similar to watching a tennis match. Taking another sip of her drink, she wondered if she were the ball. Taking advantage of Will's concentration on his hosts, she ogled him thoroughly.

Definitely no gargoyle, no extra ears or fingers, and he was even charming, somewhat. The man had a high paying job, judging by his car. It made her wonder why his fiancée left him, not only to play with the other team, but also to be the other team. "So, why did your fiancée dump you to get her own johnson?"

A collective indrawn gasp filled the room. Tonya was sure she gasped, too. Wait, she was the one who made the remark. Using one finger, she pushed the martini glass away from her. *Get away from me Milky Way Martini Devil.*

Lynne erupted into a babble of excuses. "Can't hold her liquor. Ignore her. Don't answer."

Will sighed. He rubbed one long-fingered hand over his face.

"Truly, I'd like to explain. A lot of speculation and very little truth has circled around the matter."

Holding up her hands to ward off the explanation, Tonya dithered. "Oh no, don't explain. It's me. I ask stupid questions. You have so much going for you that any woman would be crazy to be hooked up with you, and…" Her face reddened as she realized what she was saying wasn't making it any better.

Marc covered for her slightly by announcing, "I'm off to get the vegetables." Not a great announcement, but it saved her from saying anything worse. Lynne followed her husband, mumbling something about bread. They were in the kitchen making emergency plans for the dinner party that suddenly imploded.

Taking advantage of their absence, Will spoke. "Erica really wasn't my fiancée. We never made any plans or anything, but we were best friends. We did everything together. I guess people assumed we would be a couple in the end."

"Um, so, um did you, ah." Tonya bit her bottom lip, knowing she was drifting back into forbidden territory.

Her discomfort caused Will's lips to tilt upward. "Did we sleep together?"

A quick head bob confirmed her prurient interest. She shouldn't want to know, but a part of her did. Was he so bad in bed or lacking in technique that Erica thought she could do better? Not in finding another beau, but literally could perform better?

"No." He shook his head side to side in case she hadn't caught the word. "It really wasn't that kind of relationship. I thought it would be at one time. We were both healthy, attractive, single adults. Even kissed, but nothing happened. We did everything together from movies to sporting events as friends."

"Really?" The surprise in her voice was genuine. "Marc was afraid you were all broken up about not attracting women."

Marc stood in the doorway with a serving bowl and turned around before Will noticed him.

"Oh." Will's brow furrowed as he looked down at his plate. Not looking at her, he asked, "Is there anything you don't know?"

"Don't feel so bad. You know I can't hold my liquor, and I might lose my job. That's more than my mother knows." She tried for her standard work smile, but it felt more like a grimace. Picking up her fork, she decided to eat, but before she could, Marc grabbed her plate.

He picked up everyone's plate, stacking them along his arm demonstrating his prior experience waiting tables. "I will reheat everyone's plate. It's cold now."

Marc disappeared into the kitchen. He could be finicky about food, but it was odd that Lynne stayed in the kitchen unless they were attempting to give them time to talk. Well, she could assure them that it wasn't working. Maybe she should tell them. Her chair didn't slide out well on the Oriental rug.

"Don't go, I'll explain." Will reached for her hand, detaining her and treating her to another electrical jolt. If she were wearing wool or silk, she could blame it on static electricity. It was just as well because she wasn't too sure how steady her walk to the kitchen would be.

"Go ahead, I'm all ears," she said to encourage him. He removed his hand, leaving her hand cold and abandoned on the tabletop. Using both hands, she lifted her chair a bit as she scooted it back to its original position.

"As you heard, I spent a lot of time with Erica." He reached for his drink and finished it in two swallows. "In the beginning, I thought we might develop a romantic relationship. When that didn't happen, we were already in the habit of doing everything together. It didn't leave much time for dating. I tried a few times. Most women didn't accept that I had a gorgeous friend who also happened to be a woman. They were either jealous or suspicious I was a player."

"I would be," she said the words, unaware she'd verbalized them until they were out.

Will directed a look her way, compelling her to explain. "It isn't natural for men and women being friends outside of a romantic relationship. Those other women knew that. The only reason a man pretends to be your friend is to start a romantic relationship."

Marc and Lynne chose to peek out of the kitchen, but withdrew their heads as soon as she noticed. It looked like dinner might be a long time coming.

"You're right. I started seeing Erica because I thought we'd have a relationship. When it didn't work out, we hung out like two buds. Of course, I never realize how true that comparison was until now. I spent almost eighteen months hanging with Erica. When she decided to go off and do her man thing, I had no one. Most people thought I was devastated because she left. I would have still hung out with her, I mean him, but Eric was into a completely new lifestyle. Work kept me busy. Plenty of men advised me to get out there and find a new woman. I wasn't looking for a new woman. I lost my best friend, not a woman. Does that make any sense?"

"It does. Yeah, more than you know. It was odd just cutting you off like that. It's happened to me before when a friend got married, moved away, or changed jobs. It made me wonder if I ever mattered, or if our relationship was just convenient." Memories of the former company she visited six weeks after she changed jobs came to mind. Her cool reception surprised her.

Will picked up his empty tumbler and tilted it. Lynne swooped in with a full water glass and left it, causing him to blink before commenting.

"Would you say our hosts are acting a bit odd? I know Marc is my friend, but even for him, this is different behavior." He angled his head to the doorway where they knew the two were listening.

His remark created a break in the tension. Laughter served her as a partial answer. "Yeah, I think they're worried about us. Marc is worried about you not dating. As for Lynne, I'm not sure what about me has her worrying. Trust me, there's a list."

Rubbing the back of his neck, he half-heartedly chuckled. "I doubt it could be that bad. As far as dating, it's not that I don't want to. I've gotten out of the habit. My line of work makes it hard."

Lynne mentioned something about his being a lawyer. "You only work with men?"

"Oh no, I see plenty of women, usually angry women who hate men, in general. I'm a divorce lawyer. Tends to depress me when it comes to relationships since clients come to me with crushed dreams and betrayed trust. I'm grateful for the invitation from Marc and Lynne to see what a happily married couple looks like."

A murmur of approval came from the kitchen, indicating they were listening.

No doubt his view on womankind wasn't exactly high. Not the type to be understanding about Clint spreading her photos on the Internet. Nope, he'd probably see it as a natural consequence. Too bad. Will had potential.

"Do you ever represent women?" If he did, it would give him a chance to see a woman's view of a disintegrating union.

A long whistle greeted her inquiry. "That's mainly all I do. I trained in corporate law, but this opening occurred in a major firm. My mentor advised me to take it since he knew the senior partners and could give me the bump over the other candidates. I did."

Crossing her arms, she considered that it must be nice to have people to help you into sweet jobs. "What happened then?"

Will pushed back a little from the table. Finding the same resistance, he settled for tilting the chair back on two back legs. "Clifford and Barrows had a real estate division, which was my original goal, but first I had to learn divorce law. It didn't make sense, but as a newbie, the senior partner took me through a harrowing experience of dealing with couples who'd experienced love gone wrong."

At least she never had to divorce any of her exes. Divorce might make the break final and keep her exes from troubling her. If so, she regretted not marrying if only to be able to divorce. Sure, she knew it was a stupid thought, but anything to get rid of Clint would be welcome. Whatever happened to the previous woman he left her for?

A sighting of him at a local barbecue restaurant with his arm around another woman told the tale when he stopped coming around over a year past. Yeah, she could identify with a deceived wife. Will settled his chair back to four legs, and she wondered if it was her turn to respond. "Been there, done that."

"You're divorced?" Will's eyebrows shot up with the inquiry.

Did he mind? The firm name she'd recognized from their provocative billboards with airbrushed models lounging about in various stages of undress. The slogan was something about life being too short to endure a bad marriage. There was also some other line about hiring them before your spouse does. "Um, no, never married, so I couldn't be divorced. I meant about love going wrong."

"Oh, that." Will gave her a brief smile that didn't reach his eyes. "The women I've dealt with wouldn't admit to any love for their husbands. All they wanted was to make them pay for eternity. Anything that would heap extra suffering and embarrassment into the settlement, they wanted that, too. If a husband valued something from a dog to golf clubs, she wanted it, just to be spiteful."

"Dinner, again," Lynne sang out the words while Marc returned with their reheated plates, a towel protecting his arm.

Their reappearance signaled the start of the meal, and the end of their current conversation, but Tonya was unwilling to give it up. Will thought the women he represented were somewhat reprehensible for wanting revenge. "I understand that the women want to make their husbands pay, but don't you think they want a physical payback for emotional pain when they were ignored or cheated on?"

Marc's body interfered with her ability to see Will's face as he placed the plates on the table. She heard his voice without seeing his expression.

"Most people would think that. It's been my experience that the women overwhelmingly sue for divorce and not because the mister has been stepping out, but rather that marriage didn't suit their expectations. Many have prenups they try to break, and others are the cheaters, but still blame the husband."

How depressing. She slumped in her chair, thinking it sounded bad. "No wonder you dislike women so much."

Marc moved around the table, pouring wine into the goblets. Her remark resulted in him overfilling his wife's glass.

"Marc, look what you did! My grandmother's Chantilly lace tablecloth."

Lynne ran to the kitchen with her husband complaining as he followed. "It won't stain. It's white wine."

Tonya's eyes followed the departing couple, wondering if her appearance was straining one of the few happy couples she knew.

Rubbing a hand over his face, Will sighed. "It's not that I don't like women. I realize I see them at their worst. Sometimes, I wonder if my clients even have a good side. Their husbands married a trophy wife without expecting the blowback they'd get when they moved on to a newer version. Plenty of wives dumped husbands that aren't up to par, too. One woman listed the way her husband ate as an irreconcilable difference. Part of my attitude comes from not practicing the type of law I want."

Lynne returned with a tea towel to mop up the spill. Marc followed, still apologizing. Unfortunately, his apology wasn't about the wine.

"How was I to know my friend would dislike yours and would start fighting like the Hatfields and the McCoys?"

Catching the reference to herself, she caught Will's eyes. His mouth fell open, mirroring her own shock.

"Hey," she interrupted the two, who were glaring at each other. "I like Will just fine. I don't think we were fighting, were we?" She directed the inquiry to Will.

"No," he agreed, then added with a genuine smile. "Tonya is the first woman I've met who's not afraid to spar with me. Most women who find out I'm a lawyer either get dollar signs in their eyes or tell me I'm a cancer on society. I've found our discussion," he waggled his eyebrows, "stimulating."

Lynne, holding her wet towel, returned to the kitchen with a befuddled expression. Marc hit his forehead with the palm of his hand. "You lawyers, your courting rituals are so different from us humble culinary geniuses."

Courting, did anyone seriously think Will was courting her? The thought made her sit up straighter, pushing the girls out into prominence. It took some pushing since she was, at best, average. Clint once told her she was smaller than most of his previous lovers. The sudden insertion of Clint in her mind deflated any hopes she might have had about Will. Sometimes she forgot she was the one with a malignant growth called Clint that made her unacceptable dating material.

Her hands balled into fists. Even now, despite how much she tried to make it otherwise, Clint was controlling her. It wasn't fair to bring another man into the circus she currently called her life. Not everyone could be like Brian, unaware of all the undercurrents. In fact, she didn't want another relationship like that. She had a better relationship with Sebastian, her dog.

Marc, Will, and she laughed at the oxymoronic pairing of humble and genius as Marc intended. Lynne hurried into the room with her forehead knitted. "What did I miss?"

"Your husband was entertaining us with the idea he was humble." Tonya grinned, suddenly feeling the return of her good humor that had slipped away at the thought of Clint's machinations.

Once Lynne sat, Marc raised his glass. "A toast to new beginnings."

Lynne and Will lifted their wine glasses while Tonya decided between an empty wine glass and a full water glass. Grabbing the water glass, she held it up to clink gently with the other glasses. The last thing she needed was to bust a wine goblet. Good chance the glasses were family heirlooms, too.

The group took a collective sip from their glasses before settling back into their seats to a truly excellent meal.

The sound of cutlery on china and satisfied murmurs mixed in with the sound of guitar music drifting from the nearby speaker. Tonya took advantage of the excellent meal, especially since it would cost more than she could ever rationalize paying at the restaurant. So far so good. A quick glance at her handsome pseudo-date demonstrated he too was lost in the delicious cuisine. Her eyes lingered on his face as he chewed.

Strong jaw line, she always liked that in a man. Overall, he appeared to be a decent, sexy man. His only real drawback happened to be a job hated. They had that in common.

"Whatever happened to your aspirations of going into real estate law?" It had to be less acrimonious than divorces.

Will stopped chewing at the same time a pointy-toed shoe connected with her ankle. It came from the side. Lynne met her accusing stare with her own meaningful look, while mouthing the words, "What are you doing?"

Luckily, Tonya had mastered lip reading years ago, due to her deaf paternal grandmother. Not that she needed to lip read, but she wanted to understand her granny's world. Her only issue was she often spoke her thoughts aloud when she thought she was only mouthing them. "I was asking a legitimate question."

Placing his fork down, Will used his napkin to dab at his mouth. "Fair enough. I started at the law firm with a promise I'd switch to real estate law as soon as an opening became available. At the time, they didn't have enough divorce lawyers to fill the demand the advertising created."

Did the advertising create the demand? Were there that many people dissatisfied with their life partner choice?

"About the time I was hired, several other young lawyers came on with the senior partners guiding them. One day, when we were having a board meeting, I noticed the senior partners sitting by their protégés. Each young lawyer, dressed in stylish clothes and sporting a fashionable haircut, was a younger version of the senior partner."

"Why was that important?" Lynne asked.

"Well." He wrinkled his nose in distaste. "It took me forever to figure it out. Maybe you've seen the pictures of the team in magazine ads. Those enhanced photos make everyone look fabulous. Somehow, the idea of an attractive lawyer titillates a scorned husband or wife. There's also irony in your soon-to-be ex's lawyer, who is fighting against you, to be the same sex. As ridiculous as it seems, there's the illusion that some divorcing spouses play up sleeping with the lawyers, just to ratchet up the hate factor."

Lynne made a sound of distaste. Marc, close enough, playfully punched his friend. "Another perk of the job, huh." This earned him a narrowed eyed glare from his wife. He hurried to amend his statement. "Not that I'd consider it a perk, being married to the hottest and most awesome woman in the world."

The obvious flattery brought a lazy smile to her friend's face.

Picking up another slice of rosemary peasant bread, Tonya wondered how many potential divorcées enticed the handsome lawyer into a pre-divorce fling. It hadn't gotten past her notice that he'd hadn't answered Marc's quip about it being a perk. "Do you get many come-ons from the soon-to-be divorcées?"

It was an awkward question. Just one in the series she threw out tonight. Unfortunately, the food and water sobered her up. She couldn't claim drunkenness even if she wanted to. Instead of answering immediately, her tablemate flushed, making her contemplate what answers he considered.

Lynne emitted a harsh bark of laughter, similar to a seal. "Just ignore Tonya. Joking, you know." Then she had the nerve to fist her hand with her thumb out moving it toward her mouth in meaning drink, but could also translate as drunk.

Well, that chafed. Besides, she could be home right now with Sebastian catching up on her shows. The idea didn't appeal as it did earlier. Will looked at her and raised one eyebrow.

"I wasn't joking." She picked up her water glass and drank before she said anything else that might cause her hostess to tap dance on the table topless if it would distract attention from her latest inquiry.

Her eyes met his over the top of his water glass. In the tiny instance, she knew he'd answer her question.

Pushing his empty plate away, he placed both hands on the table. Tonya's eyes immediately went to the ringless left hand. Even though she knew he was single, her instinct was still to look. How cliché.

"There are a lot of lawyers at the firm much more attractive than I am. In fact, I would say all of them are."

Lynne stood, excused herself, and headed for the living room. Maybe the conversation topic made her uncomfortable. It had a similar effect on Marc, who stood clearing the empty plates. With their audience gone, she shyly admitted, "I find that hard to believe, you're a very handsome man."

"Really?" His eyes widened a bit while his lips tipped up into a grin.

"Of course." Sober or tipsy, blatant flirting all the same, but she wasn't, not really. "I imagine you had your share of female clients hit on you."

He looked down at his hands splayed on the tablecloth. "There haven't been that many."

"Aha, now you admitted it." While she felt a small sense of triumph getting a lawyer to admit anything, she cringed at the thought of women with augmented features and perfect hair running their acrylic tipped fingers over Will, especially when their purpose was revenge.

His lips formed into a straight line, then twisted to one side as he exhaled slowly. "It's not like it means anything. Any man would do. I'm smart enough not to take them up on their offers."

That was different. She figured most men would, especially since they knew it was strings free or was it? Some women would see a single, available man with a decent income and suddenly they were in need of such a man.

Yeah, some women who always had to have a man. A few of his

clients were probably like that. *Wait, I am like that or used to be, which totally explained the Clint Fairweather fiasco.*

"As a lawyer, I could lose my license if I got involved with a client and even be named in the divorce proceedings." He shook his head the same time Marc carried in the dessert and placed the domed creation in the center of the table.

"Hurry up, Lynne. I'm ready to light it."

The click of her heels announced she was rushing. Her hair looked slightly tousled as she flourished a magazine in one hand. "Found it."

"Found what?" Marc's frown hinted at impatience. He held the lighter above the brandy-soaked crust.

"The ad for the law firm. I thought Tonya would enjoy seeing it." She pushed the open magazine across the table. Her index finger pointed to a beautiful ad with half a dozen blonde-haired women in tight skirts and four movie-worthy hunks in suits behind them. Talk about Photoshopped—she wasn't even sure which one was Will. Turning the ad toward him, she asked, "Where are you?"

He stared at the ad for a while. "Not in this photo, that's for sure. None of these people works at my office. It's a stock photo. Any company can buy it if they need gorgeous people in suits."

A click of the lighter announced that dessert was ready. A sudden flare-up of flames had everyone jumping back until it shimmered into a blue halo and sputtered out.

A series of oohs and ahs accompanied the flame out. Marc used a chef knife to cut into the frozen dessert, plating each serving while Lynne distributed them.

The night ended for entertainment purposes right about then. Everyone dug into the dessert with gusto and audible appreciation. It had been a delicious meal and her dinner date superb, not that she expected to see him again. Her behavior could have been better on all fronts.

Marc refused any help with the dishes, and the last thing she need-ed was more liquor. It looked like it was home for her. A quick glance at her watch showed she had a couple of hours to spend with Sebastian before bed. Thanking her hosts, she palmed her car keys, ready to walk out the door when Will made his move.

Chapter Three

WILL STEPPED IN front of Lynne, who was prepared to walk her out. He smiled at Tonya. "Can I walk you out to your car?"

"Yes. I'm surprised you want to after all my weird questions. I might have more."

"This is true." He acknowledged her statement with a nod. "I'll have to take my chances." His hand cupped her elbow, guiding her out the door.

The touch of his hand ignited heat that raced from her elbow up her arm and spread to the other extremities. The man certainly had the right pheromones to flip her switches. Carefully watching her feet, she made her way down the stairs.

"Are you safe to drive?" His question echoed her inner thoughts.

Here she thought she'd sobered up. If two martinis put her under, it would make her look like a lightweight drinker, which she was. "I think I'm good."

His grip tightened on her arm as she almost missed a step. Great, now he'd think she was drunk as opposed to clumsy. A series of sharp barks pierced the neighborhood stillness.

"Tell you what, if you don't mind, I'll drive you home."

Her first reaction was to protest her sobriety before she realized she could extend their time together. "Okay." She held up her keys and allowed him to remove them from her unresisting fingers.

Will's hand stayed on her elbow as he guided her down the few steps to her car. An actual lawyer could help her with Clint if she handled things right. "Are there any cases of blackmail among your clients? I know in television shows, the divorcing spouses are always threatening one another."

Will wrapped his arm around her waist as they made the final step onto the driveway. "A person has to notify the police to stop a blackmailer."

"Oh." She liked Will's arm around her. Anyone else helping her might get a cutting remark about how she wasn't his grandmother. The firm masculine grasp suggested safety. Lord knows she hadn't had that from any man. *Wait, what about the police.* "If it's that simple, why don't more people go to the police when blackmailed?"

Instead of replying immediately, he snorted, then attempted unsuccessfully to turn it into a throat clearing. They had reached her car, which meant it was time to go. Looking down, she opened her purse to search for her keys only to remember giving them up. Will took the time to lean against her car, and boxed her in with his other arm once she looked up. He kept his torso a good foot and half from hers by the benefit of his long arms, slightly curved to make a cage around her with the car serving as the fourth wall.

The porch lights threw his face into relief, all angles and dark hollows, but she remembered his hazel eyes and sincere countenance that would allow him to sell ice to Eskimos. His behavior didn't intimidate as it might have if she didn't know his most recent history. The angle of his head and the decreasing distance between their lips had her pulse fluttering.

Will was going to kiss her. It might help him get his dating mojo back. Who was she kidding? She wanted to kiss him, too. His lips came closer as part of her brain played with the blackmail issue, reminding her he never answered her question.

His lips were almost on her. Then it happened, a sudden halt to the romantic proceedings, due to her half-whispered words. "Why don't people go to the police when they're being blackmailed? You never explained." *Damn multi-tasking brain.*

The lips that were millimeters from touching hers pulled back. Instead of kissing her, Will dropped the arm embracing her and leaned back against her car with a sigh. "Why are you so intent on knowing about blackmail? Are you writing a mystery?"

It sounded like an easy way to explain why she needed the information. "That's it. Could you help me?"

His hand shot through his hair, then rubbed his neck. "Okay, I'll help. You'd be surprised that people who once professed to love and honor the other will resort to blackmail. Sometimes it is to get something, such as a shared possession or even the kids.

This wasn't something she'd considered. Were people dissatisfied with love always out to make the other pay? If so, it made the idea of romance a very scary prospect. *Yeah, like I hadn't figured that out already.* "What do they use to blackmail each other?"

Will slapped the car lightly with one hand. "Often one of them is engaged in an affair. The cheating one makes concessions to keep his current squeeze out of the limelight. Maybe one of the parties participated in some unethical business practice. There might be a criminal record or something the other wants to stay hidden, say, plastic surgery procedures or even the true parentage of their children."

"Do they go to the police about this?" Would the police even care about such things?

"Nope. Divorce lawyers work about the same as priests or therapists. People don't want to air their dirty laundry, even if the police would stop another person from extorting money from them. Mainly, they're afraid it will get out, which it often does. The other reason people are blackmailed is because whatever they did was a crime."

It would be hard to confess the blackmail was the result of suggestive photos she had made. "If someone were being blackmailed by email or photos, would the police need to see them?"

Will pushed off the car, stepping into the light and revealing his quizzical expression. "Sounds like you're into this book. The emails and photos are evidence. Of course, the police would have to see them."

"Damn," she whispered the words, but could tell by the jerk of his head that Will had heard them. She'd done her best to destroy the evidence. No way would she ask Richard to retrieve the message and attachment. A cop would look at the photo and then at her. The idea sucked. A female cop wouldn't be any better.

Nope, she already heard in the office lunchroom how other women regarded those who took boudoir photos: Skanks, whores, and women who had some twisted desire for attention. She wasn't like that. Her brief period with Clint wasn't about attention. It wasn't even about love, although she kept telling herself it was.

It was more about proving herself worthy of love. Yeah, and all she got out of it was a persistent stalker and a handful of provocative photos she'd paid good money for. Clinton had the photos now.

Nothing to present as evidence, the weight that had left her shoulders not only settled back, but also gained another twenty or thirty pounds.

Will moved closer, softening his voice. "Tonya, are you in trouble?"

"Not yet." She inhaled deeply, hoping her words wouldn't prove to be prophetic.

She looked up into his shadow-shrouded face, wishing she could somehow hand him her problem and allow him to do his legal magic. He might be able to do something, but he certainly wouldn't want to go out with a woman who had a slimeball ex and made profoundly stupid choices. Her photo didn't appear in the dictionary next to the definition for discerning.

His right hand curved around her cheek and chin, angling it upward. "I wish I could help." His lips landed on hers, firmly and with a hint of promise.

The kiss lasted only seconds. It warmed her. It reminded her that he wasn't for her until she'd broken free of Clint's threats. God, she prayed she could without everyone in the company finding out that she didn't have any tan lines.

Her right hand rose to trace his face with her fingers. "I wish you could, too." She sighed deeply, aware she was melodramatic. A trait she always hated in her co-worker. *Suck it up, girl.* "Time for me to pull on my big girl panties and take care of the situation."

"I'd like to see that. Not the situation, just you in the big girl panties." He playfully leered at her, lightening the moment. Her elbow to the ribs had him backing up. Even aware he was joking, it still struck her as wrong.

The car keys jingled in Will's hand. "Remember, I'm driving. Marc will pick me up."

That's right, she forgot. A coyote yipped in the distance. It sounded like some canine commentary to her, similar to laughter. Here she'd used her best departing line, but the man still had to drive her home.

Marc came out on the stoop for an update on their plans. He agreed to pick up Will, but he might be fifteen minutes behind, wink, wink, nudge, nudge. Nothing would happen in that limited time, she wanted to say but didn't. For once, she kept her mouth shut after she rattled off her address.

The radio played low on her favorite love songs station. She closed her eyes after watching Will competently handle her car. No fears for Natalie, her car.

A lawyer in the car, she should pick his brain. Yawning, she made sure to cover her mouth. "It's not you. I'm tired. Lynne told you how things were at work. People are always on edge. Makes for a tense day and hard to sleep at night. Everyone at work is trying to secure their job in this economy."

His calm baritone seemed out of place in her car. "Are you worried?"

"Hell yes, you have no idea. Even have someone trying to blackmail me, I think." Oops, that was more than she wanted to confess. What was it about Will that relaxed her?

"Hmm." He turned onto her street. "Blackmail constitutes a threat if you don't perform a certain action or pay. Does this sound like your situation?"

"Yes, it does. I don't know what to do." Boy, she'd let that cat out of the bag. Still, maybe an uninterested third party could help.

It was close to nine. Energy raced through her veins, waking up parts that wanted to slumber. The possibility of not worrying about Clint and his threats made her feel like she could do anything, even dance.

Will's headshake was visible in the dimly lit car.

"What? Why are you shaking your head?" She thought he'd be a hero and pull some solution from his magical lawyer hat. Now he morphed into a shadow man telling her no.

He glanced at her, but the dark made it hard to read his expression. "We already discussed this. Those martinis must have hit you hard."

Maybe the alcohol made her a little loose-lipped, but everything seemed to be riding her hard of late. Tonight, her foundation cracked. Too bad she didn't know how to shore it up.

Will continued, not getting a reply from her. "You have to take the ball out of the blackmailer's court by doing whatever she is threatening to do to you."

Her teeth gnawed on her bottom lip. The man probably thought there was some girl drama at work. There usually was, but she wasn't part of it. She'd already said more than she wanted anyhow. Pretending to consider his words, she plastered on a smile. "You're right. That's exactly what I'll do."

Yeah, I'll pass around the racy photos of me to all the employees. Maybe a group email will do the trick. That way Clint will have no hold over me. It won't make me any less unemployed.

Will sat up straighter and pushed his shoulders back as if pleased by her faked gratitude. *Geesh, men were easy to fool. Why do I waste so much time being honest and authentic?*

The familiar shape of her brick house came into view. Pointing to it with one arm, she directed Will into the driveway. "Here it is. Home sweet home."

Her hand was on the door handle ready to make a run for it and leave behind all the embarrassment of the evening. Her eyes shot to her keys hanging out of the steering column. Well, she'd need those. The keys disappeared underneath masculine fingers as Will removed them and swung the car door open.

What could she do with the man? It would be rude to leave him outside just because there was no way she could add another layer of craziness to her already entangled life. Her car door had swung open before she'd formulated a plan. *A gentleman. How rare. Maybe I should rethink this whole men are too much trouble.*

Sebastian's frenzied barking and the rippling of her window sheers signaled they were in danger of shredding. Ignoring Will's proffered hand, she vaulted out of the car and scurried to the front door, only to remember she didn't have the keys.

Will followed at a more leisurely pace, unaware that the sheers she'd paid eighty dollars for on clearance were meeting their demise under the anxious nails of her puggle. "It's okay, Sebastian," she yelled into the crack where the door met the frame. "Mommy's home."

He probably thinks I'm a nutcase talking to my dog. He already thinks I have some drama going on at work. The handsome man hurrying toward her with a smile shouldn't be so appealing to her, but he was.

"Here you go." Will handed her the keys. "My self-esteem is hurt that you ran away from me."

Driving her house key into the lock, she twisted the door open. Sebastian wiggled through the opening to dance between the two of them. At least she could always count on her pet to be happy to see her.

A growing puddle near her feet reminded her that the other thing she could always depend on was Sebastian's ability to pee when excited. At least they were on the porch. "Do you want to come in until Marc arrives?"

His lips lifted into a wide grin. "Sounds great. Maybe I'll discover a little bit more about you."

Her hand rested on the door handle while she fought an urge to pull it shut. A teetering pile of mail on the foyer table, along with abandoned shoes, would be the first thing he'd see. Great, he'd find out her secret slob factor.

Holding onto the knob, she forced a smile while blocking his entry. *Project sincerity.* "Oh, there's nothing unusual about me. I'm boring. Go to church on every Easter and Christmas Eve. Feed the homeless every second Saturday. I collect pop tabs for the Ronald McDonald house. My life goal is to visit every one of the states in alphabetical order. I am up to Colorado. Had to skip Alaska, since it was so far away."

Will laughed a big, booming sound. Probably thought it an enormous joke.

Her fake smile ached as she tried to keep it in place and pretend his laughter wasn't hurtful. "I'm telling you the truth." Pain colored her response, but she hoped Will hadn't noticed. His smile vanished as his face grew somber.

"I'm so sorry. I guess… I, ah, I thought… Well." He stumbled to a halt, not making any sense.

"Ah yeah. I know what you mean." She pushed the door open, seeing no way to keep the man on the porch, especially since Tina, her closest neighbor, had a diamond pulled into her blinds. Instead of being a sweet old lady, the stacked divorcée resembled a raptor with false eyelashes, dragging home various men, only to reject them hours later. No doubt she checked out Will thoroughly.

The only reason she invited Will in was to save him. *Yeah, that's right. Not on the hope he might kiss me again.* He walked past her without the slightest attempt to pull her into his arms. Just when she decided, or more honestly her hormones did, she wanted to play, he didn't.

Hands in his pockets, Will strolled along the perimeter of the room, examining her wall art. "I like the Caribbean water colors."

She did, too, but recognized it as filler chatter. "I'm sorry if I embarrassed or upset you somehow by describing my life. I guess you didn't realize Brenda Boring was your date for the night. Trust me, it's an image I've been trying to break free of for some time."

Will stared at her and raised one eyebrow. "That explains your lack of alcohol tolerance. So far, you're doing well as far as breaking free."

"Yeah, maybe I've been working on that for the last couple of years without any real success." Ah yes, there were other things she did, trying to become something she wasn't.

Sebastian ran into the house; she knelt to scoop up her furry pal. The puggle looked at her with his big glossy eyes, and then veered away from her reaching hands to Will. Sebastian never cared for anyone she brought home. In fact, she tried to keep the males in her life separate.

Will walked closer before squatting to be at Sebastian's level. He gently patted the dog's back as he spoke. "He's got you wrapped around his paw. What male wouldn't enjoy a beautiful woman ruffling his hair?"

Her eyes met his, and then traveled up to a lock of hair that fell into his eyes. Did he want her to ruffle his hair? Tempting. The last thing she needed right now was the emotional upheaval of a love affair. Their fingers touched as they both continued to pet Sebastian. Her fingers stilled underneath his. Despite her awkward half-bent pose, she was almost sure Will was going to kiss her.

A low growl rumbled under her fingers, warning her the friendly hound was about to display some of his less desirable behavior. Sebastian shot out from under both of their hands, making a sharp turn to face Will. He barked once, before latching onto Will's suit pants with his teeth. The dog shook the pant leg while growling.

Tonya, horrified, dropped to her knees and grabbed her pooch. "Sebastian. No. Stop it!"

Her words had no effect on the dog, who continued to growl and pull on the pant leg. "Stop it, now. Bad dog."

Outside of prying his mouth open, she didn't know how she'd calm her dog. He'd been difficult in the past with male visitors, which resulted in her putting him in the garage.

"Do you think he knows I'm a lawyer?" Will asked, looking mildly amused.

Instead of outrage that her dog was destroying an expensive suit, he acted more entertained. Well, at least Will had a better attitude than her previous guests did. How could she get Sebastian to stop? "Sebastian," she tried to put enthusiasm in her voice that she wasn't feeling, "do you want to go for a walk?"

The dog halted his clothing assault and looked up hopefully. She moved toward the kitchen, keeping her eyes on her dog, unsure if he'd turn and go back to biting Will's trousers. As she passed the key rack, she picked up his distinctive blue leash. Sebastian's hopeful mien transformed into doggy euphoria as he pranced up to her, waiting for her to snap on his lead.

Feeling a little guilty for tricking her dog, she led him to the garage and pushed him in the dark space that smelled like gasoline and soured milk. By the time she'd let Sebastian back in, her garbage would be scattered everywhere. Sebastian was the reason she kept the trash out of the house.

The miscreant taken care of, she leaned against the door for a few seconds, buying time before she handled Will. Unfortunately, the man followed her into the dark kitchen.

"Does your dog object to all your dates?" His warm voice sounded mellow, not the least bit upset that Sebastian had made his pants into a teething toy. The shadows hid his expression.

"Well, um." She stalled, caught on the word date. Goodness, a date, well if it were, most men would have ended the evening much earlier with some excuse about working the next day. "It's hard to say. True, he's not a fan of men, but he's a rescue, and a man could have abandoned him."

"Maybe," Will readily agreed as he drew closer. "I'll tell you what I think."

Tonya watched his approach, aware she needed to do something to discourage him. It mystified her that despite her inappropriate questions and a minor mauling by her dog, that the attraction still shimmered between them.

True, she wasn't an ogre, but she hadn't tried too hard to play up her good features tonight. His arms were around her before she could think of a suitable answer; then again, it might just be a bootie call. *Oh, what the hell.* Forget overanalyzing the situation. A hot man had his arms around her. Before she could say anything to ruin the moment, her body responded for her. Somehow her fingers were in his hair, playing with the tendrils as she inhaled his scent—a trace of fading citrus cologne, along with an underlying note of a pine soap or deodorant, mostly, but the major note was aroused male.

His lips started at her ear, leaving a trail of light kisses as he made his way down her neck. When his hard, muscular body pressed up against hers, a gusty sigh sounded, making Will chuckle low and deep. *Was there anything this man did that wasn't sexy?*

How nice it was to be with a real man as opposed to the fantasy version she'd been making do with for the last six months. A slight buzzing sounded on the edge of her awareness, but it didn't seem to fit into the scenario. Peculiar.

Will's mouth left hers, allowing her enough time to refuse the unspoken request made by his erection growing between the two of them. Instead, she stood on her tiptoes, rubbing her cheek against his beard stubble.

A familiar voice came from the living room. "Tonya, I don't think your doorbell is working? I tried it, but no one answered the door."

Marc, of course, he was Will's ride back. How could she forget that? The buzzing she heard was her doorbell.

Will cursed softly into her hair before loosening his embrace. "Don't make the mistake of thinking this is the end. I found the only genuine woman in the city. I'll be damned if I'll let you go."

Genuine, so that was her appeal. Well, no way she could have faked tonight. Grabbing his hand, she raised it to her lips and kissed it. Her spontaneous reaction to his words made her blush a little. No reason it should, but it carried more emotional impact than simply kissing. Not knowing what to say to Will, she chose to answer Marc.

"I think you're right. The doorbell must be broken." She walked into the bright living room, blinking a little in the light.

Marc had his arms crossed, leaning against the door with a smug smile. No doubt he'd heard the bell and might have even stepped into the kitchen to search for them.

"That's why I let myself in, but I'll warn you to lock the door after I leave. Good neighborhood or not, it always pays to keep your door locked."

Will wandered in behind her. Marc's eyebrows shot up in surprise. "What happened to you? To think I was worried about Lilac."

Why did Marc act so shocked? The fact he compared her to Lynne's little sister was a strike against him for sure. She turned slowly, expecting that somehow Will had changed in the few seconds they were apart. Still as sexy as ever. The lock of hair that'd been threatening to fall into his eyes had. Sure, her fingers rumpled his hair, but not too bad. What was wrong with Marc?

Will looked good to her, very good. Her perusal continued across his fitted dress shirt down his legs to his knees where his pants were torn. The exposed leg showed signs of dried blood.

"Oh my God, Sebastian bit you." Here she'd been playing suck face, when the man was bleeding because of her unpredictable pet.

Marc asked the question that was on her mind. "How did you not notice this?" It was hard to tell if he was asking her or Will.

She was clueless. It must have happened sometime, but there were so many pheromones flying around the room, she hadn't even noticed. Her only goal was to get her dog out of the room. With any luck, Will would kiss her, which he did. Would she have noticed the bloody calf when they were lying naked on her bed? She might not have looked that far down. If she had, she would have kissed the abused leg as if she could make it better with her lips. The thought heated her already warm body.

How did Will interpret the event? He shrugged his shoulders. "I was, uh, preoccupied."

Marc laughed and took a few steps to his side to slap him on the back. "Preoccupied, uh, that's what they are calling it now."

Tonya felt her face heat with the words. The darkened kitchen called to her. At least she wouldn't be the butt of any jokes in there. Marc tried to shepherd Will out the door, murmuring about a side trip to the hospital, which Will refused.

"Sebastian has all his shots. He doesn't have anything." No reason for the man to worry about catching some canine disease.

Will shook his head. "I'd say he has a bad case of puppy love and is reluctant to allow anyone close to you."

Her half-opened mouth failed to refute his words, but she realized they might be true. After all, Sebastian was used to it being just the two of them. His aim might be to keep it that way, if possible. The dog might even think he got rid of Brian. "Maybe."

Marc swung the door open. "I'll give you two a few seconds for your goodbyes." He stepped out onto the porch, but his silhouette was visible through the front window.

A couple of steps brought Will to Tonya. Using the edge of his hand under her chin, he brought her eyes up to him.

"Remember what I said. I meant it." He winked, then turned and walked out the door. She could hear the men talking on the porch. Marc referred to her as a loose cannon, which disturbed her, but not enough to forgo any of his specialties.

Biting her bottom lip, she eased closer to the front door, trying to hear Will's reply.

"Sure, she's complicated, but maybe that's what I need. I'll tell you one thing, something bad is riding her."

Complicated didn't sound like a compliment, even if it was true.

She'd all but told him about the stalking—well, not the photos—but everything else. He was willing to try, despite clear warning signs.

"Your funeral, pal," Marc laughed as he slammed the car door.

She so had to call Lynne and tell her to dope slap her husband. He had it coming for the last remark. An image of her grandmother warning her that eavesdroppers never hear good about themselves came to mind.

Chapter Four

SEBASTIAN WHIMPERED, REMINDING her of his location in the garage. Might as well let him out. It wasn't as if Will was coming back. Chances were she'd never see him again. The anxious pup shot through the door as soon as she opened it. Instead of greeting her, he ran past her to search every room with his nose to the floor.

"No worries, pal. The sexy lawyer is gone. Doubt there will be any future visits after your conduct." Sebastian wagged his tail as if he understood.

Tonya shook her head. Was it too late to train him? As long as she lived alone, it wasn't a big deal. Honestly, he wasn't that well behaved. Her shoes resided on the top shelf of her closet. The more expensive the shoe, the better her pooch liked it. Sebastian didn't go for style, but the suppleness of the leather. Turned a pair of Prada pumps that she'd skipped takeout for six months to buy, into an expensive chew toy.

A flick of her hand turned on the kitchen light, illuminating the clutter on the kitchen table. Her nose wrinkled at the sight of the old newspapers, debris left from a purse switch, and more junk mail scattered across the maple trestle table. "Thank goodness the lights were off in the kitchen."

Grabbing the trashcan from the garage, she waded through her mail. A quick review of the envelopes usually earned them a spot in the circular file. Brandishing an envelope near Sebastian, she spoke more to herself than the dog. "Look, an organization that pairs up homeless dogs with children. Why don't they just give the dogs to the children wanting a pet, as opposed to taking money in the process?"

The offending envelope dropped into the can with the others. "The way things are going, I might have to set up my own charity to keep you in dog food."

Even though she meant the words to be a joke, they still hit home. *What am I going to do if I lose my job?*

Her phone chimed before she could fall into a full-blown pity party. Before she even considered the possibility that it might be Clint, she'd swiped to the right. The number revealed it was Lynne. "Hey, girl, what's up?"

The familiar voice released the tension in Tonya's shoulders. She decided not to complain about Marc's behavior. After all, she hadn't been a peach tonight. Her friend's voice boomed through the phone receiver, indicating she may have had a few drinks after they left.

"Guess what, Will likes you. He came back with a big smile on his face, talking about how real you were, not fake like everyone he usually meets."

Real, yeah, not sure if that rated as a compliment. "You want real, I'm your girl."

Lynne half-snorted into the phone. "Please, don't try to act like you're not interested. Marc told me he interrupted a pretty hot embrace."

"Aha, I thought he came into the kitchen."

"Tonya, no one was answering the door. What did you expect? He thought of slipping out without saying anything, but he figured it was better if he interrupted for both your sakes."

She didn't like the sound of that. Was she an infection that Will might catch? Her voice grew shriller with each verbalized thought. "Did Marc think he was saving Will from a fate worse than death? That I'd take advantage of the naïve lawyer?"

Her words painted an ugly, uncomfortable picture, which propelled her into pacing the kitchen with determined strides. Sebastian, familiar with her moods, shoved his way between chair legs to his sanctuary under the table. He tended to be anxious whenever emotions grew heated. About half the time, he was the culprit behind her upset.

Lynne sounded less giggly and more reasonable. "Don't get your panties in a wad. He did it for you and Will."

It made her wonder how out of control she sounded. Leaning against the counter, she lowered her voice in order to sound reasonable. "How's that?" It didn't make much sense to her.

"You're upset right now, like a kid who had her candy stolen right out from under her nose, but try to look at this like an adult. There's chemistry between the two of you. If you both managed to do the deed, then that would be the end. No more future dates or anything."

"*Well.*" Tonya stretched out the word because she didn't want to agree. What she wanted was the charming man back in her kitchen. "He didn't strike me as a booty call type of guy."

"How old are you?"

Lynne's question disturbed her. Was she hinting Will wouldn't be serious about her because of her age? "Hey, you managed to snag a younger man. I'm thirty-six. Same as you."

A heavy sigh carried across the line. "You're missing my point. You're acting like a smitten fourteen-year-old declaring the man loves you for your soul. You're both attractive, single people, who probably haven't had sex in a while. Are you following me?"

"Yeah," she agreed but wasn't really following a hundred percent. "Are you saying he'd take a booty call if I offered?"

"Wouldn't you?"

Of course, she would. Marc not only interrupted the moment, but also took the moment bringer with him. "Yeah, I kinda hoped to make good on it tonight."

"Exactly, that's why Marc did you a favor. Things would be weird if you did sleep with him. Will might not call because he'd be afraid you thought he was a horn dog, or he might think he was just another man you fell into bed with."

"Exactly." Tonya rolled her eyes before continuing, "There's been so many that I have to keep a white board attached to the wall by my bed for tally marks, in case I lose count."

"You know what I mean. How would you act if you decided to test the mattress before you knew each other better?"

Damn. She hated it when Lynne was right. Maybe it was not so much her friend being right, but more that she was wrong. Wasn't she just reenacting the fiasco that turned Clint into her stalker? Not every man she ever slept with felt the need to obsess over her. Most married someone else and forgot her easily enough. Her mistake with Clint was thinking he was something he wasn't...a normal man. Time eventually demonstrated what she refused to acknowledge, despite the various warning flags.

Instead of answering immediately, she exhaled, wondering for a second if Will had the characteristics to become a problem, opposed to a flirtation. "Ah, you're right. I might want to go out with him, but since I'd already slept with him, everything would end up being a booty call. You have to admit he's pretty hot."

"I refuse to answer that as a married woman. I'm glad you liked him. Marc's worried you might use him and cast him aside."

Tonya could hear masculine laughter in the background.

"Is Will still there?" A sense of mortification swept over her, picturing the handsome lawyer eavesdropping on the entire call.

"No. That was Marc laughing. Will left almost immediately after Marc brought him back. My husband thinks he likes you, if that makes you feel any better, but I think you issued your own test about that."

A series of giggling and smooching sounds carried over the phone line stirred up envy in Tonya's heart.

A breathless Lynne managed to say, "Got to go. See you at work tomorrow."

The phone went dead before she could even reply. She placed the cell on the counter and walked back over to the table to shuffle through the remaining junk. Sensing the emotional mood had swung back to neutral, Sebastian crept out from underneath the table, knocking a chair over in the process.

Quick reflexes allowed her to catch the chair before it hit the floor. "Boy, when will you ever learn you aren't a puppy anymore?" The dog trotted off down the hallway on his way to pre-warm the bed for her, another reason why she couldn't consider getting involved with anyone.

Too much baggage. Still, didn't everyone have baggage? The bills earned a place on the table while she used her arm to herd the remainder of the mail into the trashcan. Her phone chimed again. Couldn't be Lynne. A chill chased up her spine, imagining it was another threat from Clint.

The possibility drew her to the phone as much as it repulsed her. Better to know than be unprepared for Clint's next stunt. The number was unfamiliar. Her eyes dropped to the glowing text.

I enjoyed meeting you. Hope you might consider going out with me.

Will. What a relief. Her finger hovered above the keyboard as she wondered what to say. What if she replied and it wasn't Will? It could be a devious trick by Clint. He'd obtained a new phone number when she blocked his old number.

Feeling stupid for doing it, she had to make sure.

Will?

Once she pressed send, she felt like ten kinds of fool.

Yes, it's Will. My friend and your friend tried to fix us up tonight. You drank too much and asked me why my girlfriend wanted her own penis. Does any of this sound familiar?

Just reading the words made her cringe. Despite her obnoxiousness, he still wanted to see her. Could be because he was a lawyer, and most people avoided the whole profession. Probably afraid of being slapped with a lawsuit due to a breach of promise or whatever. Still, how could she sound any less weird than she already had?

I've been getting wrong numbers lately. Just wanted to make sure whom I was replying to. That sounded almost normal, even if it wasn't true.

Can I call you?

The idea of him calling had merit. It would end the evening on a better note than wondering what Clint's next move might be.

Yes. Give me ten minutes.

Her thumb depressed the send button, and she sprinted for the bedroom, agitating Sebastian, who barked energetically from his spot on her bed. Not enough time for shower, a quick trip to the bathroom to wash off her makeup and brush her teeth consumed most of her time.

A quick spritz of perfume made her feel sexy as she jumped naked between the sheets. Will would never know, but it stroked her libido knowing she'd be nude on the phone while she talked to the hot lawyer who liked her. That was a wonder in itself.

A glow from the hallway indicated a light left on. Damn, that meant she'd have to go turn it off. The way her finances were recently, she couldn't afford to leave a light burning. Her eyes cut to the phone, calculating how much time she had. Not much. She didn't want to miss his call after her somewhat weird text message. Her goal was to talk to Will, and then drift off to sleep. With any luck, she'd skip the nightmares that troubled her lately.

Tonya glanced at the phone lying on her bed before she made the mad run down the hall to turn out the light. A few long-legged strides brought her to the living room where she turned off the problem light. "Done." She stood in the dark catching her breath. A distant chime came from the bedroom.

"Oh no!" She ran as hard as she could to the bedroom, thinking this must be what it feels like to be a streaker. A sense of freedom, the forbidden, and a huge chunk of exhibitionist thrown in. Tonya jumped on her bed, rattling Sebastian, who gave her a disgusted look. Apparently, he wasn't a fan of her pushing her boundaries.

The sheets felt cool as she slid under them. Of course, she'd call Will back. What excuse could she use? A finger tap brought the screen to life. No missed calls. Strange, she'd heard it chime. A text. Odd, when he said he would call. Another tap opened the message.

Sweet Dreams. I must say you are looking good.

The message made her grin a little even though it perplexed her. He said he was going to call, but the fact he chose to text was peculiar. It was late, and they both had to work the next day. That could be the reason behind the text. It didn't matter if he called or texted. Her efforts to reassure herself fell flat. Might as well put Will's name in her phone so she'd know when to answer the phone and to ignore any possible Clint messages by different numbers.

She'd considered changing her number, but with the possible loss of her job, she'd already started nosing around for another job. Couldn't afford a number change at this moment. Clint already demonstrated he could uncover any number changes. What would stop him from getting a new number?

There should be a warning for women to never date a man who worked for a security agency. That's what his agency called itself. Back in the day, it might be a gumshoe firm. All she knew for sure was it had dozens of ways to dig up dirt on people. Clint used to entertain her with the tricks played on unsuspecting employees, like revealing medical records to addresses without having a clue they'd been played. That might have been the first time she wondered if she was dating a jerk. What kind of person does that?

Her fingers stopped typing Will's name as her skin chilled. What if the text hadn't been from Will? The number was unfamiliar, but that didn't mean anything. Scrolling up, she found her previous exchange with Will. The number was different. The thought of Clint sitting out in his car, watching her run through the house naked, cramped her belly, causing her to dash half-bent to the bathroom. *Damn. The man wouldn't even let her hold onto a superior dinner.* She stayed kneeling, resting her head on the toilet seat until Sebastian walked in to investigate.

He cold nosed her calf. His way of saying, 'What's up, buddy?'

Tonya pushed herself into a standing position, if only to reassure her dog. She rinsed out her mouth and splashed water on her face. No longer feeling sexy and carefree, she donned her winter flannel pajamas. Her sense of exposure didn't abate, which resulted in her donning her father's old, ratty, plaid robe.

Clint had threatened to burn it, which made her cling to it that much harder. The stained, worn robe bothered him because it wasn't sexy, slinky, or revealing. To Tonya, it reminded her of her father and the pancake breakfasts he always made on Saturdays.

Sebastian beat her back to bed. He watched her with suspicious eyes as if she might perform another unexpected action, causing him to abandon his spot again. "No worries, friend, I'm in for the night."

She slid under the covers, exhausted. Her grandmother was fond of saying that a person never had more than they could handle. Well, that old axiom sucked big time. Her eyelids fluttered closed while she contemplated turning off the light. Normally, she slept with it off, but the darkness made her vulnerable. She exhaled deeply. Make that more vulnerable.

Didn't most people in those movies of the week call the police when stalked? Of course, that would put her back to playing show and tell with her boudoir photos. Technically, she did nothing illegal. Plenty of women paid good money to take provocative photos for their husband or sweetheart. Then again, they didn't have her family or employer either.

Hellfire and damnation were predicted when she moved away from home. This issue would only prove them right. It was hard to determine which was worse, Clint shadowing her every move or her family using her as an example of what happens to a woman who exerts free will? Yep, she'd set the females in her family back a couple of centuries. The phone's ringing levitated her a few inches off the mattress.

Her heart stopped for a second. What now? Her thoughts bumped up against each other like students exiting on the last day of school. Surely Clint wouldn't be ballsy enough to call her. She wouldn't give him the satisfaction of answering. Wait, it could be Will. The phone stopped its incessant ringing. She patted down the covers trying to find it. It was close to Sebastian, who blinked when she felt under him for the missing cell.

The number was the same one Will used earlier. It was too late to call. A glance at the clock revealed it wasn't yet eleven, but the time hadn't changed. She had, almost forgetting for a brief moment that she was a woman with too much baggage to have an ordinary life. The phone chimed in her hand. A text.

It's okay if you don't want to talk. I understand.

Apparently, the man thought she was rejecting him. Did he think she usually tongue tangoed with strangers and then threw them aside? Of course, she'd be doing that if she ignored Will's call. Great, now she wasn't going to get any sleep.

She sat up and slipped out of bed, earning a disgusted look from her canine, who flopped back onto the comforter.

Knowing the luck Will had recently, he'd conclude he was a turnoff to women. Not that she, Tonya Smiley, served as a one-woman crew who propped up men's sagging self-esteem.

The oversized Amish furniture she'd inherited from Granny made it hard to pace in the small room. Will was a decent fellow. The devil's advocate reminded her that she'd thought Clint was a decent fellow, too.

"No, I didn't. I just thought he was hot and had too much to drink. I only added decent to get you off my back."

Her eyes caught her reflection in the mirror. Here she was talking to herself, and Will still wanted to date her. What were the chances she'd find another man who accepted her as she was? Up to now, she hadn't met any. People might talk about women wanting to make men over, but her experience was that men wanted her to be something she wasn't. Ironically, they never saw anything wrong with asking her to wear flats, dye her hair, and lose weight, or use 'baby talk' when they were in bed.

The same men might complain if she asked them to be taller, have more hair, or grow a pair of balls. Here she was going to throw away the first semi-normal man she'd met in a long time. Maybe she could call and explain why she couldn't date him. Her eyebrows went up as she imagined the conversation.

I like you, Will, a lot. Your girlfriend becoming your boyfriend doesn't faze me. After all, my boyfriend became my stalker.

Yeah, sounded great. Just the thing to win a man over. Maybe a cup of herbal tea would help. Lemon Zinger might not give her inspirational thoughts, but it would clear out the residual taste of vomit.

Tea in hand, she settled into the rocking chair in the dark living room. She didn't dare turn on the lights, not knowing who might be outside watching. The embroidered sheers didn't shield her from prying eyes. Blinds, shades, something to cover the windows were on her immediate to-do list. She never bothered before because she never thought she'd be doing anything in the living room that she needed to hide from prying eyes.

Wrapped up in an excess of material for the temperature, ensconced in her grandmother's rocking chair, and tea by her side, she might be ready to call Will. Comfort items checked, except for her dog. Unfortunately, he appeared to have enough of her roller coaster emotions tonight or could just be holding a grudge because she shoved him in the garage. Sebastian would play the wounded canine until she emptied out a box of dog treats, trying to earn his favor again.

With no luck winning over her four-legged friend tonight, she'd call Will. The continual ringing in her ear indicated he wasn't picking up. Could be she waited too long. The man could have given her some time limit known only to himself if she hadn't called back, then she was history.

The phone continued to ring. Why didn't it go into voice mail? If it did, she wasn't sure if she'd leave a message. What could she say? *Sorry, I missed your call. My personal stalker dialed me up to freakout mode. Okay now, if you still want to talk.*

If it went into voice mail, she'd hang up. He'd know the number. A click sounded, and then an almost panting masculine voice answered. "Hello. Is this Tonya?"

Goodness, what had the man been doing? An unsavory image filled her head of him with another woman. What nonsense considering Marc fixed him up with her? Well, actually Lynne did. "Yes, it's me." Before she could think twice about her actions, she asked, "What makes you so breathless?"

Did she just say that? Talk about sounding needy and clingy.

"Tonya." Warmth imbued the one word. "I'm so glad you called. I didn't think you would, so I jumped in the shower. I thought I heard my phone ringing, but figured it was wishful thinking on my part."

Instead of imagining Will with some bimbo that wandered by his place and happened to ring the doorbell, her mind's eye conjured up a wet, naked Will standing in the dark kitchen talking on his cell phone. No, make that a well-lit kitchen. It was her imagination. She wanted to ask him what he was wearing but didn't. That would make her no better than the stereotypical male.

"Yeah, it's me. Surprise." That sounded stupid. Help would be nice here. Could she look up on her computer a script for phone conversations with a man you like, even though it might not be the wisest choice? There probably wouldn't be any. If there were, it wouldn't include the word surprise.

"Actually, it is a surprise. Wasn't sure you'd call me back. I think I did almost everything wrong. My inactivity on the dating scene shows."

"Seriously. What did you do wrong?"

"Everything."

"I think that's my response. Explain. I couldn't see anything."

A low laugh teased her ear. "You're too kind. I suspected Marc might attempt to fix me up. He's been more worried about my love life than I am. Even though I knew what was going down I still lingered at work. Could have gone home and changed clothes to be more approachable."

"You looked great. The loosened tie and all had the sexy lawyer persona going for you."

A relaxed chuckle greeted her comment. "That's another thing. I talked about work. There's no bigger dating turn-off than a divorce lawyer."

Mentally Tonya agreed, but wasn't about to admit it. "Hitman?"

"No, there's that extreme bad boy angle that many women would consider hot."

Damn it, the man was right. "Ah, but you're not the bad guy. You usually represent women to help them get what they deserve."

"True. Sometimes, more than they deserve, although that isn't the way most women see it. I represent the breakup, the heartache, the worst time in a person's life."

"You're a regular grim reaper of relationships."

"Hey!"

"Oops, sorry." Her eyes rolled upward at her verbal stumble. "I didn't say you were. I was following your imagery and provided some of my own."

"All right. I guess it's easy to pull lawyer metaphors out of the air."

Time to bite her tongue and not agree. "I think you're a great guy. What else did you think you did wrong?" Silence answered her question, making her wonder if he had put down the phone and tiptoed away.

"Inane dinner conversation."

"Oh, you mean something worse than my tipsy comments."

"Yeah, that was bad." The smile was obvious in his voice.

"Hey!" She pretended outrage, but she was far from it. A slow heat spread through her that had nothing to do with tea or her flannel cocoon. She could really fall for this man. Besides being easy on the eyes, and a great kisser, he was transparent. No masks, he was what he was. Refreshing.

"No worries, Marc and Lynne were more upset than I was. Personally, I admired the fact you were able to say what you thought, even if alcohol loosened your tongue a little."

"A lot." She smirked at the phone as if he could see her.

"I was wondering," he started.

Here it comes. She sucked in her lips while reminding herself that she didn't need any more complications in her already complicated life.

"If you'd consider seeing me again."

Remember to let him down easy, where he doesn't think it's him. She knew what to say, something about not being over a previous breakup. Instead, she said, "Yes, I'd love to go out with you. When?"

For a second, she watched herself from the corner of the room as if she were a type of hovering spirit. Maybe her consciousness, or id, or ego, or whatever that term from psychology class was. The animated woman rocked with vigor as she wrapped a tendril of hair around her finger. Her flushed cheeks and enlarged pupils served as textbook examples of arousal. There was no way she was going to say no to Will. Just as well he was across town. The talking self may have forgotten the evil ex, but she hadn't. Out there in the dark lurked a man who had decided to make her life a living hell. There was a chance he'd make Will's the same.

The woman in the rocking chair sighed a little after bidding Will goodbye. Her hovering self zoomed back into her physical body. *Put up a sheet or a blanket over the sheers. No reason to give Clint any free shows.*

The disturbing thought had her rifling through the linen closet for flat sheets. Standing in the dark on a chair, she tried to drape the sheets over the curtain rods, but they kept slithering to the floor. Disgusted, she stepped off the chair, throwing the puddle of sheets an irritated look. "Why does the victim have to do all the work to maintain some privacy?"

A stalker who didn't know where she lived would be much better. Even better would be a stalker she hadn't slept with and posed for a number of cheesecake photos for, but it was what it was.

An idea occurred to her as she walked into the kitchen and gathered up all the bag clips she could find. Ten minutes later, after a few failed attempts, and one stubbed toe, the sheets hung haphazardly secured by chip clips. It wouldn't win any home decorating awards.

Lifting up a sheet, she placed her hand under it, feeling the thinness of the fabric. Better chance with the living room light on that she'd be a shadow show. It would be easy to tell if she was home. Don't be home seemed like the immediate answer. It was a ridiculous one. It was her house. How would she care for Sebastian if she never came home?

If she didn't look like she was home could be a solution. That meant cleaning out her garage to pull in her car. *Another thing Clint is causing me to do with his ill-conceived pursuit. Still, I'm not sure he wants me back. The man could be lying in bed with a new girlfriend. He has looks, surface charm, and an over-inflated ego that makes him stalk previous lovers. The jerk walked out on me. Now that he's done with the girl of the week, month, or whatever, he expects me to welcome him back with open arms. He goes all nutzo when I don't. My life could be one of those news magazine shows where the woman never realizes her sweetie is a serial rapist or killer.*

The thought made her stumble into the bedroom doorframe in her dark hallway. "Ow!" She rubbed her forehead vigorously, heading off any possible bruising. A large bruise on her forehead would stand out on her future date. Will would ask. How could he not? It would be like showing up with a black eye or a broken arm.

"Oh, that bruise. That's from walking around my house with the lights off at night to convince my stalker I wasn't home."

Yep, it sounded as demented as she thought it would. Still, she couldn't be the only woman with a stalker ex. Most of the stories she read online had bad endings with the woman murdered, mutilated, and the new boyfriend attacked. Losing her job would be a slight consequence compared to what could happen.

No workplace wanted a woman who presented a threat to the other workers. Tonya climbed into bed, punching her pillow in disgust. "Why did I have to be needy enough to take up with Clint?"

Sebastian opened his eyes from his prone position on the bed. He blinked twice, and then closed them again. No answer. Why should he when she didn't have one?

Her eyes rolled upward to the popcorn blown ceiling. A cheap way to finish a ceiling and it attracted dust. If she turned off the light, then she wouldn't see the dust. Her hand hovered near the light. Was Clint out there? If he saw her light go out, he might go home thinking his work was complete. It would be nice to sleep without worrying.

A bottle of sleeping pills sat on her nightstand along with a bottle of water. It was sad she drugged herself every night, but she needed sleep to function the next day. Otherwise, every sound convinced her that someone was trying to break in or was already in the house.

Her tumble into slumber was swift. Her last coherent thought revolved around whether she should mention the stalking, for Will's safety.

Chapter Five

WET, SLOPPY KISSES on her face gradually awakened Tonya. Her lips tilted up, while her eyelids remained closed, feigning sleep. With Will's looks, a person would think he'd be a better morning kisser. Maybe that was the real reason Marc fixed him up. A small sigh escaped her. It would be a difficult job, but she'd tutor him.

A thought tickled at the back of her mind. Today was a workday. She remembered that much. Didn't make sense for Will to have stayed over. Carried away with the heat of the moment, plus too much alcohol and the desire to block out the reality of Clint did not equal a connection. Her eyelids popped open just in time for a right eyeball to get a thorough swipe from Sebastian's tongue.

"Ugh!" Grabbing the sheet, she wiped at her face. "Sebastian, how many times have I told you that is not the appropriate way to wake me up?"

The overlarge adoring eyes and a wagging tail prevented her from being mad at a creature who loved her so. "I get it. You want to go out."

Her arm served as a restraint to keep her pup's kisses at a distance as she slid out of bed. Her flannel pajamas made her grimace. "Good thing Will didn't stay, considering my bed wear."

Sebastian danced in front of her and gave a yelp as if agreeing. She shook her head at the coffee maker as she passed it to open the back door. Steam wafted off the carafe of hot water. When she failed to add the coffee, it didn't do a person much good to have an expensive automatic coffee maker. "A sign of how my day's going to be."

Her brows lowered at her words. Didn't she know any better? Hadn't she heard on one of those talk shows that you spoke your day into existence? Her hand reached up to push her hair out of her eyes. She expected the worst and inevitably got it. Today would be different. What could she speak into existence? There was the possibility of becoming a millionaire, but it bordered on the greedy side, even if she could use the money.

Besides, when you spoke things into existence, weren't they supposed to be something that could happen? Tonya bit her lip while wrestling with options. Sebastian trotted toward the door after initiating as many flowerpots as he could. Normally, she'd yell at him, but this year she'd never even planted anything. Empty pots were the targets of Sebastian's urinary efforts.

Her initial wish was for Clint to find someone else to obsess over, but she abandoned it as being too cruel to some unknown woman. She swung the door open while announcing her wish. "For a change, I'd like to have mind-blowing sex."

Tina, her neighbor, looked up from watering her pots of glorious cascading petunias. "You and me both." She saluted with her right hand as her left clutched a leopard skin spotted watering can.

She heard her. Tonya almost slammed the door before Sebastian reached it. The dog, aware of the vagaries of his owner, made a dart for the opening. Canine inside, she leaned against the door. Well, that was rude of her. Should have at least said good morning. Still, it was hard to find a follow-up statement after she announced to the neighborhood the state of her love life.

What else could happen? After filling Sebastian's bowls, she turned the radio on. Strains of a soft rock ballad filled the kitchen. The tune had her waltzing around the kitchen, imagining Will holding her in his arms and singing gently in her ear. The man would be a wonderful dancer. Unlike so many men who refused to dance, he'd take every opportunity.

Sure, she was making up her own little fantasy, but wasn't that why they were called fantasies? The song ended, and a perky deejay came on. "Rise and shine, if you're heading to work you might already be late. It's nine o'clock."

The cold cola she'd just opened dropped out of her hand, hitting her big toe. Hopping, she scooped up the rolling drink can. "God, what else?" Her hand slapped over her mouth before she could even finish the statement. *Nothing else, please.* Sebastian licked up the sticky trail of soda left behind. "Don't do that." She gave a shrug. "Go ahead. I don't have time to clean."

Breakfast forgotten, Tonya rushed through dressing. With any luck, she'd park in the rear lot, sneak in the back door, and slip up to her office. No one would see her, and if someone did, she'd claim car trouble.

All her usual work standby clothes were at the cleaners or dirty. She didn't have the time or energy to create some new outfits from what was left. Instead, she donned the black dress hanging in the back of her closet. It was her funeral, graduation, or other boring occasions that being a relative made it necessary to attend, dress. The plain dress made her feel somewhat like a pilgrim. It also reminded her to visit the dry cleaners.

On her way through the kitchen, she grabbed a new cola and a granola bar for breakfast. Since she'd already be late, that would cancel out lunch. Great, she hadn't fixed her lunch, either. She pushed another soda and granola bar into her oversized purse. Not very healthy or delicious, for that matter. She included a bottle of water. Just call her Miss Nutrition.

Dark clouds loomed overhead as she headed out the door. The clouds bunched together, possibly planning a cloudburst about the time she had to exit her vehicle. If the person in front of her tried to drive at the posted speed, she'd arrive before the storm. The urge to pass was strong. The shape and size of the sedan shouted undercover cop. Not the day to press her luck.

Tonya replayed the night before, reliving each moment, including the delicious dinner. Too bad she acted like a pig and ate everything. It could have been lunch today if she'd shown some restraint. Easing up on the alcohol might have helped her make a better impression, too. Still, could she help it if she had no real tolerance for alcohol? Will, strangely, liked her despite her offensive remarks. That made the two of them slightly damaged in the relationship department.

A hot metal smell filled the car. What was it? The sedan in front of her turned, but the odor remained, which made her a little nervous. Any information she knew about cars came from a radio auto talk show that featured more jokes about the brothers' lives than useful car tips. Could it just be the stale smell of dog? A couple of weeks ago, she did haul Sebastian to the dog wash.

The out of place odor didn't have the damp wool smell of wet dog. Her eyes dropped to the thermostat whose needle was veering into the red. *Damn it. Seriously?* Tonya signaled and pulled over to the shoulder of the road.

Smoke, or possibly steam, snaked out from under her hood. Never a good sign. Her auto expertise consisted of pulling over whenever anything appeared wrong. Her father had drilled that point home after she continued to drive the family car without oil, and it seized up. In her defense, how would she have known it was out of oil? Of course, her father pointed out the light and the knocking noise the car emitted before dying.

A red and blue drugstore entrance sign squatted near the curb about fifty yards away. It might be better to park in there, but how would she get to work? Lynne would already be there. A quick glance in the direction of the store revealed her co-worker, Michelle, leaving the store with a drink and a bag probably filled with snacks for the day. For once, her fellow worker's tardiness worked in her favor.

Opening her car door, she jumped out and waved her arms. "Michelle, Michelle." Her co-worker looked up and waved back. It looked like the woman was going to get into her car and leave her stranded.

"No, wait!" Her heels aerated the soil with each step as she lurched in a Frankenstein fashion. Michelle's head was down, while she fiddled with something in the car. Two more plodding steps brought her to the car the same time her co-worker's engine turned over. Her hands landed flat on the hood, startling Michelle, whose head whipped around with her jaws still chewing.

The driver's window slid down. "Tonya. Mercy. What are you doing here?" Her co-worker looked surprised to see her, despite the fact she'd waved earlier.

"Yes, it's me. I need help. My car broke down." Tonya leaned on the car as she pulled her heels out of the mire. There was nothing to wipe the soil off her shoes, so she tapped them on Michelle's car bumper.

"Didn't see you there. I'd expect you to be at work by now." Michelle took a pull on her drink and gave her a quizzical look.

"You waved at me when you were coming out of the store." Michelle's behavior confused her, but most of what her co-worker did mystified her.

"Oh. That was you. I couldn't tell for sure. You don't normally dress like one of those religious missionaries. I thought you were trying to strike up a conversation in an effort to convert me."

"Would a missionary know your name?"

Her co-worker shrugged. "An ambitious one would. Then there was your dress."

There was a reason she never wore the dress except when family occasions demanded it. Resting one hand on the car, she worked her way to the passenger side. Instead of asking, she opened the door and slid into the passenger seat, brushing several items to the floor to do so. "I was hoping to bum a ride to work."

"That's what I figured when you climbed into the car." Michelle parked her drink into the cup holder and slid on her sunglasses.

"Might want to move your car off the main road first."

"I'll do that." Her hand on the door latch, she hesitated. What if Michelle's motives were to get her out of the car? Truthfully, she never had very charitable thoughts toward her co-worker. "You're not going to leave me?"

"Goodness." Her head shook back and forth slowly. "While I knew you didn't have the best opinion of me because I come in late more than I do on time, I sure thought you might have trusted me some." Her oversized sunglasses hid her eyes.

It was hard to read her mood. Her co-worker could be playing her, but it was difficult to say. Not knowing what to do, she decided to go with the truth, or as close to it as she was willing to reveal. Spearing a hand through her hair, she mussed her semblance of a style. "Michelle, I never asked you for a favor, never needed to, and prided myself on doing things on my own. Right now, today, you're the only person who can help me out. Neither one of us can afford to be late to work with management slinking around trying to decide who to fire. I'm begging you, please, get me to work."

Instead of speaking, Michelle gave her shoulder a friendly nudge. "Go move that car. Don't have all day."

Tonya jumped out of the car, but instead of punching holes in the turf with her heels, she removed them once she hit the grass. Later, she'd figure out what to do with her car. Maybe Lynne could give her a ride home. Might even be able to prevail on Marc to give her some automotive advice. Her feet slipped on the damp grass, but she was able to catch herself before she fell. One positive as far as her crappy morning went.

Five minutes later, her fingers wrapped her seat as Michelle sped through a stale yellow light and switched lanes without signaling. How could she, since her cell phone was up to her ear, leaving only one hand free for steering? Occasionally, that hand would beat out a rhythm along with the radio. From what she could hear of the one-sided conversation, one of her children left an important project at home. It was difficult, but she managed to cross her fingers under the seat while clutching it.

From the sounds of it, her co-worker's insistence she couldn't bring the project to school weakened. *Let the kid take the consequences. Be strong.* Tonya doubted telepathy would save her. Michelle did have family in the area. "Maybe grandmother could pick up the project."

Michelle's head whipped around in her direction the same time a dump truck headed their way. "Good idea."

"Truck," she shrieked the word, causing her co-worker to swerve right into the shoulder. Luckily, no cars behind them allowed Michelle to guide the car back onto the road while calling her mother. If they ever got to work, Tonya would be willing to buy her co-worker a blue tooth for her phone.

Ten stressful minutes later, the sedan bumped into the parking lot. "Thanks," Tonya threw the words behind her as she vaulted out of the car. She abandoned the fanciful idea of kissing the ground as soon as it occurred. No time. She rushed for the door, finding it open. Today, she appreciated the lax security.

Her only goal was to get to her office without anyone spotting her. She could pretend she'd been there all the time if Michelle didn't mention picking her up. If she did, then she'd go with the car excuse. The halls were empty with the distant sound of typing and conversation. Slipping off her shoes, she tiptoed up the stairs.

Her office was in the far corner. The interior light outlined the closed door, which caused her breath to catch. There should be no one in her office, considering she was in the hall, and Michelle wasn't far behind. Her steps slowed as she tried to decide what to do. Probably would be best to go in with shoes. She stepped into her shoes and tucked her purse near a trashcan the better to pretend she'd only been in the copier room. Her fingers pushed a wayward tendril behind her ear. She opened the door to discover a woman wearing a hat typing feverishly.

Seriously, she couldn't be more than thirty or forty minutes late.

The company already replaced her. Her teeth clicked together, grinding her back molars, reverting to a habit that wearing an oral positioner to bed had extinguished. Over a dozen people quit and no one replaced them. The woman, hearing her entrance, glanced over her shoulder, revealing a familiar profile.

"Lynne. What are you doing?" Her friend had shoved her trademark hair under what looked suspiciously like a fishing hat.

Her friend spun around, pulling off her hat, and shaking out her hair. "That's the thanks I get for saving your butt. Where were you? I know Will didn't stay over, unless he made a return trip?" Her eyebrows raised in an inquisitive fashion.

"No, he didn't come back. He did call. I fell asleep without setting the alarm. Excuse me. I have to get my purse." Returning with her purse in hand, she continued the conversation as if she'd never stopped. "If that wasn't bad enough, no coffee, no breakfast, and then my car breaks down on the way to work."

The door stood open, allowing her to see Michelle coming up the hall without the least attempt to be sneaky. Anything private needed discussion quickly. True, she felt a little more congenial toward her work mate.

Lynne stood, allowing Tonya to take her seat. The open document got her attention. Several lines of twelve-point font that read *I don't know why my friend isn't returning my phone calls. After all, I wasn't the one who got tipsy and made all the offensive remarks. Overall, she still managed to walk off with a handsome lawyer. Way to go, chickee. The way I see it, you owe me, considering your lack of dates. Makes me wonder why you're not answering my calls.*

"What calls? I talked to you last night." A quick movement of the mouse highlighted the text and deleted it. Not exactly what she wanted management to see as they went through their security searches. Nina, in accounting, commented that they were reading personal emails. Not sure why, since the company didn't have any top-secret information or recipes.

Her friend tapped her nose. "Checking to see if it grew? I called about every five minutes after nine. You usually beat everyone else in."

Peculiar. An unpacking of her breakfast and lunch colas, plus water bottle, and granola bars got her a little closer to finding her cell. Surely, she didn't leave it at home.

"Goodness, I'll expect you to pull out something interesting, like a dildo or a gun."

Tonya continued to paw. "You're out of luck." A corner of the familiar cow spotted phone case peeked out from underneath a tampon and a half-used gum pack. She pulled it out and flourished it. "Aha, I found it."

"That doesn't explain why you never answered my calls." Lynne fisted her hands on her hips. "I even wore Ernie's stinky hat for you."

The name of the building custodian had her wrinkling her nose as she tapped her phone on without any luck. "You get friend of the year. Not sure how you got the hat off Ernie's head."

Her friend demonstrated by throwing her shoulders back, and her chest out. "I was wondering if I could borrow your darling hat for a few minutes."

"Yep, that would probably do it." She hit the cell with the heel of her hand. "I don't think my phone is working."

"Did you charge it last night?" Lynne asked, peering at the phone. "Looks pretty dead."

Her friend's words matched her thoughts. "No, this is the worst time in the world for me to have a dead phone." If Clint was going to do something stupid, she needed to be one step ahead of him, doing preventive measures.

"Why? I know it's never good to have a dead phone, but what makes today worse?" Her friend took a step back and gave her the once-over, starting at her feet. "I get it. You're going to phone in a fashion emergency. Here I thought no one would believe you'd wear such a hat, but..." She grabbed the cap and tried to place it on Tonya's head.

"Stop. My hair already looks like crap." Her friend desisted. Michelle entered the room juggling her phone, drink, purse, and goodies sack.

"Hey, did Tonya tell you I was a regular life saver went she broke down on 38?"

Lynne's eyes cut over to her friend. "Not yet. Good thing you were there since her cell phone wasn't working."

Her co-worker's entry gave her another reason that having a phone was a necessity. "I need a phone to call someone about my car. Maybe you can drop me off at the drugstore on your way home. That would be grand." She waved at Lynne, expecting her to leave.

"Okay," Lynne agreed, but her forehead still had the puckered look that didn't bode well. "Let me call Marc. If it is something simple, he might know what to do. Why did you stop?"

"The temperature gauge flickered into the red zone." Tonya wanted to quit talking about her unreliable vehicle and get a peek at her email. Despite her attempts to block Clint, he knew ways to get around simple blocks. All he really had to do was develop a new email. Her friend continued to debate how to take care of her car as she opened her email and scrolled through the addresses. No obvious Clint email, but there were a few she didn't recognize. Fear, which was becoming a frequent companion, squeezed into the chair with her.

Lynne murmured. "Probably out of coolant." Grabbing the hat and picking up her coffee cup, she brandished it. "My excuse for wandering the halls. Out of coffee. See you later."

"Yeah," she agreed, making brief eye contact before zeroing in on the three unknown emails. Her hands wrapped around the monitor, angling it away from the door and making it impossible for any visitor to get a casual glance. Snippets of conversation indicated her co-worker was hard at work getting the forgotten school project where it needed to be. Maybe Michelle had a hard time saying no, but her relatives apparently didn't.

The first email was a pharmaceutical ad for Canadian drugs. One down. The other one declared she'd already won big. Her impulse was to delete it, but the subject line could be a joke that was only funny to Clint. It was an ad for the Irish Sweepstakes, which she hadn't entered. No way she'd won big. The third was a bit of a rambling letter from a junior executive from a sister company. The missive confused her a little. It contained no requests for information or action. A nothing letter that made her wonder about the sender, a tall, shy fellow who had the look of sheer terror when she talked to him at the last inter-company conference in Columbus. At the time, she was making conversation, not hitting on him. It seemed prudent since they both did the same job in different buildings.

A perusal of the letter, looking for hints, didn't really yield any-thing. Apparently, the man was only establishing contact. Could be he wanted communication for similar reasons, or he could be flirting. The deadly serious letter failed if it was a flirtation device, but who knew? It did reflect the personality of the sender. Sucking her lips in, she considered deleting it, but that would be wrong. Wouldn't bother replying today.

Nothing from Clint. A long sigh escaped as she leaned back into her chair.

Michelle must have heard her and misinterpreted her relief. "Don't stress too much. You have to ask for help sometimes instead of always trying to do everything on your own. People will help you if you ask."

"Yes, you're so right." She managed to stretch her lips into a big, wide smile, although she couldn't do much about the rest of her face. "After all, you brought me to work."

Her co-worker agreed, then shook an index finger at her. "You got to trust other people. Let go of the reins. Other people not only can help, but they want to."

Was she still smiling? She wasn't sure. True, Michelle meant work. Still, it would be nice if she could share her Clint issues with Lynne or even more with Will since he had the legal brain. The most she did was hint to Richard that someone might be harassing her. The man showed her how to block both phone calls and emails.

As much as she wanted to cry on Lynne's shoulder, she refused. The embarrassment that she was foolish enough to have taken up with Clint decided her. Her best friend's vocal opposition to Clint resulted in the romance becoming an almost covert one. The only fact she readily shared with Lynne was that he dumped her.

Enough wallowing in her bad choices. Stacks of reports to check and legitimate emails awaited her. Michelle had a point. Still, from the one-sided conversation she'd overheard about the forgotten homework, no one rushed to save the boy's grade willingly. People say they'll help, but when you ask them, there's always excuses.

Tonya grimaced as she picked up a heavy statistics binder. Data entry fell to the entry-level workers, but unfortunately, they were the first to leave when rumors of a cutback started circulating in the break room. Easy for them to find another job since they earned little more than minimum wage. Plenty of companies, not in the red, needed drudges to input data or answer the phones.

The black binder fell open, exposing blocks of text, mind-numbing chunks of info for her that needed cross checking against their online records. Part of not reaching their annual revenue goals came from the misplacement of a decimal. The revenue they thought they had, they didn't. Unfortunately, the company spent the non-existent money. A click opened the needed file. The screen bloomed with long rows of data and drew out a long sigh.

"Great."

Michelle called across the room. "What's up?"

Everything, or would that be down? Right now, everything sucked. Her mouth twisted to one side as she gestured to the book. "The book of doom. I have to recheck all the info. Ya know, whoever made the decimal disaster is long since gone, probably in the first wave of resignations."

A grunt signaled agreement as her co-worker sucked on the straw of her oversized drink.

"Now I have to check every column, every figure." Makings for a self–pity party assembled in her mind—spent years working for the company, hard work, long hours, and now she got monotonous work, best done by educated monkeys or possibly a computer program.

A screech of her desk chair announced Michelle's movement in her direction. The squealing desk chair never bothered her co-worker, but it grated on Tonya's nerves. Several times she swore to herself she'd oil the chair. So far, she'd never made good on the promise.

Her co-worker's shadow fell across the open binder. "I wanted to see the book that got Mary Ann canned."

"Mary Ann?" Her eyebrows went up. Mary Ann was a pleasant older woman who'd worked in data entry forever. "What happened?"

"Heard from the custodian, she fell asleep on the keyboard."

The words sent a chill up her spine. What if she fell asleep, or worse, made a mistake? Clint's threats might not be the impetus that relocated her and Sebastian to a refrigerator box under the bridge.

Lynne breezed into the room, clutching her accustomed cup of java. "I heard you got the book." She angled her head in the direction of the binder.

"Yes." Tonya groaned dramatically. "It might be easier just to pack up my desk now, instead of lengthening my torture." Her right hand shoved the keyboard up against the monitor. The downward slide of her body in the desk chair spoke more than words could.

Lynne grabbed the back of the chair and spun it around, squatting slightly for eye contact with her friend. "Stop that! You're no quitter. Why not scan the pages and have the computer compare it? That's what they're for."

The hopelessness settled onto her shoulders, pushing her deeper into her chair. The kneehole in the desk tempted her. All she'd have to do is slide down a little farther and crawl into the small space, curling into a fetal position. Lynne's voice sounded tinny and thin, as if it were coming from far away.

The only problem with the kneehole solution was eventually someone would take her place or her desk—probably Roberta in personnel, since she resented the fact that Tonya's requisition form for a new desk over two years ago got the go-ahead while her own went nowhere. Roberta's desk wasn't that old while Tonya's dated back to pre-Civil War. The avaricious woman would sneak in after hours with her malleable husband to switch the desks.

Lynne's voice continued, interrupting her expanding scenario of Roberta and her husband tripping over Tonya's body as they moved the purloined desk. What was she saying? Computer? Computer scanning something? The words floated through her ears, not even lingering long enough for her to analyze them. A needle-sharp pain in her forearm brought tears to her eyes. She blinked hard, trying to hold back the tears. The close-up view of Lynne's face came into focus. Her lips moved.

"Are you listening to me? Earth to Tonya?"

Her open hand pushed Lynne away. "Boundaries. Personal space." Her friend stepped back, but put both hands on her hips. The ever-present coffee cup was missing from her friend's hand. "What did you say about the computer?"

Michelle's face replaced Lynne's. "Thank the good Lord. You checked back in. I wasn't sure if I was going to have to empty a pitcher of water on you."

A pitcher of water? The more genial relationship that had sprung up between the two of them after the shared ride splintered a little. "No water, please."

Lynne's eyes danced above the hand she held in front of her mouth. Her friend pointed in the direction of the binder. "You scan each page on the printer, and then load the digital file for comparison using a digitized scanning software."

"Digitized scanning software," she repeated the words softly, reverently. "Where could I get this software?"

"Accounting already has it. The company has multiple licenses for it. Ask Richard to install it for you." Lynne smiled, picked up her coffee cup, and lifted one eyebrow.

Let Richard install it, yeah right. The man she most recently begged for info on how to block her persistent stalker from sending unwanted missives. Good chance the last favor depleted her quota for the year. It would be better if Lynne asked. Most men liked her friend. Not in the *I want to jump your bones* way. No, they enjoyed light banter with a woman out of their league, but her marital status kept them safe from the inevitable rejection.

It also left them free to spin fantasies about how she might have really fallen for them if she wasn't already married. It resulted in the majority of the male staff eager to perform small favors. A smile, murmured thanks, or a pat on their shoulder appeared to be reward enough. Tonya managed her best sad puppy dog expression by widening her eyes and letting her lips open slightly. It wasn't hard to look sad and pathetic when she felt that way.

A snort and a long sigh answered her unspoken question. "Knock it off. I'll do it. You're spending way too much time with your dog."

True. When it came to males, he always delivered unconditional love. An image of a smiling Will tempted her. It would be nice to believe there were actual normal men out there.

Chapter Six

THE BIG HAND on the clock hadn't budged in the last ten minutes. It must be broken. Tonya walked over to the clock and placed her hand on it, feeling a slight vibration under her fingertips. Surprise, it ran. Initially, she thought scanning the binder would be a big help as far as keeping her mind occupied, not the gateway to insanity. The arrows on the printer designated where each page should go. Done wrong and the painstaking process would start over. She did it enough to know the drill. A helpful grade school student could do it. Well, for about five minutes. She had lasted maybe ten minutes before her gratitude fled, and monotony set in.

The plain beige walls of the copy room shimmered as if moving. God, she was losing it. Her hand crept up to scratch her neck where her stiff collar rubbed. Her first challenge came in the form of page numbers. Made three copies of seventeen, skipped eighteen, before heading onto nineteen. Grabbing a pencil, she wrote down the latest scanned page.

Lynne stuck her head into the room. "Ready to go yet?"

An audible click signaled clock movement while she mentally cheered. Glory be it was five. Finally, she could stop counting pages. Black dots danced in front of her eyes, blinded by the copier light when she forgot to put down the lid. "Past ready," she mumbled, her finger aiming for the power button on the machine.

"Stop!"

Her finger hesitated a centimeter above the button. "What?" Didn't her friend tell her it was time to go? She twisted her head to glance back at Lynne.

"You haven't saved the scan. You'll lose everything if you just turn off the machine."

Whoa. Taking a large step away from the machine, she collapsed into a folding chair. The thought of undoing hours of menial work had her resting her head in her hands as her friend stepped up to the machine and typed on the copier screen pad.

The mechanical whine of the machine shutting down brought her head up fast. "Um, you saved it, didn't you?"

Her friend placed her hands on her hips and lifted an eyebrow. "Seriously, you have to ask. Of course, I did. I saved it creatively under Tonya S. It will be there when you start again tomorrow."

"Yay." Her unenthusiastic tone reflected her attitude. "I can hardly wait." At least she'd have a night to recover.

The room's overhead lights snapped off, leaving her in the dark. "What the?" The silhouette of her friend stood in the doorway.

"Hurry up. I have a book club meeting tonight. I need to get refreshments."

The dim light limited visibility, causing her to knock into a table before she found her purse. "I'm not sure why you have to be that way. If you don't want to take me home just say so. Besides, you have a chef for a husband. Why do you worry about refreshments?"

Lynne clapped her hands briskly. "Hurry."

They walked down the hallway, past closed doors and dark offices. Unlike Tonya, most people didn't stay long hours. They put in their eight and headed out, possibly to job interviews.

"Why can't Marc whip up something?"

Her friend grimaced at her words. "That's what everyone thinks in my book club. I imagine some of them are even excited about coming to my house because of the superior refreshments." Their heels clicked in tandem as they descended the stairs. The ghost of stale smoke hit them as they turned.

"I wish Jon would smoke outside like the other smokers. He's not fooling anyone." Tonya returned to the subject at hand. "Oh, I imagine the snacks are the highlight of the book group considering the gloomy books you guys pick."

A door slammed in the distance. The building turned creepy once everyone left. She should know since often she was one of the last to leave.

Lynne playfully hip checked her as they reached the ground floor. "The book we were reading when you visited was on the dark side, but they aren't all."

"Does tonight's book provide a satisfied feeling that several hours hadn't been wasted throwing the reader into a deeper funk than when she started the novel?"

Her friend didn't speak immediately, which was answer enough. "Well, the narrator is dying from some incurable disease and is reflecting back on her life."

They both opened the exterior doors at the same time, stepping out into the sunshine. A few hours of daylight remained. Lucky her. She could use them to get her car towed somewhere if Marc couldn't get it started.

"Hmm, sounds like a feel-good story. I appreciate Marc looking at my car, too. It's no wonder you have to make refreshments." Her friend's laughter puzzled her. They headed toward the blue sedan, one of the few cars left in the parking lot.

"Me, bake? No way. I'm heading over to the gourmet bakery on the south side."

An electronic chirp unlocked the car, allowing them both to slide into the sun-warmed interior. A twist of the key brought the car to life, complete with a jangly commercial and heat blasting out of the vents. Lynne adjusted the dials until the air conditioning kicked on. "It was cold this morning."

It wasn't, but Tonya didn't feel like debating it. There was too much to do. Messing with a contrary vehicle had no place in her timetable. Laundry topped the list unless she wanted to reuse underwear. Nope, rather go commando than sink that low. If things went well, maybe she'd hear from Will. A text would be welcome, considering her rotten day. Nothing where she'd have to look decent, especially since she was as far from that as possible.

The drugstore came into view, and Lynne clicked on her turn signal. Her undependable vehicle sat with the hood up and the bottom half of a male body extending from it. Something poked at the back of her mind. *Not right, not right,* the words kept lighting up in big red letters similar to the symbolism in subtitled movies. Having her car break down wasn't right.

Her eyes focused on the tight ass and long legs attired in dress pants. Nice. She couldn't say she spent much time ogling Lynne's husband's rear view, but she knew it wasn't his butt. "Lynne. That isn't Marc."

"Oh, I didn't mention there's some meltdown at the restaurant?"

"No." Her hand slid over her hair, feeling the disarray of escaped tendrils. It probably resembled a bird's nest. "Who's under my hood?" The question sounded strangely provocative.

"Have a breath mint." Her friend shoved an open roll at her.

She chewed one vigorously, well aware of the need. "Thanks." She growled her appreciation, aware disaster day had a few more jolts left. Will backed out from the hood and waved at them. His tie tucked into his shirt, his sleeves cuffed, and a few sizable grease spots decorated the front of his blue dress shirt. The man looked good, even dirty.

Tonya's hand depressed the door handle, wondering how she could delay the encounter when Lynne spoke. "Get out there. He's waiting for you, and I have to get to the bakery before it closes. I preordered Napoleons and éclairs."

"I'll remember you forgot to tell me Will was my road service crew and then you had to brag about the yummy desserts I wouldn't get." She hoped her words would make Lynne feel guilty.

"I'll save you an éclair."

"You better or else," she mock threatened while smiling at Will heading her way.

Her friend drove off with a spritely beep and a wave for both of them. Coward. However, it would be a hard drive to reach the bakery in time. A less caring friend would have had her take a taxi.

Will grinned at her while offering her a greasy hand in greeting, then pulling it back. "I'm dirtier than I realized. I do have good news, though."

"What's that?" She rooted through her purse until she found the plastic wrapped tissues and handed them to Will.

He struggled to extract the tissues from their plastic sheath without success. Tonya grabbed the package back. "Here, let me do it." Their fingers touched, sending a hormonal alert through her body. Tiny little hormones suited up in yellow slickers and raced through her body screaming something about blast off. Okay, her fifth-grade teacher was right about her overactive imagination. The chemistry was still there. Did he feel the same?

She handed him several tissues for his hands. Her tissue wrapped fingers dabbed at his shirt, only smearing the grease into a larger, very noticeable smear. "Great. I made it worse."

Will's eyes flickered downward, checking out the damage. "It's not..." He stopped as he considered. "...anything that won't come out in the wash."

By biting her bottom lip, she stopped herself from mentioning most people wouldn't be able to remove a grease stain. "You had good news?"

"Yes, I do." Will looked back to her car. "From what I was told, I figure it was the radiator. It was. Did you loosen the cap before you left for work?"

Even though she knew nothing about cars, it sounded like a stupid thing to do. "I'm not even sure if I know how to get my hood open. I know, hopeless stereotypical female." She rolled her eyes. "My total automotive knowledge is when a car does something unpredictable, stop driving."

Will stuffed the used tissues into his pocket. His eyebrows lowered as he considered her words. Did he think she sounded like an idiot? It sounded that way to her. Too late to say something else as the man slowly shook his head, probably wondering why he ever thought her desirable.

"It doesn't make sense that the radiator cap was loose. The lid on the reserve was open, too. The system can only work if sufficient pressure is present to circulate the coolant. Without it, like this morning, the car overheats."

Her eyes slid over to her car, noticing a bottle of coolant on the ground. "You had to refill it?"

"Yep, no big deal. The drugstore sells coolant. What puzzles me is why the caps would be loose?"

She could almost hear the wheels whirling in Will's head.

"These things don't loosen themselves unless you do a great deal of rough driving."

She shook her head. "Unless you consider my work commute with a side trip to the grocery and the mall rough." An overheated car would leave her stranded somewhere on the road, an inconvenience at best, and at worst, left her vulnerable to whoever came along.

"No." Will gestured back to the car. "Jump in and see if it will start."

An air of menace rested on her car that hadn't been there this morning. While to most people it was just a car—transportation—to her it was more, part of her identity. The car represented freedom to go wherever she wanted. Her hesitant feet carried her to the car where she tugged on the handle. Locked. Of course, it was.

Will slammed down the hood and waited.

"How did you get the hood up if the car was locked?" She made a point of locking her car every night. No reason to help Clint in his campaign of terror. Her crowded garage contained treasures her mother bestowed on her before moving south. The boxes sat undisturbed for the last six months, leaving her car outside.

"There's a latch under the hood. Come here, I'll show you."

Great, she learned how Clint violated her car. She stood beside Will as his fingers ran under the edge of the hood. He pulled his fingers out and reached for her hand.

"You have to put your hand under the edge to know what you're looking for."

She moved closer to Will as she ran her fingers under the rim, feeling nothing until her fingers bumped up against a protrusion. "I feel something."

"Hmm, you should." Will stepped close enough to brush against her side. The scent of his spicy cologne washed over her, along with the acrid smell of sweat and automobile.

"Push it to the left."

Her two fingers exerted a moderate bit of pressure until the hood popped with a click. It didn't fly open, but it did unlatch. So simple, even Clint could do it. Forget Peeping Tom, the man sabotaged her car. She'd have to clean out her garage tonight.

"Now you've learned something." Will's voice took on a suggestive tone as he spoke into her ear.

Locking the car, and blocking his calls still left her vulnerable. Who set this world up where women were always the ones in danger? Afraid to walk dark city streets or enter a subway car filled with only males. Not too many men worried about old girlfriends stalking them, not that there weren't a few embittered females out there. Most never took physical revenge, but settled for making snarky comments on social media. Even heard there was a site to rate dates.

Her fingers remained under the hood rim as she angled her head to reply. The whisper soft kiss surprised her. Two teenage boys hooting nearby tainted the moment. "Work it."

The catcall had Will backing away. "Sorry. Not the best place to kiss you. I couldn't help myself." His lips tilted up with his excuse.

Stupid boys ruined the moment. Why did she care what they thought? Hands free of the hood, she stepped toward Will, wrapping her arms around his neck. "There's never a bad place." She rocked forward on her toes to reach his lips, ignoring the loud remarks from across the parking lot.

His lips followed hers with a sensual leisure that melted any remaining resistance. What was the reason they shouldn't get involved? One of the teens, probably egged on by the other, yelled, "Get a room."

The thought had merit. *Whoa, girl.*

She allowed her heels to drop, breaking the kiss. His hot gaze threatened to set her ablaze. The expected kiss didn't come. Instead, he stepped back, as a slow, wicked smile grew.

"Start your car. If it catches, I'll follow you home to make sure it's okay."

Her eyes remained on his face until he winked. Oh yeah, follow me home. Why did it take me so long to get it? A quick paw through her purse unearthed her car keys. A chirp from her fob opened the door. Here's to the car running. Part of her worried that somehow Clint damaged her car beyond repair. That would suit him and his nonsensical plan. Without a car, she'd definitely lose her job since she couldn't depend on her friends to tote her everywhere. Not that she'd ask.

The motor caught, alleviating her automotive fears. The temperature gauge needle remained in the cold zone. The good counselor knew his car issues. A metallic clang startled her. Will waved at her from the front of her car, where his hand rested on the hood. Re-latching the hood, that's all it was. God, when did she get to be so jumpy? No need to answer that. She knew.

The view outside her window bested her thoughts. The dress pants tightened over a prime ass as Will bent, picking up his suit jacket off the ground. The man must work out, or run, something. Then again, he hadn't even hit thirty yet. Men didn't age the way women did, constantly fighting off the effects of gravity.

The man in question sauntered to his car, epitomizing everything that was good about the male gender. Kindness, intelligence, and sex appeal, the man had it all. With any luck, she could take inventory of his attributes. A sigh escaped her lips. Listen to her, thinking of reasons to get involved when she knew better. Wasn't that how she ended up with Clint?

Her ten-year life plan didn't include being single forever. By this time, she'd mapped out a perfect future with a sexy, romantic man who set the sheets on fire and brought her coffee in bed, along with the newspaper. Children hadn't been a part of her plan right away. Instead, the two of them would take exotic trips, take tons of photos, post them on social media, and make everyone else jealous. A honk reminded her of the waiting man, as if she could forget.

The speedometer needle barely passed five as she crept out of the parking lot. The motor could drop out of her car. Who knew what mischief had happened to her car? "I'm sorry, Natalie."

Yep, she named her car. Didn't most women? Natalie sounded like a good friend name. Maybe a stronger name would have discouraged Clint from messing with the sedan. Something like Greta, Bertha, or Brunhilda might work. A bigger, tougher vehicle is what she needed: one of those pimped out trucks with huge wheels and a vicious dog in the cab wearing a spiked collar. Besides not being able to afford it, driving might be difficult since it would take a ladder to reach it.

A glance in her rearview mirror showed Will following at a safe distance. Didn't she read something about a man's driving behavior being an indication of his prowess in bed? Those who careened through the streets running red lights and rolling over curbs demonstrated a me-first attitude they brought to the bedroom. A considerate driver equated to a thoughtful lover. Her seductive thoughts came to a screeching halt when she remembered the laundry and garage cleaning. What she needed was an assistant to keep her clothes ready, her house clean, and her shopping done.

How could she send Will home, especially after she'd indicated that she'd be very happy to render a more personal thank you? With the laundry, garage cleaning, and her need to keep the delicious lawyer out of the current cesspool that constituted her life, honesty had merit. "Natalie, as a car would you recommend me coming clean with the man with the wonderful hands?"

A laugh bubbled up at the realization she'd just asked her car for advice. The main issue with being secretive was you couldn't tell anyone. The car made an ominous knocking sound and hesitated for a second. It almost stalled, but the engine caught again. Her laughter stilled. It sounded like her car answered with a resounding no. Of course, it did.

"I thought honesty sucked, too. Dinner might be a nice thank you, although he might be expecting something served a little more horizontal in nature."

The entrance to her neighborhood came up fast, forcing her to turn on her blinker. Almost home and no great excuses to hurry her sexy Good Samaritan on his way. All she really wanted to do was peel off her funeral dress, then she'd start on Will. The car made another ominous knocking sound. She wasn't sure if Natalie commented on her plans or worse, Clint did something to her fuel. Didn't people put sugar in the gas tank? Wasn't sure what it did, but the result was the car didn't work.

No sign of her hot-to-trot neighbor. Good. If she had to push Will out of the house, he would make it to his car. Her hand hesitated in switching off Natalie. What if she didn't start tomorrow? She'd get up extra early in case she needed a taxi.

Will appeared beside her car door to hand her out. Impressive, she almost wished her neighbor observed. It would only make the woman more determined to sink her claws into him. Tonya stared at his outstretched hand for a second. Oh yeah, there were actually men who assisted women from cars who weren't carjackers. *Get a grip, girl. Act like this is something I'm used to.*

Her hand rested lightly on his as she stepped out of the car. A cacophony of barks greeted their arrival. Ah yes, Sebastian, her faithful hound, and occasional relationship preventer. Her teeth slammed down on her bottom lip, causing a small pang of pain. No way would Will enter her house after his last canine encounter. That solved the problem of how to send him on his way.

The smell of garlic drifted on the breeze, reminding her of the nearby pizzeria. Sharp nails on glass scratching indicated Sebastian destroyed her impromptu sheet curtain. Damn. Couldn't just slap a blanket up over the front window without causing questions. Another reason Will needed to go. "I bet you're not looking forward to seeing my dog."

"You'd be wrong." He rattled a small sack. "I brought a secret weapon."

"I'll put him up, so you won't need a weapon." Her back stiffened as she tried to tug her hand out of his grasp, but he held on.

"Stop it." He angled his head until they were eye to eye. "Seriously, you'd think I'd hurt your dog."

Well, not now, Tonya had to admit with him looking at her with a mixture of incredulity and horror. "Um, no, not you, of course." His expression didn't change. "What's in the bag?"

His face relaxed as he explained. "Last night, I went online to figure out why Sebastian took such a dislike to me."

"I wondered that, too." The fact he went home and immediately searched for ways to win over her dog impressed her. Most men would insist she get rid of the ankle biter or at least cage him. "I'll need my hand back to open the door."

His face flushed as he dropped her hand and took a step back. *What was with that? Men thought women's actions were incomprehensible. Yeah, right.* The house key released the lock, allowing the door to open enough for Sebastian's nose to work its way into the tiny sliver.

"No, no." She reached down to push her dog back inside.

Will squatted and opened the sack to shake out decorated dog treats. They looked like gourmet bakery cookies, but cost even more. Tonya priced them at the Pet Bakery at the Fashion Mall. She decided she didn't love her dog that much, or more appropriately she couldn't afford the treats. With her luck, Sebastian might expect the luxury all the time. Might even go off his grocery store brand dog food in protest.

He used the dog treat, gesturing in the direction of the door and squatted with the treat in hand. "Let him out. This is neutral territory. He considers the house as much his as you do. I came into his house without even a proper introduction. My appearance brought out the guard dog in him."

Sebastian provided companionship on lonely nights, but it never occurred to her he might object to company. He could be jealous. Her fingers cautiously pushed the door open, expecting the worst. In his current position, there were so many other places Sebastian could bite Will. Her puggle plunged out of the front door, dancing on feet too small for his sturdy body. His dance abruptly halted when he spotted Will. His large protruding eyes focused on the treat in Will's out-stretched hand. He took one step in Will's direction before looking back at her. Was he asking permission?

Will waved the cookie slowly back and forth. Pushing it closer to Sebastian, then pulling it back. "Come on, boy, closer and you can have the cookie."

Tonya wanted to stop the cautious bonding session before her dog did something regrettable. Before she could utter her objection, her pup made a rush for the treat, snapping it out of Will's hand.

Sebastian carried the cookie almost a foot away, scarfing it down in three bites. His long tongue rolled out searching for any missed crumbs. Finding none, he eyed Will speculatively. The canine's rigid walk highlighted his natural reserve as he approached the still squatting man and sniffed his open hand. "Yeah, get a good sniff. I'll be around a lot. Might as well get familiar with the scent."

The keys she'd worked out of the lock dropped to the porch with a metallic clatter, scaring the dog, who hid behind Will. That might be progress of some sort. "That's all I can take." Will rocked to his feet and shook out each leg.

The white bag remained on the cement near Will's legs, but, more importantly, close to Sebastian. The dog moved almost silently toward the bag. It was as stealthy as her overfed pooch had ever been. Her expectation was for him to grab the bag and run, akin to a cartoon character. Before he could enact his impulsive plan, Will picked up the bag without even a backward look.

"I'm holding onto the last dog treat since I'll need it later."

Need it later. Hmm, someone thought he was staying. "Thanks for following me home. You'll probably want to get home and eat."

His silence rattled her, causing her to ramble, filling the empty space between the two of them. "Yeah, I have to do laundry." No sign he took the hint. "I'll have to clean out the garage to get the car into it tonight." Nothing. "I know I should invite you to dinner, but…"

He placed two fingers on her lips, stopping her babbling and effectively wiping her mind clean of any coherent thought. "Invite me in."

His fingers still rested against her lips. Using her right hand, she pushed open the door behind her. His hand dropped as he walked past her into the house. Sebastian followed in a rush, not even bothering to glance at her. Tonya scooped up her keys and followed. What just happened?

The cell phone in Will's hand caught her attention. "What's the closest pizza place?" he asked with one lifted brow.

"Delmonico's."

He repeated the word into the phone.

"What are you doing?"

"Getting ready to order. Pepperoni okay?"

Any idiot could recognize the man was ordering pizza. Still, she wasn't sure how he managed to get into the house after she'd decided against it. It was the last thing she needed with the unpredictable Clint lurking around her. "Yes. Pepperoni is my favorite. Banana peppers, too."

He ordered the pizza, giving the right address without even asking her what it was. Will turned and winked at her.

"Thanks for letting me get dinner without some huge fuss about wanting to fix me some grand meal since I rescued your car."

As if. She wasn't even sure what she had in the pantry besides rice cakes and peanut butter. Many nights it served as dinner. "Can you take a rain check?"

His eyes twinkled, announcing his amusement. His head dipped, and he kissed the top of her head. "I was teasing you." He spoke into her hair, sending a tiny chill down her neck and across her shoulders.

"I knew that."

"Sure. Go get changed. We have thirty minutes before dinner. Enough time for you to start on laundry while I carve out a car-sized shaped space in the garage."

The man went alpha on her all of a sudden. It wasn't totally off-putting, but surprising. Weren't they at the stage where they tiptoed around one another? "Why would you do that?"

His chin went down as his eyebrows went up. The look conveyed disbelief.

"Explain it to me. Obviously, I'm missing something."

His head shook slowly side-to-side as he held open his arms. "Come here."

Tonya had no problem walking into his embrace and resting her cheek against his chest. His arms closed around her. It had definitely been a hug-worthy day. He spoke next to her ear. The words took her a second to decipher what each one was.

"I'd do just about anything to spend time with you. Imagine you figured that out by now. As for the garage, I don't want your stalker undoing my automotive work."

Stalker. The word had her stumbling backward, breaking out of the embrace that seconds before she'd never wanted to leave. "Stalker? How did you know?"

Chapter Seven

TONYA'S HAND SLAPPED over her mouth as she stumbled back. He knew and didn't leave the house as fast as possible. Not quite the reaction she expected. Instead, he offered to clean her garage. "How?"

The living room furniture consisted of a rocking chair and a small loveseat. Will wrapped an arm around her waist and pulled her to the loveseat.

Her world, as she knew it, must be contained in a human-sized snow globe. Fate, destiny, or a mean-spirited giant shook it hard, almost daily these past months.

It would be good to share the burden with someone, even if a potential lover was not the ideal person. It would only make her sound like a poor dating prospect: someone who couldn't pick out a decent companion. Didn't people assume like attracts like? However, there were plenty of couples to disprove that theory.

The loveseat, or more likely the dress, irritated her, chafing her legs. She wiggled one way rolling up on one hip, but not relieving the discomfort. Will regarded her with some interest and a great deal of amusement.

"I'll give you the short version, and you can go change out of your torture dress."

There had to be something semi-decent she could change into, even if it was her yoga pants. "Go on, how did you know? No one else knows."

A sound between a snort and a cough emanated from him as he folded his arms behind his head and stretched his long legs in front of him and crossed them at the ankles. "Ya know they don't allow any stupid boys into law school."

His eyes rolled up a bit, and then he coughed for real. "I think I should clarify that statement. Plenty of stupid boys get into law school, but they don't have the smarts or determination to pass the bar. There's only so much that money and Daddy's connections can do."

He held up one finger, stalling what she was going to say. "Never mind. The example wasn't a good one. Let's just say I realized you're on the edge. Whenever the phone chimes, you tend to jump. You're worried about your job, but Lynne insists you're the hardest worker in the entire company. She may have mentioned a deadbeat boyfriend, also."

"She did?" A heads-up would have been nice on that one. "Why did she do that?"

Will reached for her hand, intertwining their fingers. He studied the joined hands as he spoke. "I think she was trying to encourage me in a backhanded sort of way. I mentioned something about how someone like you wouldn't be interested in me."

Oh no, she could imagine the scene all too well. Someone else might have played it more aloof, encouraging the man to shoot for the moon and he'd still end up among the stars. The combination of Marc and Lynne listing bad relationships or dubious choices she'd made probably made her sound like a four-star loser. The truth was they didn't even know the worst of it.

"You must think I'm a mess." Her first instinct was to go lock herself in the bathroom, but eventually she'd have to come out. "Friends." She grumbled more to herself. "I told her I liked you."

"I know." Will brought their joined hands up, tucking his under to brush a light kiss across her knuckles. "I like you, too. She didn't say anything bad. The stalking thing I figured out on my own. With all the questions about blackmail involving photos and emails, I knew it had to be about you. The car was a definite cheap shot."

Her urge to hide vanished as he explained. In his rich, soothing voice, he made it sound as if everything would work out. He brought her hand up for another lingering kiss, allowing his tongue to slip out and lick the sensitive skin between her fingers. The unexpected sensation tickled and made her forget about everything but living in the moment.

The doorbell rang. No way the pizza could have arrived that fast. No loud delivery car idling in her driveway. Will stood and motioned her back to the bedroom. "Go get changed."

Something wasn't right on the other side of the door. Sebastian stopped in his efforts to reach the dog treat bag to glance at the entrance. Mesmerized by the possibility of a snack, a reluctant growl was his only response. As the homeowner, she should open the door, but free-floating anxiety pushed her toward the bedroom more than Will's words.

What kind of person allowed Will to handle what could be a messy situation? A tired person. It could be a dedicated church member inviting her to their storefront church, or possibly the FedEx man delivering a gourmet omelet pan that a late-night infomercial had convinced her she needed.

The door opened and closed, but she heard no voices. The thought of Clint standing on her porch made her tear off her dress, forgetting the side zipper and ripping it in the process. Good riddance. A black V-neck T-shirt and black yoga pants would serve for yoga class, a poetry slam, or if she chose a life of cat burglary. Tonight, it would work as she entertained a surprisingly complex man.

Barefoot, she padded down the hallway, unsure what she'd find in the living room. The lack of sound might indicate Will left on his own or with a little help from her neighbor. Sebastian, the white treat bag pinned between his two front paws, was chewing his way through the bag and making a huge mess in the process. It surprised her that Will would let him. She figured he'd take the bag from her pooch even if only to establish dominance and prevent a slobbery pile of shredded paper.

His back was to her and his head bent. All his attention was focused on something in his hands—an object she couldn't see. A delivery box normally wouldn't fascinate the average person, unless the mystery of a woman on the verge of losing her job ordering unneeded gourmet cooking tools captivated him.

He grumbled to himself, unaware of her entrance. "What asshole leaves something like this?"

The words reignited the sense of unease she thought she'd put to rest. "Leave what?" Her curiosity piqued, she moved closer in an attempt to look over his shoulder.

Will spun, shoving the object behind his back, bumping her in the process. "Oops."

Tonya made a grab for Will's arm to keep her balance. Realizing her predicament, he reached out to hold onto her before she fell. A thump drew her attention. Whatever object triggered Will's irritation tumbled to the floor. Secure in his embrace, she closed her eyes for a second, enjoying the warmth, the stability, and even the motor oil smell wafting off him.

The shirt needed stain treating before it became unsalvageable. The memory of her predicament forced her eyes to open and look to the floor. A crude doll lay face down on her floor. A doll, how odd. It made her wonder if some child had lost her dolly. Even from this distance it was obvious that it was handmade, and not by a skilled craftsperson. It resembled a sock puppet with rubber bands on it making an indentation for the head, arms, and body. The tiny purple floral dress it wore resonated, stroking a memory she couldn't quite bring to the forefront of her mind.

"It's only a doll. Nothing to get worked up about." Why anyone would leave it at her house didn't make sense. The neighborhood mainly consisted of retired autoworkers who had lived in the same house for the last forty years. Years ago, kids ran the neighborhood, but they long since have grown up. The few new faces included herself and the amorous divorcée next door. Young families preferred the newer neighborhoods with homeowner associations and commons with playground equipment.

His embrace tightened, keeping her from picking up the doll. "It's not important. I'll get rid of it."

"Yeah, okay." She agreed while wiggling in his arms. At first, she thought his arms tensed because of desire, but his set face didn't resemble a lover's. A fierce mask of determination shaped his features. His entire demeanor changed when she left the room after the doorbell rang. It had to be the doll or the deliverer.

The floral pattern clicked, but she needed a closer look. Instead of struggling, she went limp and slid out of Will's arms. An unwholesome dread penetrated her fingers as she grasped the doll.

A masculine grunt behind her indicated her would-be guardian had dropped to his haunches along with her. The material retained a silky feel she remembered. The doll was still face down as she brought it up to her nose. A citrus perfume wafted from the fabric. A loud gulp filled the silence. It took a second for her to realize she swallowed.

Why didn't she immediately realize the doll's dress came from her favorite shirt still bearing residue of her Happy perfume? When had the shirt gone missing? The color and bust twist made it a go-to shirt for weekend wear. It made the girls more apparent without resorting to a hydraulic lift bra. Its disappearance nettled her, even causing her to go online to find a copy, which she hadn't. Her fingers loosened, dropping the doll.

No exact date came to mind, but she did know it hadn't been too long ago. Someone had been in her house. Her suspicions crawled over her skin as if tiny invisible bugs, leaving hairs up in their wake as they moved on. "Clint." She growled the name.

What else had he done? He could have installed cameras or microphones, recording their very conversation. She saw it once on a television news show. Her eyes cut to Will's concerned face. Good thing she hadn't given in to her initial attraction last night. No reason to give Clint a free show.

His hand under her elbow steadied her as her thighs ached from their squatting position. His breath brushed past her cheek as he spoke. "I don't know about you, but this crouching is getting to me. Why don't we sit down and talk this out?"

A grunt of agreement escaped her lips as she pushed forward on her toes to rise. "Yeah, let's do that." Her shoulders drooped as she stood. Any energy she'd felt at the unexpected appearance of the handsome lawyer drained away. Clint stood between them as real as any person, separating her from Will as effectively as a quarantine notice. One bad decision made on a night she'd felt especially lonely would ensure her single status.

Anger slowly slid across her skin, replacing fear, as she sank into the overstuffed loveseat. The soft snuffling sound of a dog treat decimated fanned her resentment. Her head snapped in Sebastian's direction. She shook her index finger at the canine. "You were supposed to be some sort of protection. I imagine you were had for the price of a pig ear or a pork chop."

Sebastian's survival instincts produced a hesitation in consuming the cookie, or it could have been a thoughtful interval. On a normal day, his momentary stop might be regret, but not today. No, today was the no-good rotten day where everything went wrong. Technically, things had been wrong for a while. Unfortunately, today threw the spotlight on it. The doorbell rang. What now?

Will stood, reaching into his back pocket for his wallet. "Pizza."

The loud rumble of a car without a muffler or a crumbling one, idling in her drive provided reassurance, along with a lively knock. The door swung open to a red-shirted teen holding a pizza box. Nothing to fear, unless she considered calories. Right now, she could benefit from some comfort food. The teen left with a whistle at the sizable tip Will bestowed.

Tonya headed into the kitchen to clear off the table and retrieve a bottle of red wine. Too bad wine was all she had. Something stronger would help blot out the morass her life had become. The urge to feel sorry for herself overwhelmed, but she couldn't succumb: couldn't fall apart while Will was still here—too much to do, which now included scouring the house for bugs and cameras. Calling a locksmith would be on the list, too. In the end, she had no one but herself to depend on. Getting drunk wasn't an answer, especially with work the next day.

Two pieces of pizza and a glass and a half of wine later, Will approached the elephant in the room topic. "Tell me about your stalker."

"I'd rather not." She'd rather place her hand on a hot burner than discuss her need for human companionship that resulted in a mistake that would haunt her indefinitely.

His hand covered hers, stilling her nervous nail drumming. "I know. The truth is we have to examine everything to know how to keep you safe. What might he do next? You need documentation of what he has done to obtain a protective order."

Clint respecting a piece of paper? That would never happen. Rules, legal or otherwise, were not for him. Still, Will was a professional. "You do have a point. So far, all I've been doing is reacting to Clint's latest bombs."

"Understandable," Will replied and ripped off the flyer from the top of a pizza box. He flipped it over to its blank side and pulled a pen from his pocket. "Let's start with his name."

Goodbye romance. Nothing kills a budding relationship more than discussing a psycho former lover. "I appreciate your help, but I'm only going to cooperate if you let me wash your shirt. I need to start a load if I want clothes tomorrow."

His answer consisted of loosening and pulling his tie off slowly. In other circumstances, she'd find the move seductive. Even now, her lips canted up on their own as he unbuttoned his shirt.

"Don't get too excited," he teased. "I have on an undershirt. My grandfather was a tailor. He'd have my hide if I ruined a hand-tailored shirt with sweat stains."

Her first guess that his clothes were expensive was right. "All the more reason to get out those pesky grease stains." He shrugged out of his shirt, exposing his tightly fitted white T-shirt. She sucked in her lips to keep from whistling. If he looked that good with clothes on, her imagination ran unchecked for a moment stripping him down. Broad shoulders filled out the fabric along with a well-defined chest, not the body of a desk jockey.

He tossed her the shirt, not unlike a stripper, she thought. Shirt in hand, she headed off to the washer. The man was hard to figure out. That shirt removal reminded her more of an all-male revue move. Not that she was an expert on that, far from it. She did see one show when in Vegas for a conference. It had been, her mouth twisted as she tried to remember, four or five years ago.

The show consisted of gorgeous toned men of all different nationalities strutting their stuff, convincing every woman there that the show was her private fantasy. A tall order, considering how many screaming women there were. A couple of squirts of stain treatment and vigorous rubbing prepped the shirt. Warm water, maybe hot to release the grease, she spun the washer dial and threw some towels and panties into the load. The clothes mixing in the hot water would be more intimate than she and Will would ever get.

The sight of Will with his hands behind his head, his biceps bunched, reminded her of one of the revue dancers. He resembled one that had shimmied near her table, popping his muscles, and wiggling his oiled ass as he slid by, causing the women to shriek and wildly wave bills. She couldn't really remember the man's face, too concerned with hiding her own, in case someone was filming the entire show to share on social media.

Corporations, especially hers, took a dim view of workers having a social life, especially a fun one. A particularly vivid dragon tattoo on the dancer's back caught her eye, though not for the usual reasons. Tonya shook her head as she remembered thinking about the needles, pain, and time that went into the tattoo.

Will looked up at her entrance, put down his arms, and straightened in his seat. "Okay, let's start with some facts. See what can be done to limit his harassing behavior, then we'll hit the garage."

"Why are you so nice to me? Is Lynne paying you?"

His lips turned down at her words. "No, no one is paying me. Just because I'm a lawyer doesn't mean I'm motivated solely by money."

Whoa, stepped on a nerve there. Sebastian bumped against her leg for attention, but she chose to ignore him as she slipped into her kitchen chair. She'd get over her anger at the dog before the night was over. When she adopted him, she never thought he'd be the world's greatest guard dog. She didn't know she'd need one, never considering Clint would be an issue, especially since he peeled out of her life so fast, he left tire tracks.

The sound of the pen clicking reminded her Will was waiting. Not sure if she should apologize, she chose to anyhow. "Sorry, I didn't mean it that way. I guess I'm not used to men being as nice to me as you have been these last couple days."

Her words depressed her as she settled into her seat. Will's words were low-voiced, but she still heard them. The gravelly bite to his tone initiated a twist in her lady parts.

"You need to find a better class of men to date."

Summed up her love life in one sentence. "You're right. I'll work on it right away as soon as I deal with the worst class."

Instead of replying, Will put the pen to the paper. "Name. Where did you meet?"

Why did this feel like a police investigation or a trial? Well, the man functioned as a lawyer. Her hand wrapped around the wine bottle. Another glass of wine might make the distasteful matter go down better. "Clint Fairweather. I met him at a party of some sort. I didn't have any friends that knew him or could vouch for him. He was good looking and smooth. I drank too much and felt sorry for myself because I arrived alone. Somehow, we ended up together.

"It sounds a bit weird, but I don't even remember having a courtship. You know the usual give and take of dating. The awkward dance of drawing closer, then backing off again for various reasons. You know what I mean, right?"

The slanting words on the cheap flyer stopped as Will looked up. "Contrary to Marc's analysis of my love life, I've dated, and ran through the relationship scenario a time or two. As a divorce lawyer, I've heard dozens of how we met stories told through gritted teeth with the conclusion being, if I knew now what I knew then, I would have killed him."

The idea had merit. Her lips pursed. Maybe not killed him, but at least not taken him home.

"Explain to me how you became a couple, then not a couple."

Ah, he wanted to know something she hadn't figured out. "Not the usual way, of course. I'd love to be part of a couple: people who do fun things together, go on trips, walks, ride a tandem bicycle together, watch movies, and hold hands. That type of thing."

"You need a better class of men." He repeated the refrain.

She exhaled loudly. "No one knows that better than I do." The man made her lose her train of thought. Her fingers picked at the cold cheese on the leftover pizza. What was she explaining again? Oh yeah, Clint. It would be hard to pretty up the fact she brought home a man she didn't know from Adam. The same man somehow took control of her life. He was more of a squatter than a beau.

"Um, after we met, Clint assumed 'I'd do' as far as companion services went. It was more as if testing out a vacuum as opposed to wooing me. To be fair, I was both low and lonely. He presented himself as a prize, and my sad mistake was that I believed him."

"Hmm," Will murmured as he wrote a few more words down. "What made you so low?"

Talk about a conversation she didn't want to have. Couldn't see how it mattered, but maybe it did. It also demonstrated that fate was a fickle bitch. She delivered a handsome, caring man, then provided all the baggage that would scare away everyone. Honesty was not the best policy. Whoever came up with the saying 'no regrets' had never done anything dubious and didn't have a stalker ex.

God, she didn't even want to think about that night. "Ah, yeah. It was a holiday party. I'd just heard my ex had married, in a big splashy destination wedding."

Will opened his mouth and shut it without saying anything. He rubbed his bent index finger against the crease forming between his eyebrows.

"I bet you're wondering why I cared if my ex married. His name's Jeremy, to prevent any confusions among the exes." It never made sense to her why men didn't get my ex got married first thing. Her right hand ran through her hair, a nervous habit she'd developed as a child and had never dropped.

His lips stayed in a non-committal line while his eyes showed interest. "Did you still love him?"

"No, not at all. In retrospect, he was actually a good person, but no chemistry between the two of us. We'd been broken up for more than a year when I heard the news." The scene came back to her as if it had happened only seconds earlier.

The only reason she went to the party was Trudy would have harangued her if she didn't. The woman was such a drama queen that she would make it all about her. Tonya would be the villain in the story. In the end, she pep-talked herself into it by mentioning free food, booze, and possibly, single men. She hadn't been out in a while. It would be good to be around people. She even squeezed into her silver sparkly mini dress that always got second looks when Lynne called warning her. She wanted her to find out from a friend, rather than a frenemy ambush.

Will stared with his mouth open—the same look Sebastian got when she danced around the house. Clueless, the man was clueless.

"Jeremy married before I did."

Obviously, the man heard her, but chose not to reply immediately. Will held up his index finger. "Let's see, if I understand this. Jeremy, your ex, who you felt no emotional attachment to, married."

Tonya nodded eagerly, excited that he might be getting it.

The second finger went up as he continued talking. "News he married devastated you so much, you forced yourself to go to a party and hook up with Clint, the stalker." He shook his head slowly side to side.

Her high hopes that he was the one man on Earth who understood the trauma of an ex marrying first died a swift death. Somehow, his summary made it sound silly and a little skanky, too. Her hand shot up to ruffle her hair, but she stopped in mid-ruffle, realizing what a mess her hair already was. "I didn't care that Jeremey met someone and fell in love. He deserved to. The fact he managed to do so before I did made me the one with the issue. The unlovable one."

She hadn't meant to say all that, even if she felt it. No wonder she'd been easy pickings for Clint, especially after three cosmopolitans. Her cuticles drew her attention. If she looked at Will, he might have that disappointed look. The same one she always saved for Sebastian when he piddled on the floor.

His arms wrapping around her from behind startled her, causing her to jerk and hit his chin. She'd never even heard the man move. Definitely not the response she expected. Tonya leaned back into the hug. If only she knew what he was thinking.

"Getting married isn't some type of competition. Trust me; I'd know. The women who come through my office did compete to snag the best provider. They married early, so sure they were getting a good one. Now in hindsight, they had plenty of indications why their husband wasn't their soul mate, but chose to ignore them because they wanted the magazine-worthy wedding. Do you think that might have been part of your sadness?"

Good question. One she'd never allowed herself to consider. "I don't know. I'm not the kind of girl who made some wedding scrapbook. If I found someone I loved, I'd be content to get married in front of a judge or even fly to Vegas."

"Wedding scrapbook?" He repeated the words slowly as if they were foreign. Probably were, being a man and all.

"It's a scrapbook with pages torn from magazines of dresses, food, location, even songs for the future wedding. Some girls start their scrapbook as young as twelve."

"Twelve." Will appeared stunned by the idea. "After years of planning, no doubt the real wedding or groom can't live up to all their fantasies. No wonder so many women get divorced. It's like dreaming of being a superhero and finding out you have no superpowers."

Her familiar path into self-pity deviated as she considered Will's clients. "Are all your clients women?"

"Not all, but most, probably seventy-five to eighty percent of the people who initially filed for divorce are women. The husbands are the respondents. Now and then we'll get a man who files after having his woman tailed by a private eye."

The image of a man in the dark, taking photos of an unknown couple, made her shudder. She directed a glance back over her shoulder at the large living room window. A person could see into the kitchen if he stood at the far end of the window with his nose pressed to the glass.

Will hoisted an eyebrow at her shudder, but continued talking. "Most men don't want to divorce, even if the marriage is rocky. About the only time they'll consider it is if there's a prenup or someone waiting in the wings."

Men had no trouble leaving in her experience. The concept pulled her away from the night-darkened window. "Why don't they want a divorce?"

Will grinned at her. "Spoken like a woman. Men don't want to give up half their stuff, pay alimony or child support, but it's more than that, much more. They surrender their identity. They are no longer part of a couple. No longer a loving father because their ex makes sure to team their name with deadbeat or absentee. The career they've invested so much time into to provide for the family simply becomes a job, one they resent because all they do is work to support their relocated family.

"Inevitably, they lose the house, another part of who they are. The kids only call when they need more money. In the end, they're alone. A few men are excited at the prospect, thinking they'll be the hot stud they never were in their twenties. They soon discover middle-aged women are even fussier than their younger counterparts are. They discover relationships are almost impossible to start and difficult to maintain. That's why so many stay in mediocre marriages. Better the devil you know."

Chapter Eight

WILL'S WORDS MADE her reconsider all the stories she'd heard about horrible exes. Maybe the ex-husbands aren't always as bad as she previously thought. Any horror story she ever heard came from a bitter ex-wife. All this new insight into the male psyche made her think. She might give other men the benefit of the doubt, but not Clint. The man emanated evil. Her best bet was to be prepared for the worst.

What was the deal with the doll? Her hands flattened on the table as she pressed down to stand. Using the table made her feel a bit like her granny. Her shoulders felt as if they could belong to a senior citizen. She shimmied the offending body part, loosening it up a bit.

"What are you doing?" Will called, still seated at the table.

Tonya glanced back over her shoulder. "No worries. Just getting the doll."

The sound of the kitchen chair tumbling to the floor heralded Will's sprint into the living room. He leaped past her to pick up the doll with a dishtowel he must have grabbed from the stove handle. He held the wrapped doll away from his body as if radioactive.

"Why did you do that?" Here she thought Will had the corner on mental stability. Should have known better.

"Evidence. Need to keep it clean for the police." He walked back to the kitchen, holding the doll in front of him. There appeared to be something hanging from the doll. She'd never really examined it after realizing it sported a portion of her favorite blouse.

The reality of Clint in her house, snooping through her things and taking her favorite blouse made her blood pressure rise. "You touched it. I touched it. Clint's a private investigator. He would know enough not to leave fingerprints."

Will slipped the towel wrapped doll under the open lid of the pizza box. "Why'd you get involved with a P.I.?" Frustration tinged his words, but the accusatory tone remained.

"Hey!" She threw up her hands. Why was everything always her fault? "I did not think ahead to ask his profession. Even so, I'd never considered his profession as something that could cause problems down the road. In fact, at times I thought dating a detective made me safer. Do women ask you what you do, and then leave in the middle of the date when they don't like it?" Good comeback, she congratulated herself as she took her seat.

Instead of replying, Will's eyes were still rolled upward as if re-membering. He finally spoke. "I usually never get to the actual date. Once a woman hears I'm a divorce lawyer and with one of the most cutthroat agencies in town, most confess to a rekindled romance with their ex. One mentioned she was entering a convent. One date developed indigestion after hearing the details of my profession and had her dinner boxed up."

Tonya made a sympathetic sound. Really, he didn't strike her as overbearing or argumentative—traits she assumed a lawyer normally possessed. While he launched into a story about a vanishing date, she slid her hand under the lid of the open pizza box and snagged the doll.

"I even asked a little old lady to go in and check on her. The pity-ing look the woman gave me when she came out discouraged me from dating, which was one reason Ericka and I continued to hang out. I decided until I changed to something like Intellectual Properties Law that I'm undateable."

The doll firmly in her grasp, she turned it over. A roughly drawn face with black marker pupils, a J for a nose and a large O of a mouth.

A few loops of yarn represented her hair. The string that initially piqued her interest was a noose woven out of three individual yarn strands. Taped to the front of the doll's torso was a small yellow note. Written in block lettering to disguise his handwriting was a message.

Come back now, before it gets worse.

Her fingers traced the string noose. She never thought Clint would ever escalate this much. It was probably just a threat. Yeah, a threat, she inhaled deeply and put the doll down. Telling herself it was merely an intimidation attempt didn't stop the stomach acid from working its way up her throat.

Will's larger hand covered hers, warming it, and giving her the illusion she wasn't alone in this mess. Her hand turned under his to wrap her fingers around his. For a moment, the lyrics to some oldies song came to mind, about the two of them facing the world together. It wasn't the two of them. Will's luck ran toward vanishing dates and convent-bound females. In the book of bad dates, he'd entitled her chapter "Woman to Avoid."

Sebastian slept under the table, giving the occasional twitch and growl as he chased imaginary rabbits or dream bones that sprouted legs. Knowing her dog, more likely the latter. Will stood, pulling her up with him.

Still holding one hand, he reached for the other one. "Look at me."

His serious expression hinted at a contrived excuse to leave, not that she'd blame him. It equated no help with the garage or tangling their legs together as they slid across the sheets.

"Do you think I'd walk out on you because a psycho stalker targeted you?"

Yes, would be the correct answer, but she hesitated. Was this a trick question? "It would be the smart thing to do."

His hands tightened around hers. "No, it would be the cowardly thing. Women who don't run screaming from me when they discover what I do are rare. Besides, there's a connection between the two of us. Maybe you could use a smart lawyer on your side. Your ex may know how to break and enter, but I can nail him for it."

The prospect of retribution tempted. Her eyes fluttered closed as she inhaled. The low hum of the fridge, along with the occasional slumberous growl from Sebastian, filled the waiting pause. She wanted to believe so badly. Her eyes opened to his waiting gaze. An answer, he expected one. The selfish part of her wanted him to stay, not even walk out the door tonight. Still. "You could get hurt. I don't want you to be a target."

He lowered his forehead to the top of her head. "Don't worry about me. I'm a big boy. I even know a few moves that could put a hurting on Clint."

His toned physique did make her wonder what he did in his leisure time. In previous relationships, she was alone when it came to dealing with personal issues. Could she trust him? Often people told you what you wanted to hear, made promises they had no intentions of keeping.

Will's forehead stayed against hers as he spoke. His words danced across her face before being absorbed into her skin. "I can feel the wheels whirling in your head. Try trusting someone for a change. Let me help. You'll be doing me a favor."

Michelle had pointed out earlier today that she needed to let people help her. At the time, she thought her co-worker was referring to herself. Her failure to trust anyone was wearing her out. "Okay." She said the word softly but knew he heard when he pulled her closer for a sweet kiss. Unlike the heat and urgency of the night before, this kiss sealed an unspoken agreement. There was a promise in it. The message passed through her, warming and healing her frayed nerves. She wasn't sure how she knew, but an epiphany that everything would work out crystallized. The kiss ended much too soon.

Her right hand stroked his cheek. The beard shadow provided friction, slowing her fingers as she moved them across his temple into his hair. "What should I do first?"

He reached for her wandering hand and kissed her palm before closing it. "We have to make plans for the worst-case scenario."

Oh yay. Not what she wanted to think about, but his idea had merit. She sighed heavily. "You're right."

"Do you want to go into the living room and talk about it?" Will tried to guide her into the other room.

Tonya tugged back, refusing to move. "Not that room, he can see through the sheers."

Will looked over his shoulder, staring at the windows. "I'll take a look around outside." He dropped her hand and headed for the door. Clint could be waiting outside with a gun.

"No, not tonight. We have a garage to clean."

His eyes bored into her, probably under the impression that his sheer will would move her. "Have it your way, but while we clean, we talk. It will give us a chance to come up with contingency plans. If we prepare, then he can't succeed in his harassment campaign."

Her head nodded vigorously, glad she'd kept him from prowling around in the dark.

"You need lights around your house." His thoughts mirrored hers. "Tomorrow, we'll head out to the home store and get some."

"Money." Now was not a good time to spend money. She followed him as he strode to the garage as if he lived there. The washer shuddered, reminding her it was almost finished.

He spun around, grabbing both her shoulders. "Screw money. We're talking about your safety. I'll pay for it. We can even go with solar lights if you want."

The stern line of his lips indicated a level of seriousness she'd never yet associated with Will. He reminded her a little of an action hero ready to save the world. "What do you think is the worst-case scenario?"

Moving in with her mother after losing her job was her personal nightmare. Her mother's small house was crammed full of crystal bells. On their last visit, Sebastian careened into a display case causing the case to tilt dangerously. Swift action on her part kept the case upright, but some of the bells did hit one another, leaving small chips and a few cracks. Careful placement of the bells hid the damage. With her mother's poor vision, maybe she'd never discover it. Of course, if the three of them lived together, it wouldn't be the last such incident.

"Kidnapping." Will practically spat the word. "Assault." His brows came together as he threw out the next possibility.

Much worse than living with her opinionated mother in her patio home. Her heart skipped a beat as she tried to accept the slick investigator could resort to such measures. "I don't think Clint would do that."

His face contorted for a second before he directed his intense gaze back to her. "Do you read the newspaper? This week a husband strangled his wife. They were arguing about paint colors. One of my clients ran over her husband, breaking his leg, when they couldn't agree on dog visitation rights. Now you tell me a man, who systematically threatens you, broke into your house and left you a doll with a noose around its neck, won't hurt you? He's a textbook example of a loose cannon. Don't forget he's armed."

"I got that. Let's clear out the garage. Might want to get the car in before anything else happens." The boxes her mother left behind could possibly distract her from the frightening scenarios Will injected into her imagination. Wasn't fear of losing her job enough?

"When Mother decamped to Florida, she had too much stuff for the moving van, even after she downsized all her necessities. Apparently, the boxes contain whatever she doesn't need right away. We'll move them to the spare bedroom. It's more of a storage spot anyhow." Her shoulders raised in an involuntary shrug.

She hadn't even entered the spare bedroom in weeks. Dust bunnies and possibly spiders may have claimed the room as their own. The room's shade stayed in the down position, keeping the room's condition a secret. Five years ago, when she bought the two-bedroom house, her goal was to turn the bedroom into a joint office and guest room with a colorful sleeper sofa. Color coordinated floral prints on the walls would pick out the colors of the rug. Everything would be from a page in a decorator magazine. In her house fantasy, old college friends would visit and comment on her darling guest room. It never happened. Tonya lost touch with most of the old gang due to long hours, but mostly because she didn't want to share her life or lack of one.

Her finger stabbed at the light switch beside the interior kitchen door to the garage. The weak light fell on the haphazardly stacked boxes, along with forgotten garden tools. The garden was another one of those things she was going to do that vanished under the stress of her life.

Will waded into the mess without comment. Placing one foot in front of another, he walked toward the door, counting under his breath.

"What are you doing?" she asked. A slow perusal of the junk revealed a discarded floor light. It would help brighten up the place. Intent on plugging it in, she almost missed his answer.

"Measuring for the car and the space you'll need to swing open your door and walk around the car. Most of these boxes pushed against the walls, stacked two high might even give you the space you need."

An electrical outlet located, Tonya squatted to plug in the light. A hum announced it was a fluorescent light before showering the area with a yellowish illumination. The bulb resembled the one used in dressing rooms that made her look wan and sickly. Did the garage no favors either, revealing stained and pocked walls she meant to drywall or at least paint. Why was this turning into a walk down her failed intentions lane? "Does that help?"

Will stacked boxes close to the garage door, introducing some order into the chaos. Already, the area didn't look as bad as it did seconds ago. That could be because a sexy man muscled her stuff into compliance. His tight T-shirt revealed the play of his muscles under the cotton as he squatted to lift a box that rattled ominously. Too bad about the T-shirt, although a bare-chested Will might result in the car not getting into the garage. A single dull clank signaled a warning.

A small dark skillet showed due to the tear on the box. "Put it down, now." The whole box would crumble, spilling out the cast iron cookware her mother insisted on buying after watching a cooking show advertising it. No wonder Will was struggling under the weight. A long-legged leap fell short of reaching Will's side before the box self-destructed, throwing cornpone and muffin pans, along with a huge Dutch oven that resembled a caldron onto the cement floor.

Will jumped, dropping the empty box, but not soon enough to avoid the huge pot. "Damn!" He hopped on one foot, wincing.

The memory of moving the cookware came to mind. Instead of boxing the items up, they rode in her mother's trunk. They only ended up in the box after their arrival at her house. She remembered carrying each piece, thinking how heavy and useless it was. "Here, let me help."

Ducking under his outstretched arm, she tried to take some of his weight as he teetered on one foot. The only decent man she'd met in years got hurt helping her. "Good news is you weren't barefoot."

His shoe sat abandoned on the floor and his fingers stilled on rubbing his sock clad foot. A grunt served as his reply. He rested the wounded foot on the floor, rocked back on his heel, and wiggled his toes. "It's not broken, but Italian loafers aren't the same as steel toed boots."

The mention of his expensive shoes reminded her of the divide between the two of them. Will shifted his weight off her and dropped the arm draped around her shoulder.

"I'm glad it's not broken. That will teach you to help a woman in distress." *Babbling alert, stop now.* One part of her brain realized what she was doing, but apparently, it didn't control her mouth.

"A man in your profession probably sees women at their worst, all sneaky, and determined to strip the man of everything he has. Ranting about ruining the man in every way they can. Knowing what you know, about how vicious the gender can be…" Her mouth finally stopped in mid-sentence. *Did she say that?* Using the heel of her hand, she hit her forehead. The offending pot grabbed her attention because she couldn't even meet Will's gaze. It would either be full of contempt or a suspicion that she was one of those women who turn on a man like a coiled cobra.

"Hey, don't do that!"

The shouted warning came too late. Her foot connected with the pot before she even considered the fact she was barefoot. "Ow, damn it to hell and back and twice around the bank."

His shadow fell across her as he bent to sweep her into his arms. Tonya hooked one arm around his neck, snuggling into his shoulder. Her cheek nestled against his shoulder, allowing her to breathe in his scent: a combination of fading cologne, a whisper of dryer sheet from the T-shirt, a strong note of sweat, mixed with a muskiness that identified the man. Ah, an aroma she could grow used to. Will worked his way through the maze of boxes, into the kitchen, and carried her into the living room. He backed up to the loveseat and collapsed onto it, holding her tight in his arms.

"Pretty inventive cursing out in the garage. Can't say I ever heard that before." He chuckled as he eased her onto the loveseat.

"My paternal grandfather, Leonard, majored in cursing. My grandma usually caught him at the first damn, so he had to improvise after that." His close embrace as he carried her into the house made her forget about her hurt toe. She couldn't remember anyone carrying her. It made her feel all ultra-feminine. True, she was no lightweight, which might explain one reason she never received the delicate flower treatment. Then again, maybe she never dated the right kind of man. Her big toe took the major brunt of the collision. It throbbed, reminding her of the fact.

A closer foot inspection required resting her ankle on her opposite knee. Hard to tell if any bruising occurred with the dark purple nail polish. The reddened skin around the nail didn't reassure her. Will wrapped his hand around her foot with his thumb on her instep. "Wiggle your toes."

She did. They ached a little, but still moved. No immediate care visit required, but it would be flats for a few days at least. The thumb resting on her instep moved in an oval pattern. "Will, what are you doing?"

"Must be doing it wrong, if you don't know. Go ahead and put both feet in my lap."

Only one foot was bruised. She almost pointed out the fact. Instead, she waited to see what he'd do next. The heat from his palms warmed her foot as he massaged it.

"Oh, that feels great." She moaned the words as she pushed back into the cushions. "I pay for pedicures just to get the foot massage, but they're not this good." Her eyelids fluttered shut as she relished the experience. "You're, ah, too good."

His throaty laughter made her to open her eyes a sliver, catching a satisfied smirk on his face. *Go ahead and grin, as long as you keep those magic fingers on me.* As if hearing her unspoken command, he continued to massage her feet, taking special care with her big toe.

It felt so good after the day she had. Of course, there was no practical reason for him to be massaging her feet. *The hell with practical.* "Where did you learn to massage feet so well?"

"Would you believe I was a slave boy to a powerful foreign queen?" he teased.

She could hear the smile in his voice. Opening her eyes, she met his gaze and tried for a stern one of her own. "I don't believe any woman, queen or not, would ever let you go with those hands."

"Oh, is that so?" He winked as he smoothed one hand up her calf under her yoga pants. Tonya giggled as she playfully batted at his hand. It wasn't as if she wanted him to stop, far from it. Sebastian, who had been ignoring the two of them, glanced up at the window and growled, catching her attention and dampening her playfulness. Clint was out there, watching.

The two of them were so obvious in the front room, practically a reality show. A jerk brought her knees up to her chest, removing her feet from Will's ministrations. It put her in the fetal position without the lying down or whimpering, although she did consider the whimpering, briefly. His confused gaze lifted to hers, but she pretended not to see the question in his eyes. "So, how did you really learn to be such a great masseur?" Goose bumps pebbled her arms as she considered an unseen watcher.

"A woman was the reason behind my skills. She was a queen." Will stretched his arm along the loveseat back and angled his body toward her, moving into the area she'd recently deserted. "Queen of our household."

"Oh, that was nice." He massaged his mother's feet. It looked as if she'd uncovered his secret ick factor, a mama's boy. Good, she discovered it before making a fool out of herself. It also explained the lack of a current girlfriend. No one would meet mama's standards.

His finger touched her nose. "You wrinkle your nose when you hear something you don't like. Might as well say, that's super creepy. Why don't you listen to the whole story before making any snap judgments?"

Caught. Her skin heated under his scrutiny. A car door slammed outside, pulling her attention to the window, expecting to see a face pressed against it. Nothing. The foot thing tended to be on the peculiar side, but she should hear him out. "Go on."

"My mother was a single parent. My father dropped out of my life so early I can barely remember him. I can almost remember his voice, but not what he looked like. My mother worked twelve, sometimes sixteen-hour shifts as a nurse. It was hard on her feet and aggravated her arthritis. I wanted to go somewhere with friends when I was eleven. My mother wouldn't let me. My reaction consisted of stomping around the house and grumbling about the unfairness of life."

The image of a younger, much shorter Will throwing a hissy fit crowded out the idea of Clint lurking in the bushes. "Did it help?"

"No. I even peeked in the living room to see if my behavior moved my mom. Instead of looking sad, weeping tears of remorse, she rubbed her feet. When I saw the pain on her face, I realized how hard she worked. Did I ever say thank you? No, I threw a tantrum like a spoiled brat."

"Aha, I know what you did." She loosened the death grip she had on her knees, allowing them to relax, unfolding in the direction of Will's legs. "I bet you decided to rub her feet to show your appreciation."

"That's what I like about you. You're always giving me altruistic motives." He winked at her. Holding up his hands, he pointed his thumbs back at himself. "I wanted what I wanted. I saw an opportunity to go with my friends. That was my first foot rub attempt. It may have been more painful than pleasurable. A funny thing happened. We started talking as people, not mother and child. My goal was to take off with my friends, but my mother was telling me stuff I never knew about myself, my dad, and even her teenage life. I wanted to hear it. I discovered as long as I rubbed her feet, she talked."

"Hmm. Doesn't sound as creepy as I thought. You must love your mother a great deal. I can't say my mother and I have great conversations. Most are about how I've disappointed her somehow. Mainly, she's irked with me because I wouldn't let her dictate my life since my father is no longer around for her to order around. You're a good son." She patted his hand, moving closer to him on the cushion.

His lips twisted to one side before he answered. "I hope I was a good son. I would have made more of an effort if I'd known she had cancer. Would have gone back to visit her more, instead of hanging out at the frat parties."

"Yeah, I know what you mean. I felt the same way when my father died." Awkward moment. She did what she did best in emotional moments. Move. She stood up and stretched. "I better go check on that laundry if I want clothes tomorrow."

"You do that," Will commented as he stood. "I'll go finish the garage."

Did he just say that? Tell her what he was going to do in her house. The kitchen door to the garage slammed, indicating not only did he say that, but also did it. Tonya placed her hands on her hips, looking in the direction of the garage door. Her initial urge to tell him how it was propelled her a half-step in the direction of the door.

Wait. Think about this. He'd organize her garage. A task she'd put off for months. It would leave her free to finish the laundry. Not a bad thing, but did he have to be so alpha about it?

Her hand went to the back of her neck, massaging out the stiffness. Alpha, huh, that might not be so bad. There were times she thought Clint exhibited alpha traits, but turned out to be selfish jerk moves instead. Her cell chimed as she moved to the washer. The phone vibrated across the counter as Tonya glared at it. Couldn't be Will. Not too many people called her, outside her mother and Lynne. Could be news she'd won one of the many contests she entered. A trip for two to Miami would be nice or even the gas grill. With her luck, she'd win the year's supply of bamboo toilet tissue. She didn't really want it, but felt sad for the company since so few people had entered.

She lifted the phone cautiously as if it might bite her. Lynne's number flashed across the screen. "Yo," she answered in a raspy voice.

"Give it up, Tonya. I told you once you had a good Rocky imitation. I lied because we're friends."

She pressed a hand to her heart, even though her friend couldn't see her. "You wound me!"

"Yeah, right. You sound as if you're in a better mood. I take it Will got your car going?"

"He did." Her eyes cut to the garage door. His ears could be burning. Just in case, she walked into the living room, but feeling visible from the outside, she moved down the hall to her bedroom.

"That's not all he fixed, I assume. Did the good lawyer do some mood elevation, too?"

"Really, Lynne, we just met, but he's helping me with a huge issue I have."

"You told him, but not me. What gives?" An edge of irritation flavored her friend's tone.

Great, she'd have to tell Lynne. Somehow, Will thought it was best to tell. It would keep Clint from using the photos as leverage. It would also have more people alerted to any funny goings-on. Inhaling deeply, she rushed through the entire sordid story. She wasn't sure how her friend would react.

"Hmm, that's it. I had some shots done for Marc. Posed topless on his motorcycle. I'm not sure there aren't too many women who haven't done a boudoir shoot or at least thought about doing it. The real question is why is he doing this crap now? You guys haven't been together for over a year."

"Yeah, you're right. As you know, he dumped me to chase after another woman. Good chance that woman finally tired of him. Now he's doing his campaign of terror to chase me back to his arms. Will thinks he tampered with my car."

Will stuck his head in the open doorway. "Garage is clean. I'm jumping in the shower, if you don't mind."

She shook her head, while covering the mouthpiece of the phone. Lynne's voice rattled off questions before she even had the phone to her ear. "Yeah, he's here. Yes, he did clean up the garage so I could get my car into it. I need to go now. See you at work."

Lynne would probably harass Marc to call Will. Off-key singing mingled with running water. It was nice to have a man in the house. Her teeth sunk into her bottom lip. Correction. It was nice to have Will around.

Chapter Nine

A SMALL STACK of panties sat on the dryer. Tonya held out Will's shirt, inspecting it. Good, the oil spots weren't there. Considering how he stepped in and got a particularly obnoxious monkey off her back, washing his shirt didn't even qualify as sufficient gratitude.

The bathroom door opened, spilling out fragrant steam. A damp Will stepped out, attired in only her cartoon beach towel. His damp curls gave a boyish appeal that his toned torso gave lie to. She whistled long and low. Not her best behavior, but nothing ever came out of her bathroom looking like sex on a stick before.

He held up a wad of dirty clothing. "I was wondering if you wouldn't mind washing these for me? The pants are a washable synthetic blend."

Water droplets glistened on his shoulders, drawing attention to their width and muscles rippling beneath the skin as she reached for his clothes. Damn, how could she have ever thought he was average looking before. Their hands touched as she took his clothes. The tingle that had almost become routine zapped her extra hard. *Keep your eyes on his face.*

With the clothes tucked under her arm, she turned toward the washer. Black socks in the laundry tub, she pulled the pants inside out to negate the wear. She held up the striped boxer briefs and grinned, imagining them on Will's very fine ass. In her fantasy, she was taking them off him. The sounds of the fridge closing indicated Will's location.

"Good luck finding something edible. Popcorn might be your best bet. I keep it in the freezer." She heard the freezer door open, along with the click of Sebastian's nails. Anything connected with food interested him.

"Thanks. Hope you don't mind my helping myself. Garage cleaning is more strenuous than my usual desk jockey job. I worked up an appetite."

She held up his white T-shirt, debating if she should throw it in with the dark clothes. As long as it was on cold and quick wash, it should survive. "Hey," she called out, feeling playful. "Anyone ever tell you that you have the body of an exotic dancer?"

The sound of coughing, possibly choking, had Tonya dashing out of the laundry room. Will held onto the counter with one hand. Sebastian snapped up whatever fell to the floor. His jaws chewed rapidly as if he feared she'd steal his treasure.

Her upraised hand hesitated over his back. Laughter slipped out through the hand he had raised to his mouth. The Heimlich maneuver would not be necessary. Still, her hand landed lightly on his back. The long spread of warm skin tempted her. *Hey, I'm human.*

Her fingers felt the shift and movement of his muscles as he straightened. With regret, she dropped her hand and met amused eyes.

He motioned in the direction of her dog. "I found a cheese stick, but Sebastian ended up with it. Your question surprised me."

That made sense since it surprised her, too. Her normal habit of keeping her lips shut when it came to provocative remarks went south went she met Will. The empty wine bottle sat on the table, reminding her normal reticence probably went with the wine. "You never answered me."

"Well," he drew out the word. "No one ever used those exact words. Are you quite the expert on male dancers?"

"No, only once, about five or six years ago. I couldn't remember the name, some touring company, I think."

His eyes showed marked interest. She hurried to add. "It wasn't like I wanted to go, but all the other women were, and if I didn't..." She stammered to a stop, her face reddening, refusing to admit she more than wanted to go.

A slow, mysterious smile pulled at his lips. "Did you have a good time?"

Ah, how to answer that. A dozen gorgeous guys parading around in next to nothing, acting if they were playing a starring role in her private dreams. The light bouncing off their glistening bodies, the women screaming, the numerous empty drink glasses littering their table, and a dancer with eyes like Will smiling down at her as he gyrated his hips, inviting her to tuck a twenty in his G-string. No, couldn't be. The cartoon towel covered him thoroughly from waist to knees. She needed smaller towels.

"Odd question."

He glanced down at the towel. "Do you have anything I can wear until my clothes are dry?"

"Ah yes, I have a closet full of clothes from all the various men who have passed through my home and left their clothes behind." His eyebrows shot up at her statement.

"Of course not, but I do have a bathrobe that might work. It was my father's. I took it as a remembrance, since he spent so many Saturday mornings wearing it. It's a little shabby, but should do the trick."

"I'm not looking for anything fancy. Something that will cover me up enough for me to drive your car into the garage. Wouldn't want the neighbors to get the wrong idea."

His words made her snort. Wrong idea sounded like any romantic action went out the window. "Yeah, a robe won't give them the wrong impression."

The microwave beeper squealed. Will angled his head at it. "Started some popcorn, too."

Tonya opened the microwave door and snagged the hot bag. His feelings hadn't changed because he knew she had a crazy stalker. A steak knife made two slices into the bag and relieved some of her frustration. It would be much more satisfying if the bag bore Clint's likeness. Stupid asswipe, forcing her to take all these precautions.

"I understand that you don't want my car outside to get vandalized. Aren't you worried about yours right now? It's sitting out there, all vulnerable." Once the words were out, she wanted to recall them. Will might drive home in her dad's old bathrobe.

He moved closer, which lifted her spirits—maybe the night wasn't lost. His hand dipped into the popcorn, crushing her hopeful mood. "Not worried." He breathed the words close to her ear. "State of the art alarm system. If Clint has any intelligence, he'll know just getting close to the car will set it off."

"That's good." Sure, great for the car and okay for Will, too. When did the man go from expectant lover to home security expert? The transformation must have occurred outside the drugstore, when he realized she couldn't open her own hood.

The crunch of Will working his way through the popcorn brought Sebastian closer. The pampered pooch head-butted Will until he flipped him a popped kernel, which he snatched out of the air.

"Aha, he caught it." Will's eyes lit up. He tossed another kernel, laughing as Sebastian seized it, too.

Tonya sucked in her lips, thinking the dog got more attention than she did. Maybe she should be snapping food out of the air. The man continued to toss popcorn that her dog caught.

"Well, I'm going to shower while you two have fun."

Will looked up in mid-action, as if he might say something, but instead another piece of popcorn flew through the air. Enough already, she stomped off to the bathroom, as well as a barefooted person could. Call it walking with attitude.

A shower would be good. A chance to wash her troubles away, if only. Still, the warm water pelting on her skin would work as a mini massage. Since Sebastian and Will were bonding over popcorn, she'd take her time.

The water steamed up the small bathroom, causing Tonya to flip on the exhaust fan before she stepped in the shower. The hot water made her grateful for the larger water heater she'd installed last fall. At the time, she couldn't rationalize a larger heater. The sales representative talked her into it, claiming it would improve resale value.

A liberal dollop of bath gel on the pouf released a blackberry fragrance as she lathered her body. What did Will use when he showered? He certainly didn't smell like her bath gel. A damp bar of deodorant soap in the corner of the shower answered her question. Ah yeah, she only used it when she smelled disgusting.

She stroked the pink razor against her thigh. No real reason to shave so high, it wasn't as if anyone would notice. Didn't stop her, though. The loud exhaust fan made it hard to hear anything. No Sebastian barking, no knock on the door, nothing. Her fingers lathered the shampoo into a sudsy mess. Her eyes closed before it could burn them.

Did Will leave? That would be weird considering his clothes weren't dry. Sure, he could wear wet clothes home or the bathrobe for that matter. Did he want to get away that bad? That could explain the peculiar look on his face when she mentioned showering. Unease wrapped around her. An instinctual sense warned her she wasn't alone. Did he lock up as he left? Would it matter with Clint, who bypassed locks?

The rungs on the shower curtain clattered across the rod. Tonya squeezed her already closed eyes tighter. This was it. Her life would end as a modern-day version of the shower scene from *Psycho*. Did the actress fight back? She couldn't remember. Fear wrapped its fingers around her throat, making breathing difficult. She should know how to do this. Inhale, exhale, she mentally coached herself as everything slowed. No way she was going down without a fight. She reached toward the tub enclosure shelf where her long handle back brush rested. Might not be much, but better than a pouf. With a firm grip on the handle, she spun, opened her eyes, and brought the bath tool down with a resounding crack, right across Will's shoulder.

"Oh my God! It's you!"

He rubbed his reddened shoulder. "I guess that's what I get for sneaking into the shower without asking."

Her eyes journeyed from his chagrined expression to his abused shoulder, down to his flat stomach, a happy trail that led to a wilting arousal. The two pieces of the broken brush reminded her of her deed. No wonder she had a sucky love life. Apparently, the lousy males she left alone, but clubbed the good ones.

"I'm so sorry. Let me rub your shoulder. I can get you some ice for it." She started to step out of the shower, but Will placed a restraining hand on her arm.

"First, you need to rinse your hair." He guided her back under the stream of water. His fingers moved through her hair, lifting the soapy tendrils to the spray.

Was this really happening to her? It could be a scene from a movie, not the horror genre by a long shot. His breath tickled as his wet chest slid against her back. Ah, heaven. She inhaled deeply, missing his comment since her body went into hyperdrive about the time she opened her eyes and saw every delicious inch of the man.

"Do you condition?"

Ah, had she ever heard any more romantic words? Wait, what did he say? Condition? She managed a nod, gesturing with her right hand to the top rim of the shower enclosure where the conditioner sat.

"Got it." A juicy exhale of the bottle indicated his current action.

Once in college, she showered with a boyfriend. A popular magazine implied it would be a sensual experience. It was all elbows and complaints. True, she was the one who wanted to shower together, and it was a very small shower. Still, she thought the guy could have put more effort into it.

Strong masculine fingers worked the conditioner into her hair, massaging as they went. Her tension from her crazy day slipped away with each caress of her scalp. His hands moved from her scalp, down to her neck, kneading away the stress. She leaned back into his hands as the water cooled. No matter, she had a very hot body behind her.

"Let's get that rinsed off before the water turns ice cold." His hands on her shoulders gently directed her under the spray. His fingers lifted from her shoulders to run through her hair again. "Hard to believe twenty-four hours ago, I imagined this very moment in the shower with you."

"Really?" She turned in his arms, hooking her hands behind his neck. "You acted pretty cool tonight. Hard to believe naughty thoughts were in your head, when most of the time you were either talking home security or bonding with my dog."

The hands that rested at her waist slid down to her ass. One hand cupped each butt cheek. He flexed his fingers before pulling her into his body. "Does that feel cool to you?"

She stretched forward to breathe her reply into his ear. "Anything but." The movement nestled her closer to his desire. Her lips landed a brief kiss near his temple, before resting her cheek against his beard-shadowed face. *Paradise.* The perfect ending to a day, wiping away all the trouble it took to get here. The blackberry scented steam contributed to the dreamlike atmosphere.

Their slick skin adhered to each other. Perhaps their attraction was fateful. "It's almost like our bodies are trying to absorb each other. As if we were one once upon a time."

"Hmm." Will nuzzled her neck, making her legs go liquid. She'd probably dissolve into a puddle at his feet if her arms weren't around his neck. He pulled back, giving her the slow, sexy grin, she associated with him. "Maybe we could take this into another room?"

Her fingers played with the wet lock of hair plastered to his face. "We could do that. Were you thinking the garage, now that it's clean?"

A playful slap on her ass jolted her.

"Hey, it was a legitimate question. Maybe the kitchen. Fun with food and all that."

Instead of answering, he dropped his hold on her. Cold, along with a sense of isolation, danced up her arms and slid down her back, leaving confusion in its wake. *Am I doing the right thing? I don't really know him. Isn't this the same mistake I made with Clint? If a detective has me running scared, what will a lawyer do to me?*

The spray stopped. Will straightened from turning off the water. Noticing her attention, he winked. Her expression had to be a weird one, since she'd been considering his dangerousness as a spurned lover before they'd even done the deed. Her eyes also lingered on a tattoo she couldn't quite make out on his shoulder.

"Come on, let's get you warmed up." He wrapped one arm around her as he pulled the shower curtain back.

How could such a considerate man be bad? Oh, she knew what she was doing. Talking herself into doing exactly what she wanted, even knowing the risks associated with it. Her upraised foot landed on the fluffy bath mat. Life had dealt her such a crappy hand lately. *With my luck, I will slip and hit my head. Will would have to rush me to the hospital. The doctor will keep me overnight for observation while the rest of the staff laugh behind their hands as Will explains how the accident occurred. A couple of younger nurses would give him lingering looks when he mentions shampooing my hair. The conniving angels of mercy will slip him their numbers as the orderly rolls me away.* Her other foot made it safely onto the mat. Those nurses were going to have to look elsewhere. Tonight would be her lucky night.

Her pulse quickened as she packed away all her reasons not to fall in bed with Will. Her woeful lack of a love life status would transform in a matter of minutes, make that several minutes. A piercing squeal permeated the house. Not a siren, it could be something went wrong with the washer, but it never sounded like that before.

Will's guiding arm around her waist tensed, and then fell away. "Damn asshole is messing with my car!"

Tonya watched silently as he shoved his arms into the bathrobe, covering a tattoo on his shoulder. His tight jaw and lowered brow didn't promise a night of endless pleasure, especially when her ex was doing God knows what outside. He darted out the door before she could remind him about Clint's gun. The exterior door slammed, jolting her into action.

"Wait," she yelled the words as she ran out of the bathroom. The reflective glass of a nature scene she'd placed in the hallway reminded her that clothes might be advisable. Great, clothes, what a time waster. Indecent exposure was the thing she'd been trying to avoid. Back in the bathroom, she pulled her yoga pants and shirt over a wet body.

"Hate Clint. Hate that I ever met him. Wish he'd die. If I ran out there without a stitch, the man would laugh himself silly and probably take a photo, too. An excellent reason to get me fired."

By the time she got to the front door, Will swung it open from the outside, talking as he entered. "The jerk wad is gone. I heard him burning rubber as soon as I got outside. I'm calling the police."

The angry man strode past her. Forget her status change from lonely single to satiated female, not that she would have made it public, but still. Her shoulders dropped as she turned to follow Will.

Cell up to his ear, he spoke in staccato sentences. "Will Robinson here. Yes, that's my name. Ask the chief. He knows me. Send a car to this address. Attempted robbery. Scared off the miscreant. Yes, I know. *Send the car.*" He rattled off her address.

Police. That meant neighbors peeking through blinds and speculating on her behavior. She'd never contacted the police because she didn't want such a scenario. Clothes might be useful, especially for Will. His would go in the dryer. Her obvious nipple stand would merit a bra and a less wet top, too.

His bare feet made a slapping noise on the wood floor. The act of shoving his wet clothes into the dryer kept her busy, refusing to acknowledge his presence behind her. The police would be no help. The officers might get some titillation over the fact that sexy photos were involved, but wouldn't take it seriously. Her fingers pressed his pants into a ball before flinging them hard into the dryer.

"Hey." His comment reminded her he was behind her. "No reason to take your anger out on my clothes. The police had to be called."

Her violent pivot sent her tumbling back against the washer. Really. Decided to call the police now. Summoning up her best glacial stare, she sent it his way. He shuffled backward about a foot. "Whose choice was it to call the police?"

He placed an open hand against the sliver of chest the robe exposed. "I made the decision since it was my car."

"Your car, your precious car!" She shoved past him, jabbing him with an elbow. A childish thing to do, she knew. "I have to get dressed since the police are coming."

Sebastian had popped out from the table, his sanctuary in times of high emotion. Her brisk walk with balled fists swinging by her side sent him scurrying back under the protective forest of wooden legs. Smart dog, smarter than most men she knew, especially since she could hear footsteps behind her.

"Tonya, wait. It's not about the car." His hand landed on her shoulder.

She spun around, wanting to fight and relieve the frustration from Clint's scare tactics, her job insecurity, and the buildup to a sexual release that didn't look like it was coming any time soon. "Okay, Mr. Big Shot Lawyer, what's it about?"

The lines between his eyebrows relaxed as he replied. "You, it's about you. It's about creating a documented history of harassment. You'll need that to get a restraining order. It's about fighting back."

The intensity of his eyes faded, replaced by a tenderness that erased most of her anger, but not all.

"I don't want to fight back. It might get worse. I just want it to stop."

"I understand." His hand cradled her cheek. "I wish I knew some other way. As a divorce lawyer, I know this area. Occasionally, a spouse harasses one of my clients. In a few cases, my client was the stalker. I know the ins and outs of the legal system. We have to press back."

His profession and experience gave validity to his words. They made sense, but Clint didn't operate on logic. "I'm afraid Clint will only up the ante."

Will nodded. "That's a possibility."

The words chilled her heart. The man could work on his comforting tactics. The thumb of his hand cradling her face brushed gently over her temple. The gentle action blew on the ember left behind from their steamy shower encounter. *Why am I so upset with him?*

His lips moved, attracting her attention, drawing her. She even leaned forward a couple of inches until his comment penetrated her lust-fogged brain.

"Expect the worst. Then plan for it."

She jerked back as if a released rubber band snapped against her face. *Damn it, not what I wanted to hear.*

A series of hard knocks on the front door threw Sebastian into a barking frenzy. The police had arrived. The city's finest would naturally assume they'd been doing the mattress dance as opposed to their real activity: planning to withstand a siege from a lunatic ex-boyfriend.

The responding officer treated them both with calculated courtesy, but his irritation still showed. He may have considered the visit a waste of time. Could be he wanted to solve or prevent a real crime, especially considering his youth. He didn't have the years behind him that made a quiet night a good thing.

Somehow, despite the ratty bathrobe and nothing on underneath, Will projected an air of professionalism. He kept steady eye contact with the man as he explained the situation with three mentions of my friend, the chief. The young officer didn't start writing things down until he mentioned he was a lawyer. Odd, that would impress him more.

They both looked at her. Oh, it was her turn. Great, she wasn't sure what to say. When in doubt, act. She stood and went to the kitchen to retrieve the doll. A discarded paper napkin kept her fingerprints off it as she carried it. Both hers and Will's were already on it, but no reason for more. Instead of handing it to him, she placed it on the nearby end table.

"The doll is a threat, as you can see, but even more frightening is that the dress is made from one of my favorite tops. He came into the house and stole it from my closet. Even now, there could be bugs or cameras in the house." Her eyes went to the corners of the room near the ceiling looking for tiny cameras.

The officer pushed the doll around with his pen. "This isn't one of those voodoo doll things, is it?"

Black magic, voodoo, do I need one more thing?

Will's hand wrapped around hers, giving it a strong squeeze. He answered for her. "Oh, no, no voodoo. Terroristic threatening, yes. Breaking and entering, yes."

"Okay." Clicking his pen, the officer acted more animated as he wrote down a few notes. He asked without glancing up. "When did the break in occur and did you notify the police?"

"I'm not sure." This is why she didn't bother calling the police. It made her sound stupid. Another finger squeeze reminded her that Will believed her story. "I didn't know he'd been in my house until the doll came tonight. I'd missed the top for a couple of weeks and assumed it was in the laundry or at the bottom of the closet."

The police officer looked up, pinning her with a dubious stare. "No sign of a break in? Wouldn't the dog set up an alarm? Did he have a key?"

"No, he didn't have a key. Not sure it would matter, since he's a private investigator and bragged about his skills breaking into places to investigate."

The officer murmured under his breath. "Hate P.I.'s."

"As for the dog, he's not exactly guard dog material. He barks at everything, including falling leaves. The neighbors tune him out, no doubt. He can also be had for the price of a dog treat."

Will leaned forward, blocking the officer's view of her. "Don't forget the vandalized car."

He made a few more notes. "What's the name of your ex, who you think did these things?"

Tonya's lips twisted to the side, considering the man's tone. Doubtful, that's what it was. "I don't *think* he did it. I know it. He sends me threatening emails at work and texts."

"I'll need a copy of those emails."

He would. "I deleted them. They were on my work email." The man stared uncomprehendingly.

"Actually, nothing is ever gone on a computer. You could get your IT guy to find them."

A moan escaped her lips as she imagined asking Richard to look up the messages. All she had to do was explain it was a police matter. Maybe he might locate them before she got her layoff notice. Will let go of her arm and wrapped his arm around her shoulders.

"That's okay," he reassured her. "Do you have any of the texts on your phone?"

Her initial impulse was to state she'd erased those, too, but she hadn't. Last night had been a busy night with dinner at Marc and Lynne's and meeting Will. "I do have some. Along with the number he used."

"Good deal," the officer commented, smiling a little.

Tonya went off in search of her phone, considering how much happier the officer was once he thought there might be a real case. She shook her head as her hand closed around her cell.

After a call back to the station for procedure, the officer bagged her phone and took it with him with promises she could pick it up on the following day. The two of them stood at the door, rather like a unit, or a couple, and bid the police officer goodbye.

Will yawned as she closed the door. The earlier adrenaline drained away, leaving exhaustion behind. "I'll go get your clothes. They should be dry now."

Intent on draping his pants over a hanger with the crease in place, she didn't hear his approach. His hand reaching for the hanger startled her, making her yelp. Not like weird things hadn't been happening around her.

He hooked the hanger on the laundry room doorknob, joining his clean dress shirt. He pulled his boxer briefs out of the laundry basket. "This is all I'll need for tonight."

"What—" She abruptly stopped her question, already knowing the answer. A tiny geyser of excitement erupted, only to have worry and exhaustion tamp it down. Her hand went to her hair, which was a mass of tangled dried curls, similar to Medusa. No, she wasn't feeling sexy.

Will, sensing her thoughts, or more likely reading her expression, dropped a kiss on top of her head. "No worries. Big day tomorrow. Change locks. Outside lighting to install. You need to get a new number and focus on your new job search."

She was doing everything in her power to hold onto this job. "I don't want a new job."

"Yes, you do. You hate your current job. It has you walking on eggshells."

She allowed him to wrap his arm around her shoulders and guide her down the hall. "I do kinda hate my job."

He chuckled and flipped off the laundry room light. "I know. Remember, prepare your worst-case scenario."

The expression reminded her of a disaster movie scenario. Men with dead eyes, attired in black leather motorcycle chaps with rifles slung across their backs would fit the image. "It sounds so ominous. Like the end of the world."

His fingers tightened around her shoulders, pulling her in for a quick hug. "It's not. Taking away his ammunition. That's all."

He had a point. "I have put out feelers for jobs. If I change my number, how will they reach me?"

"Has it been more than a week?"

"Yes."

"Are you absolutely crazy about the possible positions?"

She could guess where he was going with this. "No." The jobs she applied for were the same thing she did now.

"Hmm," his lips twisted as he drew out the sound. "Either the job is filled or it never existed. Some companies run a help wanted ad to create a pool of applicants when there is no actual job."

If that were the case, she didn't want to work for them anyhow. Probably the type to fire someone for being late once. They could because they'd created a group of potential employees.

In the bedroom, he turned down the bedspread. "Crawl in. I'll go take care of Sebastian."

Tonya stared up at the ceiling. "I forgot about my dog. I'm so frazzled, but he didn't." Her last thought was she needed to stay awake until Will returned.

SEBASTIAN'S SNUFFLING BROUGHT her gradually awake. Her arm hung over the mattress, giving her pooch the opportunity he needed. His long tongue tickled her fingers, garnering her attention. "Okay, okay. I'll let you out."

Odd, her dog was on the floor instead of in the bed as usual. A masculine grunt coming from behind her stiffened her spine. What the? Her drowsy mind raced, trying to recall the previous night. Will helped her with her car, cleaned the garage, and called the police. Then there was the shower. Remembered pleasure had her stretching back her leg to feel a hair roughened leg behind her. Fell asleep sometime after the police came. It was Will behind her, wasn't it? Had to be. Concern about Clint entering her house with ease drew the hairs on her arms to attention. What were the chances of the fool slipping into bed with her?

Fear grabbed her, holding her immobile for a few heartbeats. Sebastian's panting drew her out of her panicked stupor. If Clint were in the bed behind her, would her dog act so normal? Probably not, then again, didn't he allow the man to root through her closet without

THE BAD DECISION LEGACY

much fuss?

The mattress creaked, giving her warning before two arms wrapped around her. Her scream dammed up behind her heart already lodged in her throat. Sebastian's eyes grew larger, and he wagged his tail even harder. Was Clint behind her? Had he somehow won her mercurial pup over?

"Good morning," a familiar masculine voice purred into her ear. "I texted last night I'd be taking a personal day, but I assume you're still heading to work."

Will. Her held breath hissed out, making her sound like a balloon losing air. Her body melted into the mattress. *Thank God!* She cleared her throat, managing to push her heart back down into place and coughed out the lingering fear.

"Yes, I need to go to work." Tonya rolled over and snuggled back into his embrace. For a few seconds, in his arms, she felt protected. An illusion, of course. Clint could blast through her front door. Her cheek rested against Will's bare, warm shoulder. *It would be hard leaving this.* "What did you say you were going to do today?"

"Depends on what you trust me to do." He dropped a kiss on top of her head. "My plan was to make sure your locks were changed to a key dead bolt. No using credit cards or screwdrivers to shimmy it open. Next on the list is motion sensor lights that will illuminate any tricky stunt Clint might pull. Finally, you need an alarm system. I have a friend who owes me."

With each item, Tonya mentally calculated the costs. Switching the locks was necessary. "I agree the locks need to be changed, but everything else is too expensive. What's this stuff about me trusting you? I slept through the night peacefully with you by my side." It amazed her. She hadn't awakened once during the night. Hard to remember when she'd slept that well.

His fingers came under her chin, tilting her face upward. His eyes met hers. His still looked sleepy, with the corners of his thick lashes caked with what her mother called fairy dust, but everyone else called crud. His eyes warmed as he spoke. *Why women weren't throwing themselves at his feet was a mystery.*

"Let me handle everything. I'll be earning my way out of karma payback for the divorce pain caused by my adeptness at tightening the financial noose. As for trusting me, we've only known each other for little more than two days. How do you know I won't turn out to be as bad as Clint?"

The words gently rumbled the ear she had on his chest. The vibration tickled her to the extent that she didn't catch what he was saying until Clint's name came out of his mouth. "What did you say?"

His hands moved up to her shoulders and gently pushed her away from him. He spoke slowly, enunciating each word. She knew because she watched those beautifully sculpted lips. "How do you know you can trust me? That I won't turn out to be another Clint?"

A moment of doubt clawed at her, but simple logic conquered her momentary queasiness. "For a second, I wondered, I doubted, and then I realized how stupid that would be. Two nights, we've been together. It wouldn't have taken too much for you to put your move on me. If that's what you were after. Instead, you fixed my car, cleaned my garage, and even bought me pizza." The whole thing dumbfounded her. "You're like no one I've ever met."

He pulled her in for a fast hard kiss on the lips. "Go get ready. I'll drive you to work. We can get breakfast on the way."

Will rolled out of bed as if that settled it. Tonya pushed up into a sitting position, watching the man dress. "Whoa, you're a lot more alpha than I originally assumed."

Uncertainty gathered in his eyes. "Are you okay with that?" He stretched out a hand to help her up.

Her fingers wrapped around his hand and allowed him to pull her upright. She kept her thoughts to herself until they were standing only inches apart. Rocking up on her toes, she leaned forward, whispering into his ear. "I like it, a lot."

When it looked like he might kiss her, she dropped back on her heels just to be perverse, before whirling away to the bathroom.

He yelled after her. "I did make my move last night. Did you forget? You were there."

A twist of the faucet had a noisy shower spray covering her laughter. Forget it, no way could she forget the best sensual experience of her life. Didn't need another shower, but she did need a distraction. One that wouldn't make her late to work. The preferred one might still be standing in her bedroom wondering why he hadn't wowed her with his technique. Besides, she'd need to start over with her hair, too.

The scent of coffee penetrated the steam, luring her out of the shower. Hard not to fall for a man who did so much for her. Will could have made coffee just because he wanted it, but somehow, she doubted it. "Slow down, Missy," she cautioned, catching a glimpse of her slack-jawed face in the mirror.

"Too much, too fast, is what got you into this mess in the first place." She wanted to argue with her image. Every now and then mirror Tonya was right.

Chapter Ten

THE FAST FOOD bag warmed Tonya's legs as she opened it. An appetizing aroma wafted from the bag, heavy on spicy sausage with a slight hint of grease. Yeah, breakfast biscuits weren't the healthiest food around, but she loved them. You could also eat them while driving.

Tonya handed one sandwich to Will, then unwrapped the remaining one. The buttery biscuit exerted a siren song on her, causing her to wolf it down in a half dozen bites. Her eyes cut to Will, who stared straight ahead while driving. Did he witness her gobbling down her food like a protester coming off a hunger strike? If he did, he gave no indication.

A wadded wrapper nestled between his leg and the console, indicating he'd devoured his breakfast, too. She'd never be one of those rail thin women who picked at their food, claiming they were full after a handful of lettuce leaves and a baby carrot.

"I'm normally not such a pig. Not sure why I was so hungry this morning."

A smile tugged at the corner of his lips as he slowed for the red light. "Yeah, I know. Personally, I love a woman with a hearty appetite. The bigger, the better." The sudden movement of traffic took his attention as he surged forward with the flow.

The bigger, the better. Was that a crack about my weight? Her brow beetled as she analyzed his words. At best, her weight put her in the normal category. It would be a stretch to call her Junoesque or voluptuous. Then again, he had seen everything.

Something nudged her leg. A downward glance revealed Will's right hand warming her knee. "Don't overthink it. I meant a woman who has a hearty appetite in the kitchen usually has one in the bedroom, too."

Mmm, never heard that one before. Clint complained she ate like a lumberjack while Brian chowed down so fast, she didn't have a chance at displaying her eating skills, hearty or otherwise. If she got a burger or a single piece of chicken, she considered herself lucky. Hearty appetite in the bedroom, yeah, it fit. Not that it did her any good in the past.

"Why are you driving me to work?" Tonya wiggled back into the leather upholstery, enjoying the luxury of her chauffeured ride. It was a completely different story when someone else fought the morning rush hour traffic. Will drove effortlessly, without any of the aggression she'd expect from a lawyer.

A cluster of unique shops sat on her right, including a tattoo parlor, a Mexican restaurant, and a liquor shop named Mr. Thirsty. An average commute consisted of dodging minivans driven by preoccupied mothers on cell phones, rushing red lights to get their pampered offspring to their private school. When indulgent mothers weren't almost T-boning her, she kept a wary eye out for late employees running red lights, trying to make up for a missed alarm. Now and then, people had to watch for her hot rodding it to work, but only occasionally.

A truck grill dominated the rear-view mirror. Someone wasn't pleased with Will keeping to the speed limit. The oversized truck tore around them, forcing cars in the oncoming lane onto the shoulder. They honked their annoyance as the truck drove down the street, weaving in and out of cars. Tonya glanced over at Will, whose demeanor showed no irritation with the narrow escape. Did nothing rattle him?

He used his hand to gesture in the direction the reckless driver went. "We'll be seeing our friend soon alongside the road."

"Yeah, I can see him wrecking." Tonya could imagine the overconfident driver spinning out. The short glimpse she had of him was a tight-jawed man with a thick neck and reflective sunglasses. Yeah, he'd be the type to harass an ex-girlfriend. Before she used to divide men into potential and non-potential date categories. Shame, she'd dropped to possible stalker and non-stalker.

"Could happen," he agreed. "Not what I meant, though. Friggin' maniac showed his best asshole material in front of an undercover police officer."

"What?" Her head swiveling, she peered into the windows of the surrounding cars, looking for a uniformed officer. "I don't see anyone."

A siren sounded in the distance, confirming Will's initial assessment. "He's up a little farther than I thought he would be, but in the general area. Represented his wife, who told me all the speed traps with the encouragement to tell others."

"A woman scorned is a dangerous thing." The minute the words left her mouth, Tonya speculated why she never turned bitter, the way the officer's ex-wife did, sharing privileged information. Clint had no fear of her, thinking she wouldn't do anything, except lie down and let him walk on her. No reason for him to think otherwise. She'd never really opposed him. Might not like his lame idea of a motor cross rally as a romantic outing, but it rated higher than the firing range.

"Don't I know it? Probably know better than any man around. In fact, if I had any sense, I'd avoid women altogether." He shook his head as if admonishing himself.

"Hey, I take offense at that." She placed her hand on her chest while making a mock threatening face.

Will laughed. "Not you, I'm not worried about you. Apparently, you don't have a vengeful bone in your body."

"Yeah." She added a derisive grunt. "I'm becoming more and more aware of that. It's not a good thing, either." Instead of being the easygoing one, if she played the bitch card, not only would Clint not want her back, but he wouldn't make the mistake of crossing her. "I'd like to hurt Clint." She fisted her right hand and pounded it into her open left hand.

"Whoa, what happened to my mellow kitten?" Will directed a sharp glance her way as he bumped into the work parking lot. "Here, I drove you to work as a protective measure. Without your car in the open, there's no way Clint can vandalize it. Maybe we should leave it out as bait, then you'd rip him apart like a hungry bear."

The image had some appeal. "I'm not that bad. Sure, I'm angry, but I don't know any way of striking back. Well, legally," she added with a grin.

"Uh huh, got to keep it legal. First, we have to protect you. I believe that once Clint can no longer get to you, he'll lose interest. Don't text back. Don't email. No contact." The car stopped in a parking space close to the doors. Will shut off the ignition.

Sure, he made it sound so simple, but she had to know what Clint might do next. "You don't understand. I could lose my job." Her hands went up in the air, overcoming the temptation to shoot them through her hair in frustration, knowing she didn't have time to fix her hair or even continue the conversation.

Her hand depressed the door handle, and she swung the door wide, letting in the chill of the early morning air. Will's arm shot past her, closing the door. "When you're with me, I'll open your door. Stomping off in anger is no excuse not to let me be the gentleman. As for your job, you really need to consider looking for a new one, instead of hanging onto this one. Why are you holding on so tight to something you dislike?"

A sigh escaped her as his tall form rounded the front of the car. She couldn't fault the man's manners. Why did she hold onto her position so hard? Her skillset could easily serve at a different company. One not on the edge of collapse had to be better than her present job, considering how she had to do the job of the lackeys who resigned as well as her own. Doing only one job would be nice.

The car door opened. Tonya smiled up at Will and took his proffered hand. He tucked her hand into the crook of his arm. "Let me walk you to the door."

"There's no need. I'm in plain sight." She leaned into him, hoping he'd insist despite her protest. The clouds scuttled across the sky, hiding the sun ramping up the early morning gloom factor, but her body took no notice. Normally, she'd think the sky mirrored her mood, but not today.

Car doors slammed in the distance, indicating other employees' arrival. A nearby factory's odorous exhaust tainted the air with sulfuric fumes. She couldn't remember what they made. Her nose crinkled as she sniffed. With any luck, their product wasn't edible.

His other hand cupped hers. "Think of it as humoring me. It's always smart to stay on the good side of a lawyer." His laughter sounded a little forced.

Lawyer. Yeah, right. "I thought I was on your good side."

"You are." He tightened his hand around hers, giving it a squeeze. "I wouldn't be opposed to your continuing to win my favor."

She lifted one eyebrow, while noticing they were almost at the entrance. The sound of heels meant another employee was almost on top of them. No intense goodbye scene, especially with all the security cameras.

"Counselor." She drew the word out and cocked her head to one side. "Are you asking for a bribe?"

What might he ask for? Sure, they hadn't known each other more than a few days. Still, they'd put out more sparks than any of her previous relationships combined. He grinned at her and parted his lips to speak, but a woman's voice came out instead.

"Tonya! Will. Is that you?"

Lynne trotted as fast as her heels would allow. Will closed his mouth as the woman approached.

"Ah, our dear friend, Lynne, I guess it is safe to let the two of you walk in together. I'll be here at five." He dropped a kiss on her hair before turning back to the parking lot. He waved at Lynne as he passed her.

Lynne's breath came in rapid pants as she reached Tonya. "Damn heels are a nightmare to walk in. Forget running."

She glanced over her shoulder before nudging Tonya. "Overnight date, details."

Her friend's avid expression meant she really expected her to spill. Too bad she didn't feel likewise. Discussing Will would put him into the category of men who didn't matter. At least it would for her. Sure, there were men she and Lynne dissected from hair to manners, emotional IQ, and romance potential. A few days ago, Will had been one of them. "Um, I don't want to talk about it. Will's a nice man who is trying his best to keep me safe."

Her hand gripped the door handle and pulled it, holding it open for Lynne, who smirked at her. The woman looked too pleased with herself. A suspicion formed in her head as she ran the few needed steps to catch up with her. "You didn't play me, did you?"

Lynne cleared her throat. "Define play?" She kept her eyes forward as she walked.

"Oh, you know, told me Lila bailed on you, and I was your absolute last hope. Indicate Will might turn suicidal if an appropriate woman wasn't found for dinner." They reached their landing where the combined smell of coffee, garlic, and tuna casserole battled for dominance. Lynne fanned the air, and they quickened their pace as they neared the open door of the staff lunchroom. Her friend adroitly changed the subject.

"Smells as if the cleaning staff quit, too. It's not just rats that abandon a sinking ship, obviously janitors do, too."

The tiled floors did look a bit scuffed, not polished as they usually did. "Could be. It could also be the company forgot to pay them. You're avoiding answering my question, which means you're guilty."

"Me?" Her friend brought her hand up to her chest. "By the way, I never said suicidal."

"Yeah, I give you that, but you all but implied it. I felt sorry for you, Marc, and even the man I hadn't met that you were about to loose Lila on. That's the only reason I went over." Her shoulders straightened as they walked to Lynne's office. It made her sound kind, considerate, and rather like a good friend.

Lynne's laughter shattered her benevolent facade. "Please. You came for the free meal. Probably didn't have anything at home to eat. I know you too well." She nudged Tonya with a hip bump. "Never mind, it all worked out."

"No Lila bailing on you?" She asked the question even though she was almost certain of the answer.

Lynne stood in the doorway of her office. She glanced over her shoulder in the direction of a coffeemaker located on the counter. "Thank goodness someone started the coffee. Means I won't have to wander the halls looking for a cup of java. As for Lila, she's undepend-able, probably would have bailed if I'd asked her. She did go to Vegas as far as I know."

Aha, she knew it was a fix up. "What sad story did you tell Will?" An involuntary shudder went through her body, imagining the pitiful tales that induced the handsome lawyer to come to dinner.

"I didn't. Marc did. Hard to know what he said."

"Marc, was it? Then that's not too bad." Men weren't free on de-tails. "I'll just ask Will when I see him after work."

"You do that." Lynne turned toward the coffeemaker.

Tonya headed off to her office, mentally listing everything on her to-do list. A few open doors revealed different departments. Fewer employees showed up each day. A few quit, but most were using up their sick and personal days searching for new jobs, which is exactly what she should be doing. When Will brought it up again today, it gave her a free feeling. A new job would make it impossible for Clint to threaten her. No one would give him the new employer address. Tonight, she'd start on her search.

The monotony of scanning the documents left her plenty of time to consider potential jobs. When she ducked back in her office for lunch her message light blinked on her desk phone. Anxiety had her almost not answering it, but other people than Clint called her, especially at work.

Will's voice detailed the work he'd accomplished so far, including switching out the lights and adding motion lights. His friend from the security company was swinging by later. Just hearing his voice made her feel better. A security system would make a huge difference in safety. She'd work out a timetable to pay him back.

Of course, Will sleeping beside her would be security enough, but she couldn't expect that to be a regular thing. Her lips pulled down at the thought.

The clock above the copier didn't appear to move, no matter how hard or long she stared at it. "I can't wait to leave."

"You and me both," a familiar voice announced from behind, startling her.

Her surprise subsided as she pivoted toward Michelle. Tonya sighed and leaned against the copier. "You scared me."

"I kinda figured that by the way you levitated off the ground." They both laughed at her remark. The sound echoed through the almost empty room, bouncing off the industrial gray cinder block walls.

Her eyes scoured the room, the bulletin board with the time-yellowed signs and the water spotted ceiling. The building, with its signs of neglect, could have symbolized the state of the company. What would be good about being one of the survivors of labor cutbacks?

Michelle gestured to the tall stack of scanned papers. "That's a lot. Glad it's you and not me. I was wondering—" She stopped and glanced back at the open doorway.

Her co-worker moved closer and whispered. "I was hoping you'd be my reference. I'm going for another job, but of course, I don't want anyone to know and fire me for looking. Could I use your name and email? All you'd have to say is when I worked here and what I did."

Her normally cool co-worker regarded her with an anxious expression, waiting for an answer. "Michelle, of course you can. Maybe I could use you as a reference, too?"

The woman delivered a hearty back slap that moved Tonya a few inches from her position against the copier.

Michelle waggled her eyebrows. "Got an interview?"

"Haven't even got my stuff together, but I will." Each time she thought or verbalized the words about getting a different job made the desire that much stronger. "Still, I'll need a reference."

Her co-worker's sudden wide grin dominated her face. "You asked me, instead of Lynne."

Oh, that would make much more sense, but it obviously meant more to Michelle. "Why not you? We work together." She made a mental note to use both Lynne and Michelle as references.

A door slamming in the distance followed by footsteps drew both their eyes up to the clock.

Her co-worker emitted a long whistle. "Quitting time. Pardon my dust, but I'm out of here." She matched her actions to her words.

The footsteps and conversation drifted down the hall as employees left. Tonya took the unfinished stack of paper back to her office. The last thing she needed was a bump that would send the papers flying and interrupt her scanning process. The thought of Will waiting in the parking lot hurried her footsteps.

The faster she left the better. With the looming cuts, the entire staff took on the appearance of people at a wake for someone they neither liked nor knew that well.

Talk about oppressive. Maybe it was always like that, and she never recognized it. She locked her office door as she hurried not to be the last person in the building. While the building was never a cheerful place, it became super creepy at night. Footsteps echoed in the hallways. Lately, she'd swear she heard someone else in the building, only to discover the next day that everyone had left early.

The efficient thing would be to turn off the hallway lights as she left. Screw that. If they wanted the hallway lights off, then they shouldn't have messed with the cleaning staff.

Will's car sat close to the exit. Her hand pushed the door open, letting in the scent of cigarette smoke. The smokers usually gathered outside the side door, where there wasn't a security camera recording how much time they spent smoking. Hard to believe the smoke smell extended all around the building.

Strange. The aroma reminded her of an expensive imported brand Clint favored. He griped about how hard it was to get good quality unfiltered cigarettes in the U.S. A rustle in the overgrown shrubbery sent her sprinting toward the car. Her steps slowed as soon as Will jumped out of the car. Her momentary flare of panic abated as he greeted her with a hug before opening the passenger door.

"You ran out of that place like the hounds of hell were after you."

Tonya twisted, looking back at the shadowy entrance. Nothing. "Maybe a raccoon. I'm not a nature girl." Something flickered in her peripheral vision, but no use looking back because there was nothing to see except a bedraggled building where she'd wasted a third of her life.

Chapter Eleven

WILL PUTTERED AROUND in the kitchen while Tonya sat at the kitchen table, staring at her open laptop. The sounds of meat sizzling drew Sebastian out from under the table. Loyalty fell to second place when human food competed. A glance at the stove revealed Will removing a meatball from the skillet and placing it on a paper towel.

"You aren't saving that meatball for Sebastian, are you?" Her tone had a bite of irritation to it. "My dog is the only creature loyal to me. You'll win him over easily with a few meatballs."

The words she meant to soften her earlier remark had the opposite effect. Will's brows lowered, and his lips turned down. People thought women were difficult to understand.

Sebastian watched avidly as Will picked up the meatball and held it in the air for a few seconds before popping it in his mouth. A low whine expressed her pooch's disappointment. Sure, the dog didn't need the treat, but still. "Now, why'd you go and do that?"

Will turned back to the stove, lifting another meatball from the skillet. This one he placed on a plate. He continued transferring meatballs as he spoke. "I was going to give him the meatball. Then I thought about Clint going in and out of the house as many times as he pleased without Sebastian even objecting. The man probably gave him some meat treat. If I gave him a meatball, I'd just be compounding the problem. He'll start to assume that strange men give him treats."

Ah, Will liked her dog. Didn't say it exactly, but that's what she heard. "You're not so strange."

"Ha, shows how much you know." He moved the skillet from the hot burner to one that wasn't on. "A few of my client's husbands refer to me as the devil. That was one of the nicer names."

"Yeah, but you know how people are when they're mad, saying things they don't mean and all."

Will snorted as he picked up a large pot, filled it with water and put it on the stove. Tilting the saltshaker over the water, he gave it a few shakes and used a slotted spoon to stir it.

"They meant it. Besides, I don't want Sebastian taking treats from strangers. So far, Clint has only given him non-toxic treats, but what happens if he drugs the meat?"

Drug her dog? Her gaze fell on her overweight canine, who kept watch on Will's cooking activities. "I don't think Clint would do that."

The slotted spoon in Will's hand tumbled to the floor. "You don't think he would do something like that?" His voice grew louder with each word. A quick flick of his wrist turned off the stove. He pulled out a kitchen chair and straddled it.

Tonya waited, knowing he had something to say, something important. She may not know a great deal about men, but she knew when the stage had been set for an important announcement. "No."

His large hand rubbed over his face a couple of times. "Okay. Did you think he would try to get you fired from your job?"

"No, of course I never thought that. If I had, I wouldn't have done the photos."

Everyone had a few things he or she regretted, but man, when she did stupid stuff, it bit her in the butt big time.

His arms folded across the top of the chair with his chin resting on his hands. Only his lips moved as he spoke softly, while the rest of his face stayed icily immobile. "Did you expect him to break into your house, vandalize your car, and make some type of voodoo doll in your image?"

"That's a silly question." No wonder he terrified his client's soon–

to-be ex-spouses with snapping turtle tenacity and laser eyes that peeled away any pretense.

Stupidity, lust and a whole lot of liquor got her involved with Clint. Add in a dash of loneliness, too. "Okay." She surged to her feet, knocking her laptop askew, but Will righted it before it tumbled. Great, something else she'd had to thank him for.

"I didn't know he was unstable. Crazy doesn't come with warning labels." Her voice grew shriller with her agitation, causing Sebastian's abrupt departure. His tail whipped around the corner as he sought a safe haven from mercurial humans. Her hands were in the air as if she were testifying in a Pentecostal revival. Of course, her witnessing would be about her horrible luck with men.

Will stood slowly as if wary of her. Would he leave now? Decide he had enough of helping the whacked-out damsel in distress? She didn't want to be that woman: the one who needed a helping hand, or a shoulder to cry on. She was so tired of all of this.

Will opened his arms wide. Tonya may not need the man, but she certainly appreciated his embrace. In his arms, nothing seemed too bad. He tightened his hold, pulling their bodies flush with one another. His lips landed lightly on her head. The kiss made her smile, a big goofy grin that he couldn't see.

"So, you think you're the only one who has stubbed their toe in the name of love? I've pretty much hacked off entire limbs trying to get out of messy entanglements."

Will's confession of past romantic mistakes improved her mood some. "Tell me." Her low-voiced request went unanswered. Stiffening her fingers, she poked him in the ribs. "Tell me."

"Aw, you know it will just make me look bad, and you'll throw me over."

Tonya laughed into his shirt. "Yeah, right. Like I'd throw over the man who just made my home safer than Fort Knox. Come on, tell me."

Will pressed another kiss to her hair. "It makes me look stupid."

"As if I come out as a shining pillar of feminine wisdom for getting involved with a lunatic P.I."

His arms tightened around her as he murmured. "I'll give you that."

"Hey!" Her fingers ran up and down his ribcage searching for a ticklish spot. Under his arm, deep into his pit, she found it. She knew she'd hit pay dirt when he pinned his arm to his side to prevent her wandering fingers from getting any farther.

"Stop that," he managed between chuckles. "That's so unfair."

"Maybe," she readily agreed. "I'll stop when you tell. It will help me from feeling like such a doofus, depending on how bad your story is."

His chuckles ceased, and his somber expression returned, making her wish she hadn't pushed him. An apology formed in her mind, something about it not mattering and forgetting she even mentioned it, but before she could utter it, Will spoke.

"Bella was my first client, and I was as green as they came."

A derisive snort signaled his own disgust. His eyes fixed on the wall as if seeing a memory played out on the blank surface. "Oddly, it has been about sixty plus clients ago, but I remember it like it was yesterday. It's one of the reasons I hate divorce law so much. Reminds me of an old Russian proverb that goes 'Fool me once, shame on you. Fool me twice, shame on me.' I was determined never to be fooled again."

He wasn't saying anything. Initially, she would have let him not tell her, but now that he'd gone grim-faced and stared off into the distance, he had to explain. Her right hand cupped his chin. "What happened?"

He snorted again. "What didn't? Looking back, I can see I was eager to be played. I may not have thought it, but I was. The senior partner had given me a line of bull about what a valuable service we provided. It was what I wanted to hear. Then he sent Bella my way."

"Was she a regular Barracuda? All claws and curses?" She could imagine an angry middle-aged woman put aside for a younger model.

Will turned his head slightly to kiss her hand, still cupping his chin. "No, far from it. An ethereal beauty with delicate features and long, beautiful, blonde curls. She reminded me of an Elven Queen or a fairy princess."

Her hand dropped to his shoulder, lying there like a dead fish. He said the words almost as if in awe. The same way actors in the rom-coms acted when seeing their crush, who was all wrong for them. "I hate her, and I don't even know her."

The flare of animosity made her uncomfortable standing so close to Will. She slid one foot back, then the other, creating space between their bodies. His arms tightened around her.

"Oh no you don't. See, I knew this would happen. Bella is toxic. I haven't even told you the whole story and now you're already ill."

Made her sick? "You got it all wrong. It's not you. I'm disgusted that there are women like Bella that men go all moon-eyed over. Especially when they have hearts smaller and darker than any story-book villain does."

His look shouted his disbelief. "Do you want to hear the rest of the story?" The embrace loosened as he took a step back. "I think I'll go back to cooking. It might make it easier."

"Cooking's good."

The simple motion of turning on the stove appeared in slow motion as if Will were under water. Maybe her mind drew things out. She returned to her laptop as he moved around the kitchen.

After rinsing off the slotted spoon, he began to talk in a low voice that forced her to listen carefully. "I blame Edward, the senior partner, the most. He told me this woman was a dear friend who was in an abusive marriage. I believed him, and she played the part so well, telling me detailed accounts of horrific things her husband had done to her."

Tonya opened her computer and powered it on before turning to look in Will's direction. "She wasn't? How would you know?"

He shook his head slowly. "I didn't know then. I swallowed her stories, felt outrage on her behalf, even cracked open the pre-nup agreement due to cruel and inhumane treatment. Of course, later I learned women in abusive relationships blame themselves and have no desire to talk about it. The only way you ever discover it is a trail of emergency room visits or a history of police calls."

"So, you got her a good settlement. How was that such a bad deal? That's your job."

"Oh, yeah." He ripped open the spaghetti box with more force than necessary. "An amazing settlement, considering the lying, cheating whore not only played me, but my boss, too. It also established my reputation as the go-to divorce lawyer if you wanted to royally stick it to your ex."

"Hmm," she murmured the sound, aware on some level that saying too much would stop him from talking altogether.

"Bella was a real piece of work. She'd tell me gut-wrenching stories she'd pulled off some battered spouse website. In between tales, she called me her hero."

Tonya's nose crinkled as she made a gagging expression.

"I saw that. Now the thought of how gullible I was makes me want to gag. She told me she had fallen in love with me. I was convinced I loved her. She tried to seduce me: asked me to drop by for an emergency visit, and was attired only in a sexy negligée. At the time, I excused it and left in a hurry, not wanting to lose the job I'd so recently obtained."

"Please." She stretched out the word, feeling her resentment against the absent woman flare up again. "Don't tell me you didn't suspect anything?"

The gurgle of the boiling water covered up his initial reply as he guided the spaghetti into the pot. "I intentionally misunderstood. I wanted to believe she was a woman who deeply needed my help. Keep in mind that I didn't go to college to help predatory females. Bella read me well and gave me what I wanted to believe, while she was screwing my boss."

Her fingers paused over the keyboard. "Did you know this?"

"Not at first." The spoon stirred the spaghetti as he dripped oil over the boiling water. "No, that didn't come until after the divorce was finalized. Ethically, I was free to confess my feelings for the gorgeous Bella."

"Apparently, she didn't feel the same way." She bit out the words as she pecked at the keyboard, misspelling simple words.

"Ha! Talk about an understatement. She laughed at me. Pointed out that she'd be stupid to get involved after obtaining such a generous alimony. Went on to tell me she had no interest in anyone as green as me—too ignorant to recognize when being played. She preferred older, experienced men, like my boss."

The idea of the harpy manipulating a young, vulnerable Will made her snap her teeth together, wishing she could somehow put the bite on Bella. "Yuck! Good riddance. I bet you didn't take it that way, though. I wish Bella were here so I could give her some woman to woman advice." Her hand closed in a fist that she brandished over her head.

Will's expression shifted from melancholy to amusement at her actions. "Yeah, for a time, I think I would have liked to have seen someone give her what was coming to her. Now I just look at the whole thing as a lesson learned."

"Do you?" Hard to believe the emotional trauma could be a life learning experience.

"Now I do." He managed a wistful smile. "Took a while. I think everything that hurts and takes a while to recover from changes a person. Kinda hate people who tell you time heals all wounds, but they do get more bearable the further time goes on."

Steam rose from the bubbling pot as Will peered into the cabinets. "Don't you have a colander?"

Her teeth came down on her lips. "Oh. I keep meaning to buy one. Last one I had was plastic. I melted it."

His head came up abruptly, hitting the edge of the open cabinet. "Ow!" His fingers probed his hair, possibly searching for the bump. "I was going to ask you how you did that, but maybe I'm better off not knowing."

The stench of melted plastic resurfaced, if only in her mind. She'd turned her oven on to preheat, forgetting she'd used it to store dirty dishes when her mother arrived unexpectedly one day. "Ah yeah, you're better off not knowing. No one will accuse me of being a domestic goddess, that's for sure."

In the act of lifting the hot pot from the stove, Will grunted his agreement.

"Hey, you didn't have to agree!" Hard to know what to expect from the man. Most would politely defer from saying anything. What she regarded as politeness, may have just been disinterest.

She handed Will a lid, which he pressed against the hot pot, allowing the steamy water to cascade into the sink. Not the best solution, but it worked. Will's hair formed tendrils around his face, making him look almost cherubic. "You look pretty adorable with those curls. Hard to believe anyone who saw you now would think of you as threatening in the courtroom."

"Adorable. Please." His nose crinkled up in disgust. "There's a reason I blow dry my hair. I'm a shark and can't afford to be cute. I never smile when I'm at work." He placed the lid back on the drained pasta as he reached for the jar of sauce.

Tonya considered mentioning he should have already started the sauce, but held her tongue. Relief came in finding out Will didn't do everything perfectly. Don't forget Bella, which added up to more than one thing. A perfect man she couldn't tolerate, but a man who fumbled, sometimes even fell, and got back up suited her. Then there was Clint, who apparently tried to trip her up every chance he got. What a mean bastard. Who'd want him? Apparently, no one, which was why he was her problem now. The thought had her glancing at her half-formed résumé.

"Will, I don't know what to say. I'm following the template, but it makes me sound so dull. My job is mind-numbing boring. If I'm going to get a new job, I'd like it to be less tedious."

Her eyes drifted over duties performed, necessary to almost any business and some needed a particular skill set. She was good at what she did, which enabled her to do part of Michelle's job as well. Her earlier antagonism at her workmate vanished after witnessing the woman balancing single motherhood with working. No reason to pick her up after her car conked out, especially when Michelle's day had already gathered speed, but she did it anyhow. The woman had a kind core.

"Do you think I'm a kind person?" She'd never thought about it too much, but maybe it was the reason bad things happened to her. Karma kept slapping her around because she wasn't doing her part to make the world a better place. Her intention hadn't been to ask Will, but more of a pondering aloud type of thing.

"Yes." His answer came without hesitation as he dropped the meatballs into the sauce. "Why do you ask?"

Good question, but one that revealed more than she wanted. "I wondered if somehow I made everything go bad."

"Stinky thinking will never take you where you need to go." Will placed the last meatball in the saucepan and put the lid on it before crossing over to the table and sitting down. "That's what my grandfather would tell me whenever I got down about something."

Tonya opened her mouth to speak, but Will kept talking.

"He also told me America never won a war by thinking they might not be able to do it. They went in guns blazing, hearts determined with a can-do attitude."

"Grandpa sounds pretty cool. Mine would tell me, don't take any wooden nickels, and then laugh as if it was the funniest saying in the world. Did you ever mention the Vietnam War to him?"

Will grinned at her. "Once. Never made that mistake again." He gripped her laptop and pulled it toward him. After scanning it, he made a guttural grunt before replying. "I see the problem."

"Did I use the wrong format? I'm not fond of the chronological order, but it was the one the template used." Maybe a few tweaks could fix it up, and she'd be off and running for a new job.

His head swung side to side, while his expression remained inscrutable, probably the one he used in divorce negotiations. It reminded her of playing Twenty Questions.

"What is it?"

"No passion, no dream, no drive, no heart, no guns blazing." His eyebrows lifted on the last word.

"I don't think I'll get any job with blazing guns, unless I'm going to be an international spy. I don't understand." Her shoulders went up in a shrug. Could the man be any more cryptic?

"The HR person who reads this will think you could care less for the job you're applying for. You have to sell them on you. Of course, if he's a man, he'd hire you just because you're pretty."

"Is that why they hired you?" Her teasing question elicited a thousand-yard stare as opposed to a chuckle.

"I considered that once. I met some of the candidates for my position when I was interviewing. There was an older man in the parking lot leaving, who told me he had the position sewn up. A beautiful woman in an amazingly tight business suit came in while I was waiting, demanding to know the details on when she'd start her new position. On my way out, I heard two of the associates talking about a former colleague who wanted the position. No way I had a chance—and then they hired me. I was probably one of the most inexperienced people in the group. As a newbie, they could pay me less."

"Hmm," she murmured, trying to consider how she might feel if she were in the same situation. "You've got a point. Then didn't you say your mentor was friends with the boss? Then there's the angle that most women would want to be represented by a hot lawyer?"

"Hot, huh?" He spoke while mimicking polishing his nails on his shirt. "I had no clue you felt that way."

"As if, there has to be some reason I keep you around." Pressing her hands on the table, she half-stood as she leaned over and attempted a kiss on the cheek. He swiveled his head at the last moment causing the kiss to land at the edge of his lips.

His fingers speared through her hair, holding her head in place, as he turned, aligning their lips. The playful kiss turned hot as he gently moved his lips across hers, sucking on her bottom lip and lightly nipping it. Instead of clearing the table with a sweep of his arm as she hoped, Will pulled back and winked. "Trying to distract me with your hot self."

It sounded like a prelude to the bedroom for her. Straightening, she gave him a come-hither glance under her eyelashes as her body warmed even more. Talk about a great ending to a mediocre day.

"You're cute when you go all seductive on me." He kissed the tip of her nose before going back to the stove. He grinned at her over his shoulder. "I know you think I'm playing hard to get, but once I get you on the sheets, you're not coming out for hours, maybe days. Might as well get your résumé done now, because you won't have the strength to do it later."

Her mouth dropped open as he spoke. Not the bragging about his sexual prowess, most men did that. "How do I know you'll be that good?" She purred the words in a sultry timber.

"Ha, I know what you're doing. Consider some of the most sexually frustrated women in the county have worked their wiles on me without success." He waved the spoon for emphasis before plunging it into the spaghetti saucepan.

"You go looking for sexually frustrated women? That's different. Where do you find them?" A dark, smoky bar filled with half-drunk men trying out tired lines on equally inebriated females came to mind.

"They come to me."

Whoa. This version of Will sounded more like a Dr. Feel Good. She sucked in her lips, considering her attraction to him. No way she wanted to be just another notch on what must be an almost non-existent bedpost. Something didn't make sense. Why did he tell her all that other stuff about his past if it wasn't true? The man certainly got her engine running.

"Stop whatever you're thinking right now."

Tonya put the brakes on her imagination. Good thing, it was careening into pornographic images with mouthwatering naked Will standing next to a line of smiling women of varying sizes, ages, and skin color. "Uh, how do you know what I was thinking about?" Her face heated under his scrutiny.

A deep V settled between his brows as he regarded her, then he shook his head, smoothing his forehead. "I have no clue, but it couldn't be good. You looked like you bit into something rotten, but were too polite to spit it out."

Rotten, all right, but she did not intend to share it.

Will placed the pasta in the microwave. "Dinner will be ready in a couple of seconds, and then we can work on your résumé."

Tonya continued staring at him. Somehow, the man sidestepped the large elephant in the room, or in his case, dozens of frustrated women all lining up for him. Really? Her balled fists landed on her hips.

"Whoa." Will inflected a touch of the dramatic in one word. He moved the clean plates closer to the stove just as the microwave buzzer went off. "I recognize that stance. Even though I don't consider myself an expert on women,"

Her derisive snort made him pause for a second.

"It's a fighting stance. More of an 'I'm going to kick that stupid man's ass good' pose." He removed the heated plate from the microwave with a small grimace and divided the pasta before ladling sauce and meatballs on each plate.

Despite wanting to growl out her accusations, she cleared the table as she spoke. Petulance made her sound like a child whose new toy broke. "Um, you never told me how you met all those frustrated women and worked your magic on them."

"Oh, that." He laughed as he placed the plates on the table. "Do you have any Parmesan cheese?"

"You need Parmesan cheese?" Her voice sounded louder than she intended.

Will flashed what she dubbed in her mind his 'turn knees to jelly grin.' "Yeah, forks would be nice, too, maybe even napkins. I'll open the wine I bought for dinner."

The man knew what he was doing as he baited her. She might have Parmesan cheese in a can in her fridge. She bumped into Will deliberately as she walked to the fridge.

"Hey!" His hands landed on her shoulders stopping her. "Okay, I'll tell you. No reason for you to get so out of sorts. It was a joke about my clients. I assumed most of them were frustrated in one way or another. A few ran after every man they could, once they decided to divorce. Their annoyance came from the fact that men could not make their dreams come true. They never realized only they could make their dreams a reality."

The gurgling, hissing brew of emotions turned into the placid sheen of a mountain lake. No hordes of women chasing after Will. The thought relaxed her fingers as they hooked onto the belt loops of his jeans. The last part of his statement seeped in slower. *Only they could make their dreams a reality.* Most of her life, she'd spent waiting for someone else to make her dreams a reality. Shazam! A fairy godmother would appear and grant her the perfect job. Unfortunately, the favor-granting fairy must have lost her address since she never showed.

The thought whirled through her consciousness, stirring up all sorts of debris left over from abandoned hopes. Will's hands slipped around her waist, drawing her closer as he kissed the top of her head. An energy that had nothing to do with the fact a handsome, incredible man held her, percolated through her body. Okay, the fact he held her may have had something to do with it, but not all.

"Will." She whispered his name. "I can make it happen. A better job, standing up to Clint, creating the life I want."

"You can." He placed another kiss on her hair before dropping his arms. "Let's eat first before changing your world for the better."

A sense of wonderment came over her. How many people languished in unhappy lives, certain fate had dealt them a crummy hand? Rocking to her toes, she landed a brief kiss on his lips, before moving around him to the fridge on a cheese-finding mission. Parmesan cheese can in hand, she announced. "After dinner, you and I are going to compose a kick ass summary of me that will have everyone begging to hire me."

"Preach it, sister," he remarked and then picked her up under the arms, swinging her around in a small circle. Sebastian barked at their antics, which signaled his return to the kitchen. Apparently, the emotional tide had gone out far enough for his peace of mind.

Eating got in the way of starting her new life, but she needed to do it, especially since Will went to all the trouble of making meatballs. After gathering the wine and a couple of water tumblers, they were ready to eat.

Will opened the bottle and then tilted it, starting the wine. He moved the bottle higher like a waiter in a high-end restaurant. The red liquid splashed into the squat tumblers with abandon. It would have been nicer with real wine glasses, which was something she wanted, but never got around to. That tended to be the constant refrain of her life. A heartfelt sigh punctuated the stillness.

"What is it? Didn't like my pouring?" He sat the wine bottle down and lifted an inquiring eyebrow as he sat and scooted his legs under the table.

"No, nothing like that. Just suddenly, I realized I've been living my life in neutral, never going anywhere I want to go. It's no wonder I'm stuck in a job I despise. I fell into it. Every couple of years, I'd get an urge to leave, but change requires too much work. I did nothing. Never even bought replacement wine glasses after the movers broke mine. I've been reactive, instead of proactive. Everything just sort of happened to a degree, and I let it, even though it wasn't what I really wanted." Clint and Brian both fell under that heading.

"I know what you mean. I've been considering switching jobs off and on for a while, but haven't done anything about it. After we snag your dream job, maybe we can work on mine." He lifted his glass.

Tonya tapped hers to his. "To new beginnings, going after what we really want, the realization of dreams."

The room temperature wine slid down her throat, leaving an acidic bite in its wake. She was never a fan of red wine, especially dry ones. Give her something cool, fresh, and sweet any day. Clint referred to such people as redneck wine drinkers, which resulted in her keeping her opinion to herself. No longer, it was time to stand up for what she wanted.

Placing her tumbler on the table, she glanced over at Will, wondering if she should withhold her wine summation. The level in his glass had gone down minimally at the most. "This is a nice wine, but I'm more of a Riesling or Zinfandel kind of girl."

Will stopped winding his spaghetti onto his fork. "Really. I also bought a Moscato and put it in the fridge to chill. Wasn't sure what you'd like."

"Sounds perfect." She readily agreed as he retrieved the bottle and opened it, pouring some into two new tumblers. "It doesn't make me a redneck wine drinker because I'm drinking the wrong wine for spaghetti?"

"Redneck wine drinker? Never heard that term before. The wrong wine is the one you don't like. Simple enough. As long as you like it, you're good."

Why did it sound like a no brainer when he said it, even though she'd thought the same thing? Will held up his glass of white wine and waited for her to pick up her glass. "Here's to us, believing our opinion matters."

The thick tumblers collided with a dull clunk, but to Tonya it sounded like a clear bell on a crisp winter morning. A revelation, her opinion mattered. Ironically, a jaded divorce lawyer opened her eyes.

Chapter Twelve

SEBASTIAN WHINED, PRESSING against her leg. "Almost done, boy. Can't you hold it a couple of minutes longer?" The black text on the screen somehow represented who she was. A summary of sorts, at least of her work skill set. Not getting the desired response, her pooch clawed her legs with nails that definitely needed trimming. "Stop it!"

Will walked into the room, whistled, and opened the back door, which Sebastian hurtled through in his rush. Tonya threw a grateful smile in his direction before returning to her perusal of her work history. *What just happened there?* A glance revealed Will at the door waiting for her dog's return. She hadn't asked him to do anything, and yet he flowed into the rhythm of hers and Sebastian's life. *How weird is that?*

His voice called out without his turning around, surprising her a little. "You must be done if you're contemplating my ass."

"I'm not." The words died in her mouth when she realized the night darkened sliding glass doors served as a mirror. Okay, she did check out his fine rear assets. Sue her. The man certainly had the legal expertise to do so. "I want you to look at what I typed and decide if you'd hire me."

"Glad to." He slid the door open, allowing Sebastian in. The dog pranced by the two of them and headed to the bedroom. "You wouldn't want to work at my office. It would just depress you to see so many marriages turn into vicious battle zones."

The chair scraped against the floor tiles as he pulled it out. Using two fingers, he gestured to the computer. She pushed it in his direction, contemplating what it would be like to work somewhere else. Her current job resembled an old drive-in movie she saw with zombies roaming the shopping mall. Her fellow employees' hearts and souls left the premises long ago. Only their bodies remained, moving through routine motions with blank expressions similar to the movie zombies.

"Why do you think people turn crazy when their marriages fall apart? All angry and vengeful, wanting to hurt each other as much as possible?" Clint did that, turned ugly and demanding. Weird, considering he did the leaving.

"Hmm, I try not to think about it too much." Will scrolled down the page, scanning the words. His right hand went to his temple. His fingers lightly massaged the area while he spoke.

"I used to try to affix blame for the marriage dissolution as much as the spouses did. In the end, it was never one person. Several things contributed to the break up besides simple answers such as unfaithfulness, money, or lack of communication. The length of the marriage determined the nastiness."

"How so?" Her own relationship failures made her wonder about people who managed long marriages. If you had the skill set to do that, why chuck it all?

"Ahh." He hesitated, changing something, causing Tonya some neck-stretching action. "Changed the verb there. Passive. Needs to be active." He sucked his lips as if recalling the topic. "Oh, the older women. Well, it's a completely different mindset than women today. When she married her husband, she became a work support, as well as a housewife and mother. Being the good wife was her career. Then twenty, thirty years down the line, he decides he wants a younger, different model."

Tonya imagined the shock of a middle-aged woman discovering her husband's infidelity. "I've got it," she announced, interrupting his explanation. "She not only loses a husband, her status, but her job, too.

In one fell swoop, everything is gone. The husband keeps his job, his status, and a brand-new trophy wife. It explains the wife's bitterness."

"Yeah," Will agreed and pushed the laptop back to her. "What you need is a job objective. A description of what you'd like to do. Of course, you can change it for whatever job you apply for."

Her mind still lingered on the abandoned wife. The perfidy of a husband who left behind the woman who'd put him through medical school made her blood boil. This mythical woman she named Jessica, also made gourmet dinners and chaired PTO meetings. "Men are assholes."

Will caught her eyes. "Not sure that's a job objective. Maybe for a dominatrix, but not sure what else."

Her lips clamped together. Did he think she was referring to him? "Um, not talking about you. You know those men who leave decent wives for some hot intern."

His hand slipped back to rub his neck. "Glad it's not me. The hot intern thing is more of an urban myth. Most people get busy with neighbors or even church friends, rather than some college kid. Most of the wives I see aren't saints, either. They're bitter, angry women who feel life tricked them somehow, depriving them of the happy ending they expected." His eyes rolled up toward the ceiling as he spoke.

"It's easy to see only one side." Her back felt tight as she wiggled in the chair trying to make it less stiff. The retro cat clock's short hand moved to eleven while its tail's swings counted off the seconds. Really, that late? She blinked, unsure if she'd read it correctly, ten till eleven. It explained why Sebastian headed to bed.

A sharp phone chirp resulted in Will patting his pockets until he located his cell. "Sorry." He pointed to the phone. "It's my boss." He stood and walked into the living room to take the call. Tonya saved the document with intentions of reviewing it the next day and showing it to Lynne, who might suggest something else. Will's aggravated tone carried, although his words didn't.

Seriously, divorce lawyers weren't exactly heart surgeons. Why the late-night call? Her arms stretched up over her head, she wiggled a little, releasing the cramp in her back. An unexpected yawn caught her as she lengthened her spine. She stood, more than ready for bed. Getting later all the time, her hand hit the kitchen light as she entered the living room. Will held the phone pressed up to one ear, while he opened and closed his free hand indicating his boss speaking. His fingers went into a spiral, which confused her a little. Did he mean the conversation could be ending or his boss was crazy? Perhaps both.

Tonya pointed in the direction of the bedroom and pantomimed sleeping. At her antics, Will threw her a kiss. Her hand shot up in the air with her fingers curling around the imaginary kiss. It might be all she got tonight.

Her whimsical nightshirt with dancing teddy bears reached mid-thigh. Not exactly seductive, but that train left the station earlier tonight. A book on her nightstand beckoned her as she nudged Sebastian, who slept on his accustomed side of the bed. The puggle gave up his bed without a fuss last night. Would he put up a fight tonight? She assumed Will would stay, but what was that old saying, that assumption made an ass out of you and me. Her safety didn't require his physical presence, especially since the security system called for help whenever it detected a break in or even an attempted one.

He never mentioned staying, which probably meant he wasn't. The book fell open to the bookmark she placed in it last week. Only a week ago, the antics of a nosy cooking show host turned detective amused her. It helped her relax before she fell asleep. Now, with Clint breathing down her neck, she doubted a horse tranquilizer would do the trick.

The open bedroom door allowed snippets of conversation in. "Yes, I know, Gloria. I do realize this is a bad time for you. Yes, I am taking your case seriously."

Seriously. Some potential divorcée expected a courtesy call—she turned her alarm around, displaying a glowing 11:42—at almost midnight. Probably a trophy wife who decided she could do better: a pampered diva who always had men doing her bidding.

"No, no, Gloria, that's not a solution!" Will's voice grew louder with each word. The image of the beautiful trophy wife disappeared, replaced by a wild-eyed woman holding a gun to her head. Her book tumbled to the floor as she threw back the covers. Maybe she should call the police, but where would she tell them to go. Her bare feet made almost no sound as she padded down the hallway.

Will pocketed his phone, audibly muttering, "Damn, crazy woman."

Didn't sound like the paramedics should be on their way. "What's wrong?" She slipped an arm around his waist and half hugged him before pulling back to look at his face.

"Come here." He held both arms wide. She stepped into the open embrace and buried her nose into the shirt stretched over his shoulder. The scent of meatballs and spaghetti sauce lingered, along with the distant note of pine-scented deodorant. Tonya absorbed the moment, listening to the rhythm of his breathing. The weight of his head rested against hers. When he sighed, she felt it pass through her body.

"Anything I can do?" She doubted she could help, but it didn't stop her from wanting to.

He lifted his head and brushed a kiss on her hair before answering. "Yeah, if you ever decide to marry an anal podiatrist named Charles and the two of you adopt a French bulldog, but things don't work out between the two of you because you disagree on how King Louis the 17th should be raised, please don't pick me as your divorce lawyer."

"I can safely assure you that I won't do that. Don't even know any podiatrists, let alone one named Charles." His arms tightened around her, bringing with them a sense of security she hadn't realized until now, never existed in her life.

His chest vibrated as he continued to speak, reminding her of the time a high school boyfriend insisted she rest her head on the car hood. Supposedly, the action would reveal the amazing engine underneath it. It vibrated her face, causing a recent filling to throb. Not as bad as that and thankfully no recent fillings, either.

"Then," Will continued, "don't call your lawyer up late at night, disrupting any possibility he might have of a love life with an incriminating announcement about breaking into Charles's house with the intention of stealing King Louis."

She grinned up at him. "The seventeenth. No doubt the canine would object to a shortened name."

"No doubt." His lips twisted to one side. "If she steals the dog, I'll be complicit, because I knew and didn't warn the husband. Not exactly a good place for a lawyer. Why do I get all the crazy ones?"

"Ha. That's what I usually say about the men I date." The remark popped into her head and tumbled just as easily out of her mouth. Will dropped his arms, making her look up.

"Crazy, huh?" He tilted his head. "Been called boring, difficult, slow, pragmatic, OCD, but never crazy."

"Not you." She gave him a playful push. "You're the most normal guy I've met so far."

"Normal." His nose wrinkled as if smelling something bad. "Almost as bad as crazy. It's right up there with boring, traditional, tight-laced, stuffed shirt, etc."

"Stop it." She held up one hand, not upset. "You're a wonderful, sexy, caring man. You're my hero." Standing on her tiptoes, she landed a brief kiss on his lips before dropping back to her heels, leaving him bemused.

"Coming to bed or not?" She glanced over her shoulder with what she considered a come-hither look with half-closed eyes and a knowing smile.

Will immediately followed her, but glanced at the phone in his hand. "What about Gloria and King Louis the 17th?"

Seriously, the man hesitated. Her sexy quotient took a hit, but she reassured herself that his attention to his job made him the sought-after lawyer he was. "Don't worry. Gloria's all talk. She's feeling sad and lonely. You're the only person who has to listen to her late-night ranting. The woman will throw back a shot or two of peppermint schnapps and head off to bed. No bulldog napping, no issue. Won't even remember her crazy suggestion in the morning."

"You're right. Might as well leave the phone in the living room, since I don't plan on answering any calls tonight."

Tonya's lips tilted up at the comment as she hustled into the bedroom. She nudged the still sleeping Sebastian off the bed, which wasn't easy because not only was he heavier than he looked, but he passively resisted, similar to a burr caught on the bedspread. The canine eventually jumped off the bed, but not before giving her a disdainful stare.

"Sorry, boy, occasionally my wants trump yours." The puggle disregarded the apology, settling on a pile of discarded clothing with a snort.

"Your life is hard." She opened and closed dresser drawers, pushing clothes out of the way. Where did she put the scented votives? She knew she had some. Her fingers finally encountered a squat cylinder. "Bingo."

Another search ensued, which involved moving jewelry and toiletries, before she located the matches. She dumped out her heart shaped crystal dish that held earrings and placed the votive inside. "Safety first."

The candle flickered to life before she recognized that Sebastian was the only male occupant in the room. Did irrational Gloria call again? The sound of the shower running helped her locate Will. She should clean up, too. Her fingers plucked at the oversized sleep shirt. She pulled it off, trying a different shirt to see if it might make her look more alluring. The mirror revealed that the stiff collar of her other nightshirt cutting into her neck only looked painful, and not the least bit sexy.

A dab of the exotic perfume that Lynne bought her last Christmas would be the sexiest thing she owned. *Must get lingerie*, she mentally added to her to do list. Not that she never had any before, but her bad boyfriend cleansing ritual included getting rid of anything associated with the breakup. She kept the couch and television that Brian monopolized. Replacements would be too expensive. Besides, she bought the items for her use, not some man's appreciation.

Nothing sexy, she considered wearing a black silk shirt opened with only a tiny lace thong, but it'd look contrived, since she'd already donned the nightshirt. The shower continued, making her wonder what he included in his shower routine. "Not much time left." She spoke to herself, but got a baleful glance from her canine.

Nothing to wear might as well go with nothing. Her fingers gripped the tail of her nightshirt and pulled it off. Too bad Will wasn't the one removing it. Under the covers, she debated if the skin approach took away Will's opportunity to be the pursuer. Men liked to think they were in charge. Her heart raced a little as she imagined the night ahead. A twist of the lamp knob left the room in darkness except for the tiny flickering votive. The small candle did not provide the romantic atmosphere she anticipated. If she closed her eyes, they might adapt, allowing better night vision.

The hall light would work. The shower stopped, a giggling session threatened as she waited under the sheets, anticipating the man and fingering her clit. Wouldn't hurt to get things started, but thinking about wet, naked Will started her juices to flow on their own without any manual stimulation.

A soft whistled tune permeated the air as Will opened the door. The man didn't tiptoe around trying to be quiet. Either he expected her to be awake or he planned to wake her up. Ooh, wonder how he'd wake her up. Her eyelids closed as she tried to slow her breathing to be more sleeplike. Difficult, with both her mind and fingers exciting her. Oh yeah, she dropped her damp hand to the sheets.

The sound of his bare wet feet slightly sticking to the wood floor came closer as she tried to control her breathing. His shadow fell over her, demonstrating the hall light remained on. Good deal because she wanted to see what he'd do next. *What if he thought her too tired for any mattress aerobics?*

She moaned and thrashed her legs, moving the sheet down enough to show her breasts. *Hint, hint, sexual Prince Charming, come do me.*

Will's long sexy laugh elongated her nipples, which were already tight. The man had skills.

His mellow baritone purred close to her ear. "Too bad you're already asleep. I had a bedtime dance for you."

Her eyes popped open as she scooted up in the bed. "Bedtime dance?" Will fitted his iPod into the speaker and charger unit and stepped back as her eyes devoured him. He wore a towel knotted at the waist and oddly, a tie. He didn't have that on when he picked her up today. Her eyes moved slowly over him, memorizing his features.

His hands rested on his hips as she ogled him. All lean muscle, defined biceps, pecs, and abs, her tongue rimmed her lips. "Damn, you could be an advertisement for a gym. Bring the women in droves. No exercising would get done." She shook her head slowly, thinking the women would chuck down good money just to gaze at him.

A wicked smile stretched across his face as he hooked his fingers together and stretched upward, giving a gorgeous display of his lateral side muscles. "Push play, darling. I not only worked on house safety today, but I worked up something you might enjoy."

"Oh yes!" She bounced on the bed in excitement, making the girls dance up and down, earning her a wink for her efforts. Yeah, she could put on a show, too. Planned to. Her index finger tapped the iPod, sending the sultry voice of Marvin Gaye through the room, singing about sexual healing. Instead of the bump and grind strip tease, she expected, Will's slow sensual moves mesmerized her. His eyes met hers as he loosened the tie knot, slowly pulling one end of his tie across his chest. He leaned over her, allowing the end to tickle her breasts. Her fingers tightened around the material as he shimmied backward, leaving her with only the tie.

Smooth move. Only a towel left, before she could experience skin on skin. She clapped her hands together and wolf whistled. "Take it off, sweet thing. Show me what the good Lord gave you!"

He pivoted to the music, turning his back to her as he opened the towel, but kept it tight across his ass. He stopped, ramping up the tension, before he threw a sly backward glance at her. "I thought you were a good churchgoing girl. Maybe I should stop."

Marvin continued to croon about everything he was going to do, while her mouth dropped open. Joking, he had to be teasing her. He couldn't stop. She blinked. It had to be a joke. Her eyes slid over his muscular back. God, the man was gorgeous all over. A red dragon tattoo stood out on his shoulder blade, snarling, warning and challenging her. It suited him. "Hell no, you aren't stopping. I did say I wanted to work on changing my image. Start dancing and drop the towel."

The towel rubbed across his rear before he flicked it away. He stood with his legs apart, flexing his buttocks with his hands behind his head. Drool slipped out the corner of her mouth. *Damn, he was fine.* She watched, fascinated as he alternated the cheek rolls in time with the music. Her hand slipped down to palm her mons almost without her realizing it. She kicked the sheet to her ankles and allowed him a view when he turned. The music segued into another song, something about kiss you all over.

He rolled one hip as he moved around, exposing a tiny strip of black cloth. A G-string, the man was wearing a G-string. How did she not notice that? Her eyes were on the beautiful muscle play of his glutes, not on dental floss-like fabric between those two sumptuous cheeks. Her disappointment dissipated as he shimmied nearer, displaying a very tight package. Excellent.

Her eyes stayed on the packed G-string that thrust in her direction. *Close enough to touch.*

"I brought some oil." His left hand gestured in the direction of the bedside table where a small bottle of massage oil sat. "If you want to oil me up."

"You have to ask?" She slithered off the bed, grabbed the bottle and squeezed some into her hands. She rubbed her hands together before sliding them across Will's sculpted chest, playing with his nipples as she went. She ran the oil slick hands up his arms onto his shoulders, hooking her hands behind his neck. They danced together slowly, skin sliding against skin, the oil she put on him transferred to her skin. Her juices slid down her inner thighs as she bumped against his erection.

His hands cupped her ass, pulling her closer, grinding his silk clad cock into her mons, driving her crazy. Another song came on with a woman breathlessly moaning to her lover with music in a background.

Her sudden stop brought Will's slow figure eight of his hips to a standstill. Exactly what she wanted, she dropped to her knees, thankful for the thin oriental rug that padded the floor. She hooked her fingers under the sides of his G-string, lifted it off his erection and pulled it down to his thighs, freeing his rampant penis. The tip glistened with a pearl of pre-cum. Tonight, it was good to be her. No, make that excellent.

Her nose hit his package first, nuzzling and inhaling his musky arousal. Her lips came next, peppering small kisses across his groin, gently across his tightened balls, up his length, to the crown, where her tongue lapped the pearl.

"Ah, God you're good," Will moaned the sentiment while moving his fingers into her hair, holding her in place. "Do you want to move this to the bed?"

Instead of using words to answer, she rounded her lips and slid down his length as far as she could. Her right hand wound around the base and moved in conjunction with her mouth thrusts. Her tongue worked up and down the sensitive skin, pulling another guttural moan from him.

"Sweetheart, you have to stop. I don't want to come before making you come."

Oh, she'd come more than once, but if the man wanted to make her come again, she'd let him. Her lips slowly slid up his length as she loosened her grip on his base. She stood, watching him step out of his thong. A head swing flipped her hair back. Her wet lips shaped the words, *do me.*

Tonya leapt for the bed the same time he lunged for her. The mattress caught her, well, most of her, since Will's hand tightened around her ankle, holding her right leg off the bed.

"I caught you. What should I do with you?"

He dropped her foot, allowing her to balance on her knees and wiggle her ass. "Give it to me doggy style, fast and hard." *Did she just say that?* Better yet, what would Will do? Should she roll over and act like a more traditional female?

As an answer, he smacked her rear hard enough to sting, but not bruise. It tingled, rather pleasantly. Before she could dwell on the sensation too much, the tip of his cock penetrated, waiting, as if for some unknown signal. She pushed back, shoving the wide shaft down her slick passage way. Wet or not, it barely fit, or so it felt. The slow sliding motion caused her to fist her hands on the sheet, bunching the material under her fingers and twisting.

He drove in hard, touching her womb, causing her to gasp. "Tell me what you want or I'll stop right now." His actions matched his words.

The man meant what he said. It wasn't an idle threat or pillow talk. "Don't stop!" However, he had and wasn't moving.

"Tell me what you want or I'm pulling out and going home."

What! He couldn't do that. Her Kegel muscles squeezed, eliciting a husky laugh.

"I want you." Her mind raced as she tried to piece together what she wanted. "All of you. Give me your hard cock. Every inch. Fast. Rough. Until you can't take—" His penis jerked inside her at her words and plunged before she could finish her sentence.

"It anymore." She shouted the last two words over the hammering of her heart and the rushing of her blood. The two of them exploded together, collapsing in a sweaty tangle of limbs.

A SOUND WOKE her. For a second, she stared into the dark, disoriented. The candle had burned out or Will blew it out. His body heat radiated across the few inches that separated their bodies. Even though she knew he slept beside her, she still moved her foot in his direction, gently touching his calf.

Light flooded the bedroom, making her blink. What the... A piercing squeal woke Sebastian, who barked at the obnoxious sound. Will rolled out of bed and stood silhouetted by the exterior light. Very nice, what a perfect body he had.

"Stupid bastard!" The exclamation broke through her contemplation of Will's assets. Her eyes drifted to his right hand gripping a dark object that she couldn't quite make out. Before she could ask him, he pivoted, darting past the bed into the hallway. Close enough for her to identify the gun in his hand. *Where did that come from?*

Oh my God. The image of Will shot and bleeding in the front yard spotlighted by the security light propelled her out of bed. "Stop. Wait. Don't go outside."

Her foot landed on the runner, which slid out from under her. The wood floor slapped her bare butt, sending a jolt up her spine, temporarily stunning her. Sebastian's alarmed yelps right next to her ear reminded her of the dangerous drama unfolding.

A roll to one side allowed her to regain her footing. "Will. Call 911. Don't go outside." No answer. An open front door threw a rectangle of light into the darkened living room. Her heart stopped for a moment. The man went outside. What was wrong with him? No telling what Clint might do.

Tonya darted out the door with intentions of grabbing Will and pulling him back inside before he became a target. The cold air fingered her skin like an overeager teenage lover. Damn, how'd she forgotten about being naked? Should have kept the nightshirt on. Grab Will, retreat to house, how long could it take?

Will stood under the moon, frozen on her lawn as if posing for a painting or a statue. With the motion lights on, the man might as well be on stage. Perhaps his act would be entitled *Naked Man with Gun*. The usual cars lined the night-shrouded street. No sign of Clint. As a private investigator, he would be smart enough not to park nearby. Even now, her ex could be crouched across the street behind Mrs. Lemon's lilac bushes, drawing a bead on the first decent man she'd met in a very long time.

Her lips firmed as she ran toward Will. Hands in front of her, she shoved him. He fell to the ground with a curse. Instead of the sound of a bullet whizzing overhead, she heard familiar barking and a door slam. Mrs. Lemon, the elderly widow would call the police, claiming lewd behavior and public nudity. Afraid to look up, Tonya peered up through her lashes from her place on the grass where she tumbled after broadsiding Will.

No open door, no lights in her neighbor's house, thank goodness, time enough for her and Will's retreat to the house. "Let's get back into the house before my neighbor sees us." Will rolled to a seated position, checking his gun.

"Good thing I had the safety on." An athletic lunge took him to his feet. Tonya grasped his left hand and allowed him to pull her up. In a few seconds, they'd be in the house and all would be well. Reasonably well, considering Clint was still out roaming free, doing whatever crazy thing he could get away with and apparently, that was a great deal. Memories of various questionable antics he'd shared with her crowded her memory, making her tug at Will's hand.

"We need to get inside." She thought she heard something. It could have been the whine and whirl of a camera lens opening and closing, capturing her and Will parading across the front yard in their birthday suits. "Hurry."

Only four steps separated her from the house. The motion lights on the west side of the house flickered off throwing that side into the shadows. At least no one crept around that side of the house, or remained still, knowing the light reacted to movement. Unease hunched on the edge of her senses.

Chapter Thirteen

WILL'S FINGERS TIGHTENED over hers. "Did you close the door?"

"No, of course, I..." Her eyes went to the closed door. "...didn't think I closed it." Will dropped her hand and took two steps to the door. A quick twist of the doorknob confirmed her fears.

"Locked," he spat the word. "It's the thumb lock on the door knob. It's possible Sebastian triggered it by jumping on the door."

Her arms crossed in front of her chest, chafed her arms, and tried to shield at least her breasts from public scrutiny. The overgrown bushes that surrounded her porch kept Will decent. Locked out, what were they going to do? Clint could have snuck in when they ran out. Going back in would be the equivalent of a trap, but what choice did they have? Everything was inside, including Sebastian and her car keys.

"Back door?" She offered the suggestion well aware Will spent the entire day making her house into a fortress, and she didn't lock the sliding glass door.

Will shook his head. "Nope, checked it before I went to bed. Good thing, too, it was unlocked."

Yeah, that's what she thought, too. No phone to call Lynne for help. She'd help, but probably would never allow her to live the incident down. No doubt Will and the security specialist checked and locked every window. The thought of her bare bottom disappearing over a windowsill did not appeal, but it was better than standing out on her front porch, wondering if the falling temperatures would get her before the police did.

"The garage." The upswing in his tone indicated he knew he'd found a solution. "You can stay hidden on the porch and I'll let you in. Give me the code."

The code, yeah, the one she'd never changed since taking possession of the house. "Um, 4, 5, 6, 7."

Will rolled his eyes. "You're serious?"

"It's easy to remember." Her lips lifted up in a strained smile as she rubbed her arms vigorously. The man took the hint and headed for the garage still clutching the gun in his right hand. Yeah, she'd forgot about the gun for a moment.

All she knew about guns came from movies. Clint had one, but he kept it out of sight, realizing how squeamish she was about it. In retrospect, he may have kept it hidden, afraid she might try to use it on him some day. Will's weapon wasn't the type a person could hide in an ankle holster without a suspicious bulge. Did he buy it today? The door opened behind her, startling her.

"Get in here before you freeze to death." Will grasped her arm, pulled her inside, and closed the door with his other hand. She snuggled into his half-embrace.

"Where's your gun?" Not exactly a *my hero* type of question, especially considering how he charged out of the house like a wild Viking warrior. Well, at least the way the ones in the movies did.

He tightened his other arm around her, bringing her body into a full embrace. "Hmm, weapon, huh. You want to know about that now?" Her chilled body warmed against his. "It's on the kitchen table."

"Oh good." She whispered the words next to his ear before reaching his mouth. Her lips brushed his lips lightly as she anchored herself with one hand on his shoulder and another speared through his hair, bringing his head closer.

The idea of Clint sneaking into the house worried her. She couldn't help but voice her fears against his lips. "Did you check the house?"

Will groaned a little before answering. "I did. Nothing. Even Sebastian went back to sleep. One of us must have slammed the door shut and tripped the lock with the key already in it."

His lips moved over hers, firm, dry, enticing. Even though he didn't say it, she knew the one of us was her. His tongue flicked out, teasing the corner of her mouth as his hands dropped from her waist, cupping the twin globes of her buttocks, making her forget about everything.

Oh yeah, this is what I want. Who knew it took one psycho boyfriend to sex things up?

Even now, Clint could be hiding in the house. A shiver crept up her spine, pulling her out of the moment.

"Cold?" Will purred the question against her ear. Before she could even answer and explain, he swept one arm under her legs, hugging her to his chest. "Better take this to the bedroom. I imagine I could warm you up in there."

"I bet you can." She reached past his shoulder, flicking on the hallway light. Sebastian lay on his side, legs outstretched, and mouth open. His raspy canine snores testified to his deep sleep, but something about his position bothered her.

Will stepped over the sleeping animal. "I swear your pet is a zero as a guard dog."

"Yeah, he is." Her tongue savored the saltiness of his skin as she nuzzled her way to his ear. Didn't want to defend her dog, although normally she would. A stillness settled over the house, the palpable kind that came between footsteps and heartbeats. The icemaker kicked on, bursting the bubble of fear Tonya created. *A sexy man sweeps me off my feet and into the bedroom, and I think the house is too quiet.*

Her tongue outlined the edge of his ear, eliciting a deep moan for her efforts. A vanilla aroma lingered in the air, leftover from the spent votive. The hall light created a shadowy twilight, enough to see the bed.

"Soon I'll make all your dreams come true," Will teased as his foot slipped on the crumpled throw rug. For a second, he lost his balance, losing his grip. For the briefest second, Tonya hurtled downward before Will's arms wrapped around her, and they both fell onto the bed.

"My fondest dream was to be airborne. How did you know?" She waited until Will laughed before joining him.

His fingers ruffled his own hair. "Yeah, exactly. I was trying to be smooth, and then I slipped on the rug." He directed a glare at the rug.

Her hand rested on his chest as she smiled up at him. "I don't want smooth. I want you exactly as you are." She swung her leg over his, sitting astride, rubbing up against his erection, confirming her words with her actions.

His fingers laced around her face, holding her gaze to his. "I'm glad." He lifted his head for a kiss as something fell in the closet. Tonya jerked, breaking away.

"What is it?" The muscles around his mouth tensed, not exactly the gentle lover's expression, but more than a touch of disgruntled Viking.

A sound, that's all it was. Probably a shoe falling off the shoe rack—it had happened before. The way she shoved everything in her closet, things were bound to tumble. That's all it was. Silly, really. "I thought I heard something."

"What?" his tone was mildly curious. "The house settles as the temperature drops."

She knew that, but she didn't mention it. "You're right. That's all it was. I think we were here." Her kiss landed slightly askew of his lips.

His hands angled her head so their lips met. His tongue stroked the seam of her lips, begging for entrance. A touch of mischievousness kept her lips closed until a sudden body roll landed her underneath him. The unexpected move surprised her, giving him the entry he sought. The sheets and comforter bunched under their bodies as the two of them tangled in the dusky light, memorizing each other by touch.

Her fingers struggled for purchase on his rib cage as sweat pebbled his skin. Resting her face on his chest, she licked at the sweat. "Hmm, you taste good."

His chest vibrated with laughter. "Like that? I've got a few other places you might like to explore again." She didn't think the room could get much hotter, but it did. His words stroked her already heightened senses until she writhed across the bed more snakelike than temptress. An upward lunge had her straddling his slick body.

"Enough." He wrapped one leg around hers before slowly moving her beneath him. This time the move wasn't unexpected. She'd anticipated it since the first time he turned her. A warm slide of liquid trickled down her leg, even before his fingers found her clitoris, rubbing it between his thumb and forefinger. "Ready?"

Instead of answering, she raised her hips, angling them to guide his cock inside her. A satisfied groan accompanied his penetration. Instead of the expected plunge, he rested on his forearms allowing anticipation to build.

One good hard stroke would send her over the edge and the man waits. Tonya dug her heels into the mattress and bucked upwards, shimmying up and down his shaft. "Come on."

Will chuckled before he lifted his body, withdrawing until she complained. "Hey, what are you doing?"

His sudden downward shift filled her, causing her to moan his name as she climaxed. Ankles locked behind his hips secured her seat for the ride. Her inner muscles tightened with each plunge, holding onto Will as he withdrew. His guttural groan signified his approval of her actions.

A goofy grin remained on her face as Will shouted his release. Instead of rolling to one side and falling into a deep sleep, he smoothed his hands over her breasts, starting the fingers at the outer edge and drawing them up to the nipples. The pressure increased as he went, causing her to twist. "You know," she panted the words. "I've already come twice. Once while you were dancing and just now."

"Not enough." He leaned over, sucking her nipple into his mouth as his fingers found her clit again. The friction of both his mouth and fingers brought her to a screaming finish. Her eyes opened to his intent hazel ones.

Something about his expression made her giggle. "Is there something on my face?" Having a man's full attention after sex surprised her.

His hand smoothed back her hair. "Yeah, there's something on your face, all right. A big something."

Her left hand smoothed over her face, feeling for a wayward leaf, booger, or whatever else could be stuck to her face. "I don't feel anything."

"Not sure how you missed that big, satisfied smile." He winked at her, resting his head on his bent arm. His phone gurgled, interrupting whatever else he might say.

Again. Who could it be now? She expected him to ignore it since they were in bed. Indecision flashed across his face before Will glanced at the clock, rolled out of bed and padded down the hallway. Apparently, leaving the phone outside the bedroom didn't guarantee they'd be undisturbed.

His voice grew louder as he walked back to the bedroom.

"You're kidding me. I'm your divorce lawyer, not your real lawyer. Okay, stop crying. I'll come down and straighten this out."

Will walked into the room, threw his phone on the bed, and picked up his clothes. Boxers first, then his socks, and finally his pants before she accepted the visual evidence of his imminent departure. "Where are you going?"

"My client, who you said wouldn't steal the dog, did. At least, attempted to, but got caught in the process. Apparently, I'm the only lawyer she knows." Will rounded the bed and dropped a kiss on her forehead.

"That's my fault somehow?" She yelled the words after him. Hearing no response, she forced herself out of bed, donning the nightshirt she'd discarded earlier. Double-checking the lock served as a goal, but irritation at Will's abrupt departure made her restless. The heavy metal key turned in the chamber with a solid thud, delivering a sense of protection. Her initial irritation at what she viewed as Will's desertion faded a little.

"Good, at least no one can get in."

A footstep sounded behind her.

Chapter Fourteen

A CHILL PERMEATED her body. The term frozen in place now made sense to her. Her fingers rested on the key inserted in the deadbolt lock. She'd locked herself inside, but one twist, one pull, and she'd be free. All she had to do was turn the key. Don't look back. Looking back would acknowledge the evil creeping up behind her.

Silently, she reversed the key, not even daring to breathe, not signaling in any way her actions. *So far, so good*, she mentally encouraged herself. Good thing she dressed. On some cosmic level, something triggered her decision. The sheer curtains revealed the sleeping, dark neighborhood. No one awake to help her. She doubted anyone would open his or her door to her pounding. Didn't people ignore screams, claiming they thought they were television-generated when a neighbor died outside their front door?

Where could she go once, she escaped? The oversized holly tree that soared above the Petersen's house could provide safety in its upper limbs. She could be seen heading that way though. A zigzag path through dark backyards would be her best bet.

The metallic clank that had reassured her so much previously sounded loud in the silence. Did he hear it? How close was he? Her hand pulled the door open about an inch before her body slammed against it, flattened under Clint's body. She recognized his smell, a combination of stale cigarette smoke, a musky body odor, and the tinge of hair product.

His breath dusted her ear as he spoke. The intimate act stiffened the hairs on her arm. "You'll be leaving soon enough, Tonya girl, but with me."

Her father's constant reminder about thinking before she spoke went forgotten. "No, I won't. I want nothing to do with you."

"I got that message." Clint moved his lower body, allowing a little space between them. For a brief moment, Tonya considered her forthright statement had changed the man's mind. Honesty paid off, after all.

The hard door contours pressed into her body through her thin cotton nightshirt. Clint's upper body still plastered her face and chest against the door. How could she have not seen the signs? *Closed door. Sebastian asleep on the hard floor. A sound in her closet.*

Sebastian. "What did you do to my dog?" The words came out a little morphed due to her face flattened against the door panel.

"What an irritating excuse for a dog. Drugged him. The greedy little shit took whatever I gave him."

"Oh my God, you may have killed him!" What type of person drugs a pet? Oh yeah, she remembered. The same kind who broke into your home. In the movies, women went limp and slipped out of the attacker's grasp. Be gelatin, she instructed her body, but failed to take into account his weight pinning her to the door, which kept her arms pinned beneath her.

As maneuvers went, it showed intelligence. Tonya sucked in her lips not wanting to credit her stalker with intellect, but it would be better not to underestimate him. What did she really know about Clint? Self-absorbed narcissist, who considered himself some type of action hero. He also had a healthy dislike of the police and the legal system, which always made her wonder if he'd had a run-in with both. He claimed he was a former police officer, but after a while, she accepted he tended to be creative regarding his past. Her heart pounded as she considered possible options.

The rasp of a zipper told the story of his intentions, increasing her struggles. A backward kick stubbed her bare toes with his boot. This wasn't supposed to be happening. One screw-up—Clint happened to be it—and her whole life would be over.

Damn it, she should be stronger. Should have gone to the gym, instead of watching reality shows. His hot breath feathered her ear, making her want to scrub it clean.

"I'd like a taste of what you gave lawyer boy earlier. Made me hot listening to you. Jacked off in your shoes."

A bitter mass pushed up into her throat, gagging her. She swallowed, sending it back, leaving a sourness behind. The cool air brushed across her ass as her nightshirt bunched under his hand. *Why, why now, when I've found someone decent and have some direction in my life.* A few phrases from a self-defense class came to mind.

"I have an STD." That discouraged some would-be rapists.

Instead of rearing back in horror, he chuckled. "You forgot I have access to your medical records. You're clean. I doubt you'd be doing the nasty with your boy toy if you had. You're too nice for that."

What else should she do? Her purse wasn't close with handy hairspray or keys. Wait. She had a key. In fact, it was in her hand. Her fingers tightened on it. It could work as a tiny knife if she went for his face. Her numb fingers didn't respond, especially pressed up against the door. The deadbolt lock and doorknob would leave a permanent indentation in her skin. A queasiness came over her as she considered gouging out his eyes.

Couldn't do it, but then his hand caressed her left buttock, Clint's version of foreplay. God, he was going to do it. Instead of her past life flashing in front of her eyes, her possible future unrolled in slow motion.

Clint stared at her broken, bleeding body that he'd savagely used. Her mouth open, oozing blood as she promised to tell no one. The panicked man grabbed her, cold-cocked her, and stuffed her into the trunk of his car. Her body, crumpled between camping gear, night vision binoculars, and explosives, lost all feeling as it grew colder. Her eyes couldn't see anything. Only her ears and mind still worked.

The radio played some announcement about a missing person. It cut to Will's voice offering a large reward for any information. Clint swore and started arguing with himself. One voice, she recognized as the smooth operator that charmed her when they met. The other, higher voice, was Clint's, but disturbing in its intensity.

"We must kill her," the falsetto voice declared.

"I don't know," the other Clint hesitated.

"No, now, stop the car. Leave no evidence. We'll burn her."

Tonya's heart thudded to a stop, breaking her out of the horrific future with two psychotic Clints. She felt the head of his erection probing closer.

"I think I hear Will's car." A noisy car exhaust coughed and chortled in the distance. It wasn't Will's, of course.

Clint stopped. A gun snout rubbed against her cheek. "Doubt it was lover boy, but he could come back soon. I don't want any interruptions." He stepped away from her. Loud gasps reverberated against the door as Tonya inhaled while tamping down her incipient panic.

The hall light silhouetted Clint, but she still had the pistol aimed at her face. Her face, not her heart. Clint used to inform her you always shot at the torso since it was a bigger target. At this range, no way he could miss.

Her eyes dropped down to his unzipped pants with his semi-erect member still poking out. Noticing where her eyes went, Clint laughed. "No fears, you'll still get some when we are away from here. Right now, I need you to put it back in my pants and zip it up. Remember, I have the gun."

Seriously, did he expect her to touch him gently and reinsert his dick back in his pants? Her fingers rubbed across the key. Not his eyes, but it might hurt as much. He'd shoot her, but probably intended to anyhow. She inhaled deeply. *Too bad I can't leave a note, at least a short one.*

"Glad to." She tried for a smile as she spoke, but it probably looked more like a grimace. She reached for Clint's fly, holding her palm down with her thumb across the key, holding it in place. Her other hand clutched his member until she got her fingers in place around the smooth side of the key.

"Aha, you like it." His lips were on her neck. A drop of his saliva slid down her skin, leaving a slime path behind. "I suspected you had a kinky side. Like it rough. Maybe you could go down on me while I hold a gun to your head." His half-snort laugh made it hard to determine if his suggestion was a joke or a demand.

His words gave her the impetus. Using the rough side of the key, she pulled it across his delicate skin cradled in her hand.

"What the hell?" He pushed her away, but not before she nicked his balls with the jagged edge as she fell. A torrent of curse words flew as she silently crawled away. Freedom. If she could reach the back door while he cupped his balls, she'd make it.

"Think again, bitch!" Pain erupted in her head, shocking her nerve endings and lighting up the back of her eyelids with a flash of blood vessels before everything went black.

THE SOUND OF a slipping transmission penetrated her consciousness. Countless repetitions of transmission shop commercials helped with the noise recognition. Did she leave the television on? The darkness made her blink in an effort to focus. Items tended to be vague when she first woke up. It usually took a few seconds before her surroundings grew familiar. A sensation of movement puzzled her. Could she be dreaming? Occasionally, the bed spun after a heavy night of drinking, but it never actually moved as in those possession movies.

A loud honk, then an answering honk, practically burst her ear-drums. It sounded as if she was in the middle of a street, but that couldn't be. As for dreams, this one sucked. Wake up, that's what she'd do. If she pinched herself, it would end. Tonya reached for her leg as a likely target, only her hands wouldn't move. *Were they asleep?* The rising panic forced her to twist her fingers one way, then another, without moving her wrists one iota. The more she tried the more pressure bit into them, chafing them as if tied.

The thought stopped her struggles. *What is happening?* News magazine shows filled her head with frantic relatives pleading for the whereabouts of a missing loved one. With her mother in Florida, busy with her reading clubs and Bunco groups, it would be weeks before she'd even notice her disappearance—if ever, since she always called her mother and not the other way around.

Be logical. Stay calm. The darkness and tight space meant she was probably in a trunk. A headache, along with the gagging diesel fumes, made clear thought difficult. Clint purchased a diesel sedan, insisting it was so much better than regular cars. Couldn't remember why. The memory of the key and her actions came flooding back.

Damn. The self-defense videos implied the secret to incapacitating men for minutes was an attack to the family jewels. At least long enough to escape. Should have gouged harder. Wait, jewels equated balls. Screwed that one up royally. A long exhale escaped as she considered her situation: stuck in a car, going who knows where. Clint's precarious balance between ordinary and crazy finally flipped over into certifiable. Before, she'd made excuses for his questionable behavior about bending the law as part of his profession. When he joked about killing people, she referred to that as dark humor.

What was she going to do? Her lips twisted as she realized Will would probably return to his home after their terse words.

The car slowed down, then stopped. God, please don't be the place, wherever that might be. Open your senses, pay attention to everything. A lightweight tag slapped her in the face. The car accelerated, causing the object to hit her eye. What could it be? A dangling bit of wire. What could be hanging from the trunk lid? As many times as she'd opened her trunk, she never really stared at it. A partial memory of her and Lynne power shopping came to mind. As they stuffed their many bargains into the trunk, a fluorescent tag scratched her hand. At the time, it annoyed her. Lynne warned her not to cut it because she might need it if she found herself locked in a trunk. Accidentally locked in a trunk, no chance of that happening, she remembered responding.

My *means* of escape is literally hanging in my face. If she could grab it with her bound hands, the trunk would fly open, providing an opportunity to escape. At least someone would see her and call the police. Of course, another driver might not want to get involved or think it was part of some kinky sex game. More reason she had to rescue herself. She lifted her head as the pull hit her face again. Having the location in her head, she jerked her wrists upward, only able to move them a few inches before being stopped by another rope running to her ankles. The man had her hogtied like a calf at the rodeo.

Her body flopped back onto the rough blanket. *Well, at least the man put a blanket down in the trunk. That meant he cared a little, right? Get a clue, Sherlock, that's for the dead body.* None of it made sense. Why would the man be so intent on getting her back if he planned to kill her? Oh yeah, mentally deranged people seldom made sense.

The trunk release pull bumped against her face, reminding her that escape was within reach. Sure, if she could pull it with her teeth. Her teeth! Her heart quickened with the thought.

The sound of the radio penetrated the back seat, filling the small space with heavy metal music and the reedy voice of Clint singing along. He sounded happy, maybe even convinced himself she'd be his willing slave. *See him in hell, first.*

The car moved at a good clip, maybe forty, possibly fifty miles an hour, which could mean a county highway, possibly en route to the isolated cabin in the woods. It translated to no stops any time soon. The fall from the trunk might kill her, or at least break a few bones. Broken bones—no biggie considering the alternative. Tonya snapped her jaws in preparation.

A tight strip of cloth held down her tongue and bit into the sides of her mouth, but she could still close her teeth enough to grab the tag. Clint must have been afraid she'd scream. Unfortunately, it showed more intelligence than she'd suspected. Not good, considering her goal was to outsmart him.

The turn signal clicked on, signaling not only a turn, but also narrowing the window of escape. Tonya rocked upward, snapping at the tag similar to a plastic hippo in a child's game. Despite her frantic champing, she couldn't grab the tag, which swayed wildly once the car shuddered to a standstill. She should have tried sooner.

The car's forward motion threw her back into something hard, hitting her already bruised skull. Her imagination took flight as she imagined a cement block—the better to cause her to sink to the bottom of the lake. The tires chewed up a gravel road as it lurched upward, throwing Tonya against the edge of the trunk. The other trunk items came hurtling after her. A few pelted her softly before bouncing off, but the others were heavy and metallic. Their descent was slowed by her soft flesh, but they chose to stay wedged into the back of her legs and buttocks. Her mother's insistence on wearing clean underwear would have stood her in good stead. Any underwear would shield her from the metal cylinder wedged between her thighs. *Please don't be a gun.*

The rough, nubby car carpet pressed into her face. A peaty odor with an underlying scent of manure permeated the material. Gardening, the man hauled around supplies in his trunk. Of course, the Clint she knew wouldn't have ever gardened. The cold metal chilled her leg as she carefully tried to move her lower body away from the impertinent implement. No need to take chances. With her recent luck, she'd have a gun with the safety off clutched between her thighs.

The car jerked to a stop. Tonya tensed her body, squeezing her eyes shut in the already dark trunk. Nothing. No sudden explosion. No traffic noise. A bird warbled close by while a dog barked in the distance.

Where was she? A bird, a dog… She could be almost anywhere, even a residential neighborhood, but she doubted it. The car door swung open with a creak. The car shifted with the motion of Clint getting out. Great. Now what? Tonya took a deep breath. Right now, trussed up, she didn't have options. Somehow, she'd have to get him to trust her. So far, she'd underestimated the man's abilities. Her life depended on her not making the same mistake.

A click and a metallic groan announced the trunk opening as sunlight forced her to close her eyes. "Honey, we're home," Clint purred the words close to her ear.

Tonya managed not to move as his hand slid up her bare leg. It didn't stop her skin from creeping. "Lookee what we got here. Tire iron between your thighs." He jerked the metal tool from between her legs.

Breathing slowly, she concentrated on pretending to be asleep, feeling Clint's stare on her exposed hips. Hardest thing she'd ever done. There would be even more gut-turning incidents. Her survival would depend on it.

"Come on now, you can't still be out. I didn't hit you that hard." A whine colored his remark.

What gave him the right to be peeved? Good. Maybe she could pretend unconsciousness until an escape opportunity presented itself. She felt the cold metal slide up her calf and stopped behind her knee. Her breath caught as she waited for the man's next action.

"Probably using my humble tire iron to get off. Lawyer boy didn't do it for you." An evil chuckle punctuated his comment.

Competing thoughts raced through her head. The urge to shout that Will had done a better job than he ever did started and ended before ever crossing her lips. How did he know Will was a lawyer? Oh yeah, the man camped out in her closet listening to Will wrangle with the hysterical Gloria while she complained about it. Clint might assume Will was just another wham, bam, thank you ma'am type of fellow. He wasn't. Doubt flickered at the edge of her mind. Sure, it had been a couple of days, but some people did click in that short time. That was if they continued to see each other after a minor brush up about his job.

A draft drifted over her stomach, wrapping around her waist. A suspicion triggered a slight wince. She didn't remember her nightshirt pulled up. The cold metal rubbed across her nipples. Her eyes flew open.

"Aha, just as I thought. I wondered if you were going to let me shove the tire iron up you like a dildo." His eyes took on a considering expression as he dropped the tool. "Yeah, still has possibilities."

His arms reached under her legs and back, lifting her out of the trunk. Her nightshirt twisted under her armpits, serving no purpose. Unable to endure his eager expression, she closed her eyes.

"Oh no, none of that." He jostled her in his arms, pretending to drop her, trying to get a response. Tonya kept her eyes firmly closed and mentally prayed.

God, I haven't been the best person in the world. Then again, I haven't been the worst. Rescued Sebastian. Buy Girl Scout cookies every year. That might not count because I buy them more for me. I collected canned goods for the mail carriers' food drive, too.

The hollow sound of Clint's boots on the wooden steps hastened her cosmic favor pulling. *I know I just donated all the fava beans I didn't like, but someone is bound to like them. Why else would they grow them? Yeah, I know I waste too much money on clothes, gripe about unimportant stuff, and occasionally drink too much, which resulted in this situation.*

"Damn, you're heavier than you look." His words preceded her bare ass slapping a cold metal chair. A jingle of keys and a stream of muttered curses indicated a stubborn lock had her captor's full attention. A window of opportunity for a visual observation. God, she sounded like Clint.

Her narrowed eyes took in the rosy dawn light coming through the tree branches. She couldn't move her head too much without Clint noticing, but she didn't need to. Besides the trees, she could see the open trunk car resting on a spare patch of the grass, most likely worn away by repeated parking. A rusted barrel sat on cinder blocks in a blackened clearing: a burn barrel, what people used when they didn't have the luxury of city garbage pickup.

Mold darkened the wooden porch. Jagged edges marred some of the planks, indicating it had broken or more likely just rotted through. The cabin was no one's treasured getaway. The turquoise metal flecked with rust spots that showed between her goose-bumped legs reminded her of something her grandmother might own.

The tinkling of glass shattering along with a curse announced the end of the lock battle. Was this even Clint's place? Breaking and entering didn't bother the man. The grassy parking spot and burn area evidenced a few visits, even if not recently. Gutsy of Clint to use someone else's property when the owner could return.

Of course, he wasn't staying long. Even though the man considered himself the equal to any undercover spy, he still enjoyed his luxuries. When he leaves, it will give me the opening I need. Tonya stared down at her bare legs and purple toenails. Neither were exactly suited for survival runs.

"Alrighty, got the door open." Clint's unexpected pivot had her shutting her eyes. Not that it mattered since he knew she was awake.

"Let the games begin."

His breath brushed her calves. What was he doing at her feet? His forearm went down across both feet, securing them to the porch floor. Curiosity opened her eyes as she stared down at his bent form. His right hand gripped the hilt of a knife secured in the special boot pocket.

A shudder rippled through her body at the sight of the knife. She'd remembered the night he showed her the online advertisement for the boots with a built-in knife pocket. At the time, she asked him if his plans included being a modern-day colonist, complete with a musket. Her comment hadn't amused him.

His fingers tightened around the hilt and slowly withdrew it. Would he stab it through her foot, pinning her to the porch? The image of blood spurting out of her foot until she finally died broke out a sweat on her chilled skin.

Is this it? The end of life as I know it? At least, I should make some type of effort, even if stabbing results. The pressure around her ankles eased as the rope dropped from them, hitting the wood with a dull thunk.

Clint rocked back on his heels, and sheathed his knife before pushing up into a standing position. "At least now I won't have to haul your fat ass around."

Her first response was to deny his remark—point out that if he were stronger, it wouldn't be an issue. After all, Will carried her without complaint. Every now and then, she took the smart route and kept her mouth shut. Unbound legs presented more possibilities. Her toes wiggled against the wood, working out the numbness. Hundreds of invisible needles plunged into her skin, replacing the numbness. Not the best, but it meant continued survival. The rising sun shined into her eyes, blinding her.

Normally, the sun shined or didn't shine without her thinking about it. The looming possibility that it might be the last sunrise she ever saw made it precious. Her face lifted to the light. The rays touched her all over, but unlike the stinging pain in her feet, it brought reassurance.

In the half second between heartbeats, she swore to herself. *I may not have done anything outstanding with my life, but I refuse to die at the hands of a psycho before I even have the chance to live.* Images of Will smiling tenderly before he kissed her, along with Lynne laughing, and Marc lighting the Baked Alaska, crowded her mind. Was her life flashing before her eyes before death, or was she remembering all the reasons she needed to live?

Chapter Fifteen

H ER RESTRAINED HANDS balled into fists as Clint's hand wrapped around her arm and yanked her upward. The motion had her stumbling on her still numb feet. Probably stubbed her big toe, but couldn't feel it yet. Her movement shook the oversized nightshirt out where it covered her decently. A flimsy barrier, but it was better than before.

Clint will not touch me! Sure, he had a good grip on her arm, but other than that, nothing. Her fisted hands eased a little. Balling up her fists only made the rope tighter. She needed to keep her fingers viable for when she was loose. Her eyes dropped to the knife grip sticking out of the leather boot. The knife, she needed it.

Her lunatic ex carried a gun, probably had a half-dozen stashed in his car. Still, as questionable as his mental state was, he'd expect her to go for a gun or a phone. The knife would bring in an element of surprise. An element of gore, too. This from a woman who almost wrecked the car trying not to hit a bird. The thought of the knife plunged into a major artery with Clint's blood showering her made her swallow hard.

Inhaling deeply, she steadied her resolve as she stumbled across the threshold. The deep breath netted her a lungful of stale, musty air. Dust motes danced in the early morning light, probably because there was no room left for them on the furniture. A light coating of dust rested on the navy plaid couch and easy chair. A pair of antlers hung over the creek stone fireplace, which contained a few partially charred logs. Wood smoke smell hung in the air.

How long did the smoke smell linger? A science fiction book rested half-opened on a cushion. Weird, it looked as if someone left to get a drink or use the bathroom.

Clint angled his head in an effort to see what caught her attention. His thoughts may have mirrored hers because he abruptly squeezed her arm. "No worries, sweet Tonya. Whoever left that book isn't coming back."

Why? She wanted to ask, but decided not to, realizing the answer might be something she didn't need to hear. Especially since her job was to take down scary psycho stalker. None of this made any sense. Why her? It never seemed as if he was that interested in her. She jumped through hoops doing things he wanted to do, cooking meals, doing laundry, and even dressing up in the Nazi dominatrix costume. Why she thought he was okay then, boggled her mind.

Her lips twisted as she considered her mindset a year ago. No, she never thought Clint was the one. Didn't even consider him normal, but she had considered him harmless. Screw up there. "So, what's the deal with you wanting me back?"

The searing look Clint rested on her made her realize she'd spoken her thoughts aloud. Oh well, might as well see it through. At least she might get much-needed information. "You left me to chase after somebody else, in case you forgot."

Clint grunted as he shoved her down in the chair. Never a great one for courteous conduct, but his manners went south in a hurry.

"Chased after Bridget. Not quite everything I'd thought she'd be. All show, no delivery."

The rough fabric scratched her exposed legs. She twisted in the chair, searching for a more comfortable position as she considered his words. All show, what did that mean? What happened to her?

His hand rested on the back of the chair, ready to grab her if needed. "Lola came along just about the time Bridget started boring me."

Yeah, she knew that feeling. A sense of worthlessness when he left had wrestled with a sense of relief. Lynne assured her that's how some men were, always moving on to the next woman. Of course, the story she told Lynne featured her dropping him after she suspected him of cheating. Even though he left her for Bridget, she still felt sympathy for the woman.

"Um, Lola, what about her? If he kept talking, it kept him from doing anything else. It wasn't as if the cavalry would be showing up anytime soon. No one would even know she was gone until Monday morning. A few people would suspect she bugged out like a few of the other employees who left without a written notice. Of course, they were young and didn't know any better.

Tonya stretched her back, first one side, then the other, receiving no complaint from her captor. Could be the man was mellowing out. This could all be some psychotic break, blip or something. Her posture straightened. The possibility of getting out of this alive existed.

Something flew by her head and shattered against the fireplace. "Lola. Damn whore! Not worth my time!"

Asking why didn't appear to be a good move on her part. No need to ask if Lola dumped him. Still, it made no sense he wanted her back. She sucked in her lips, knowing she didn't need to say anything else. It'd be the smart thing to do.

Her nose itched. Scratching it with her bound hands resulted in her hitting herself in the face. He must have mistaken her nose scratching for wiping away tears.

"No reason to get all upset about it. You got me back now."

The words took a while to penetrate. A chuckle welled up in her throat. Laughter would not be an appropriate response. Air born dust tickled her sinuses, turning the potential chuckle into a cough.

"No need to cry about it. I came back for you. In the end, you were the only one who treated me well. All those others were bitches, always demanding things. Take me here. Give me that. Meet my friends. The list never ended."

Tonya turned her chin into a shoulder, trying to escape the dust. The complaints half-registered as she realized she never expected or asked for anything from the man. Whatever scrap of attention he gave her, she embraced it, and held it close, never even dreaming of asking for more.

His hand slid to her shoulder, giving it a squeeze. "Now that we're back together, I think a little training is in order. Like most women, you have a tendency to chase after men."

Did he truly think she wanted to stay with him? *Be compliant. Willing.* "Ah, I'm so glad you realized." She stopped, having a hard time keeping her voice soft and pushing out the words that might get her hands untied. "All I ever wanted was you."

"What woman wouldn't?"

Her lips formed Lola's name, but luckily, he wasn't looking at her but out the window. Three swift strides took him to the window. He first peered outside, and then flattened himself against the side of the window.

"Is someone there?" She leaned forward, hoping to get a glimpse.

A quick slashing motion indicated she needed to be quiet or possibly face beheading. Screaming would garner her some attention—all the wrong kind from Clint. It would damage her compliant act, too. He shoved her to the floor before she could see the visitors and possibly rescuers.

A car door slammed. Shoes crunching through fallen leaves indicated the door hadn't shut fully. Inhaling deeply, she prepared for the scream of her life, horror movie scream worthy. Clint's hand slapped over her mouth before she uttered a peep. How'd he move so fast? Tears of frustration leaked through tightly squeezed closed eyes. *This is so unfair. Shouldn't I have a break right about now?*

Another voice joined her inner conversation. *Suck it up, girlfriend. No time for pity parties. The only action hero in the room is wearing a cartoon nightshirt. Be the answer.*

His thick fingers pressed into her face, making her jaw ache from the pressure. Too bad her mouth wasn't open. At least she could have bit him. Hard to imagine how she could have found the brute attractive.

Keeping his grip tight, he whispered into her ear. "You've always been transparent. You're worse than a child is. Not hard to see the wheels turning in your head."

A masculine voice commented close to the porch. "I don't know, man. Last time we were here, there wasn't anyone around."

"Are we going hunting or what?" The second speaker's voice held a touch of ridicule. No doubt he'd resorted to ridicule to get his way. *Been there, experienced that.* Her eye roll went unnoticed by her attacker as his gaze fixed on the sliver of open door.

Silence greeted the remark, which meant the two were probably standing with rifles over their shoulders, tantalizingly close. Who knows, there might be a little chivalry in at least one of them? Her bet was on the one who didn't want to be caught on private property.

Clint's upper body pinned her to the floor, but her legs remained free. She could use them for some type of leverage whenever the chance presented itself. Sucking her lips in, she concentrated on isolating her muscles the way her initial martial arts class taught. She visualized the move in her mind as the sansei taught, trying to ignore the fact she never made it to class two. *Must not telegraph my intentions. I'll show him who's transparent.*

"Roy, I don't have a good feeling about this. Your brother, Daryl, is in the county jail after he built the deer blind on that foreign dude's property. There's a car, which means there's someone inside who could call."

Doubts about their chivalry potential grew as she listened.

"Shut up, Lonnie. No deer blind put him in jail. The fact he shot at the man when he tried to take it down did it. Claimed it was a hate crime. Daryl would have shot at anyone who tried to take down his blind. American or foreigner."

Knowing if she heard anymore, she'd lose hope altogether, she violently kicked out with her legs, heaving her hips a few inches off the floor. Instead of jumping into a standing position as she imagined, one foot tangled with a metal floor lamp, breaking it with a noisy crash that shattered the glass globe.

"Let's get out of here!"

She couldn't tell if it was the timid Lonnie or the blow hard Roy. Running footsteps and the cough of an engine starting followed by the automotive growl as the vehicle shot back down the bumpy trail assured their departure.

Clint's grip relaxed on her mouth, then disappeared as he stood. "Damn rednecks. Your little stunt scared them off. Good thinking."

Her lips turned down as she rocked herself into a seated position. He knew good and well her intention was not to scare them off, but he couldn't resist a mocking opportunity. The scattered shards glistened in the early morning sun in a half-moon pattern around her. A few tinkled as they tumbled from her body as she switched positions. Stepping on one would hurt and slow down her escape attempt. Her bare feet scrambling through the unknown woods would be bad enough. No reason to add injury to it before she started.

Rummaging sounds came from the direction of the kitchen, which helped her locate Clint. Her eyes traveled around the room as she considered how to remove herself from the glass island without hurting her feet. Despite the dust and obvious sign of disuse, the cabin had the look of someone leaving in a hurry. A jacket still hung on a peg. Mental note, *wear the jacket*. A pair of dirt-encrusted boots sat by the door. Must have been muddy when first discarded. Then there was the open book and the coffee cup, rather like those mysteries of towns where tables were set for dinner when everyone disappeared.

The fact Clint didn't have a key for the door and the dust had been undisturbed meant he hadn't killed the owner. At least, he hadn't murdered him here. A shiver rippled over her skin, shaking free more shards that tumbled to the floor. How does a person handle a possible murderer? Her infatuation with the news magazines demonstrated that contact with a murderer resulted in death, except for the law enforcement officers who caught him.

Footsteps forced her to look over her shoulder at the possible killer brandishing a broom and dustpan. "I was going to clean up the glass to protect your feet, but I changed my mind."

Her breath stopped in the middle of inhalation. *Dead women don't worry about cut up feet. Maybe dead women don't bleed much. Something along that line that he'd laugh about, considering it sophisticated dark humor.*

"You caused it. You should clean it up." He held out the broom and dustpan in her direction. Her held breath whooshed out in a relieved sigh as she held her hands up. Seriously, had he forgotten her bound hands?

"Yeah, right." He rested the broom against the wall and placed the dustpan on the floor. Glass crunched under his boots as he made two long strides toward her. He bent at the waist, wrapping his fingers around his boot knife. "I'll cut you loose. Don't go getting any ideas. No cell phone, not that it would matter. No cell phone service. It's over a mile to an actual road. Not that you'd know what direction to head."

The knife chewed away at the thick nylon twisted rope. Each strand broke free with a barely discernable ping, attesting to the tension. Thank goodness his need to punish and humiliate her required cutting her hands free. Nylon rope was the strongest available, she knew, because Clint informed her one night after disappointing sex. At the time, she thought it a prelude to bondage, but he never followed up on it.

"Good thing I have a serrated blade," he grunted as he continued to saw away, making her glad for the wicked looking knife, too. Her gladness centered on taking the knife from him.

"As for the car, I have a security block system installed on it. No luck there. Might as well settle into the idea that the two of us are going to spend some quality time together."

His chuckle made the comment even more ominous. No declaration of love, not that she expected one. Would their quality time be a couple of weeks, days, or even hours? Whatever it was, there'd be no chance of Clint driving her back home, giving her a jaunty salute and a remark about getting together sometime soon. Nope. None at all. He'd have to dispose of the evidence, which would be her and the cabin.

Fire would eliminate the cabin. Being so far back in the woods no one would come to check before it burned to the ground. Surrounding trees might catch fire, too. Could be the plan. An arson investigator might come around, but in the end, arsonists don't leave fingerprints. The best way to get rid of a body was to burn it for an extended period at fourteen hundred to eighteen hundred degrees Fahrenheit. Forest fires and house fires didn't burn hot enough to destroy evidence. She tried not to flinch as she stared down at Clint's bent head, realizing that tidbit of information came from the man himself.

At the time, she considered his store of murder-related trivia macabre, but job related. His dark, thick hair, which she once thought his best feature, now served as a façade, masking his bizarre nature by making him seem normal, even handsome. His eyes, she considered his second best feature, where light gray. The same hue serial killers sported in the movies. Clint's gusty exhale resulted in goosebumps forming on her arms.

Her muscles tensed, waiting for the escape opportunity. Adrenaline pumped through her veins, putting her on edge and urging her to run. Fight or flight response, she knew it well since her reaction leaned toward flight. This time she inhaled deeply, controlling her instincts, which shouted at her to run.

"Getting excited, huh?" Clint stopped and leered at her, then dropped his gaze to chest level. "If I'd known you liked to be tied up, we could have started having fun so much sooner. I only left because you were boring."

He called her boring. Forgetting to placate the man, she snorted. "Me, boring?" In retrospect, they weren't the most fun couple she knew. "Maybe I was dull, but look what I had to work with."

"Me?" Clint's voice went high with surprise.

"Yeah, you." She nodded vigorously. *What the hell am I doing? Do I want to die sooner?* "Um, yeah you. Too much man for me. Too alpha." She coughed, trying to clear her throat of the bile that kept rolling up in it as she tried to form the words she knew would please Clint the most. "Too macho. Too commando."

"Yeah, you got that right, in more ways than one."

His snicker reminded her of a melodrama villain. God, when she got out of this, she'd wash her mouth out with soap to get the taste of the words out of her mouth. "I understood why you left." She'd cursed his sorry hide while stomping around the house. "A man as rich in experience as you couldn't be satisfied with one woman."

The bile came back. She swallowed again. Her grandmother always warned her that liars' pants caught on fire. The material underneath her hips heated, but probably due to her nervous shifting rather than cosmic retribution.

An approving tone colored his words as if he were praising a small child or pet. "You know me so well."

"Yes. You need a harem. Any woman would be grateful to be part of it."

"Harem, yeah, that's right." He inserted the tip of his knife underneath the final strands, nicking her skin in the process. "I'd have to agree with you, but," his voice sunk into a snarl, "Lola wouldn't. The only person who deserved a harem in her world was her!"

The last strand broke and fell to the floor. Tonya closed her eyes for a second, allowing the breath she'd been holding out in a long exhale. Getting him upset about Lola while armed with a deadly instrument almost did her in. One slit and her radial artery would spurt out her lifeblood all over the dusty floor.

When they found her, if they ever did, it would be labelled a suicide. Michelle would say her uncertain job situation sent her over the edge. Her mother's excuse to all and sundry who would listen would be she allowed Michael Heil to pass through her fingers when she could have had a life of ease as a doctor's wife. The pre-med student that she dated a few times creeped her out with his love of horror movies involving mutilation. Her mother had more interest in him than she ever did, never even questioning why a college student would want to date a teenager.

Clint rocked back on his heels, a precursor to standing. "Lola." He spat the word.

Tonya circled her ankles first, but eased back into a chair, trying to get as far away as possible. She slipped one foot under her, then the other as she moved into position, ready to vault out of the chair. Good chance he'd take out his anger at Lola on her.

A downward glance confirmed the broken glass. Clint walked across it in his hobnailed boots, scattering some of it. Her only exit, the door, while tantalizingly near, stood behind Clint.

"Damn whore!" His words came at the same time as the knife hurtled through the air. The nearness of the knife ruffled her hair before it embedded itself into the wall right behind her head. A warm trickle on her inner thigh broke her out of her frozen state. Her hands rested on the back of the chair as she pushed off, trying for more momentum to get past the glass. Her right foot landed clear, but a sharp pain in her big toe and second toe signaled she hadn't missed the glass.

Clint's open mouth denoted his surprise. "Don't be stupid!" he warned, looking at her, and back at the knife still vibrating in the wall.

Tonya froze as if playing a game of frozen statues, waiting for his next move. He lunged for the knife, she the door.

Outside, the tall pines beckoned. Her legs ate up the ground as she headed for the thickest, darkest section. Her goal was to find a climbable tree. The spindly young pines offered no protection. Most of the larger trees had already shed some of their leaves for the season. The tree mulch under her feet didn't feel too bad, but crackled every time she took a step.

Watching the ground, she tried to jump from exposed spot of dirt to exposed spot. It slowed her progress. The sound of running footsteps forced her to abandon her stealthy approach and break into a lope while evaluating trees as she ran.

Too high to reach the first branch, too weak, too little, too bare, where was a climbable tree when she needed one?

"Stop now. I have a gun. You don't want me to shoot you?"

Chapter Sixteen

THE WHOLE DOG napping fiasco took almost two hours to work out. His client's soon to be ex-husband was in no mood to write it off as a foolish prank. The irate man waited at the station with the dog. The French Bull Dog sported a sweater with tiny pink bones. At least the dog looked apologetic, but that might have been due to its wardrobe.

Will's hand scratched across his beard stubble as he hid his disgusted expression. His one attempt to reason with the man ended up with the man accusing him of encouraging his wife in her ill-fated venture. Hard fought patience kept him from retorting that the train had left the station before he ever arrived. The pair of them deserved each other. The unfortunate fact is they would both remarry and drive another spouse to melodramatic actions.

At least Tonya was no drama queen. No high maintenance tendencies, either, although the way he tore out of the house, she deserved the right to an old-fashioned shouting match. He should bring her something, a peace offering.

Stores lining the street glowed with the usual security lights, but none were open at five in the morning. Breakfast would be nice, but not even the fast food place had turned on its lights yet. Uniformed employees in the parking lot, but no bacon frying.

Besides waking up Tonya for a fast food breakfast wouldn't earn him any points. He should cook her breakfast. "Perfect." He complimented himself as he searched for an open grocery store.

He did find an all-night pharmacy that stocked bread, eggs, pre-cooked sausages, and juice. Not the fanciest breakfast, but it was the thought that counted. On the way to the register, he threw a rawhide treat into the basket. A vase of long-stemmed roses stood beside the register with a hand lettered sign advising men that they could never go wrong with roses.

It would be a nice touch. He picked out three of the healthiest roses and added them to his order.

The young male cashier whistled, then spoke. "You must have done something majorly wrong if you're out this early buying roses."

"No." He started to protest the accusation, but it was a little more accurate than he realized. "Um, yeah, something like that."

The male winked at him as if they were buds. "No problem. I know how it goes. Have to keep them happy. The bitches, they be crazy sometimes."

Will took his change and bag, not intending to reply, but did, "You keep calling them bitches and you won't have to worry about any women problems."

He half-jogged to his car, anxious to get back to the house and get his plan started. The smell of coffee would awaken Tonya and he'd be there with a smile and a rose. Better have a cup of coffee, too, just in case. If she was like most people, then she couldn't start the day without a healthy swig of java.

The house was still dark when he pulled into the driveway. Good deal. That meant Tonya was still asleep. He'd have to go through the garage using the code. Second time going through the garage, but at least this time he was clothed.

Inside the house silence hung heavy except for the raspy canine snores. Odd, Sebastian hadn't roused himself when he drove up, but then Tonya had declared him a failure as a guard dog. He placed the groceries on the table and toed off his shoes.

He passed Sebastian in the hallway asleep on the bare floor.

Strange, since the dog struck him as one that would sleep on the bed or at least the carpet. The light from the kitchen illuminated the bedroom enough for him to see the mussed empty bed.

"Where is she?"

Her absence hit him similar to a well-placed fist in the gut. Had he screwed up the best thing to ever happen to him? God, he hoped not. Maybe she was somewhere else in the house. He flicked on the bedroom light, noticing the open closet. Could she have gotten dressed and went somewhere?

It didn't make sense because her car was still in the garage. "Tonya."

There was no one in the spare bedroom, definitely not in the kitchen, the bathroom or the living room he kept passing through, frantically searching. Five minutes of endless searching that felt more like forever, he decided he'd have to break down and call Lynne.

A quick glance at his watch revealed it was only half past five, but Marc would be up. He'd also tell him if Tonya decided to take refuge there. Something was wrong. He knew it. He stood in the living room listening to the phone ring endlessly while he looked out the door into the darkened yard.

He dropped the phone when noticed the open front door. A bone deep chill swept over him along with the realization that he had fucked up big time. He winced, trying to calm his incipient panic down enough to think the matter through. A mental image of him using the key to set the dead bolt before he left came to mind. No way would the door be standing wide open, especially when Tonya knew she had a dangerous stalker.

The perimeter alarm, the lights, it could have been a distraction, something that would get them both out of the house and time enough for Clint to get inside. His heart stopped for a beat. His head swung side to side not wanting to consider the reason behind the open door and the silent dog.

He slammed the doorframe. "Damn it." His phone started ringing.

Maybe it was Tonya and she had a good explanation.

He answered the phone with a breathy question. "Tonya?"

"No, it's me, Marc. You called me, remember?"

"Yes, yes, I did." He struggled to slow his breathing. "Is Tonya there?"

There was a pause before Marc answered. "No, why should she be?"

Will related the dog napping story and how he arrived back home with an open door and no Tonya.

"Hmm," Marc murmured. "She could have gone for a walk. Weird that she didn't take Sebastian."

"That dog is dead to the world." Will glanced back at the canine, who hadn't moved.

Marc's voice confirmed a nagging suspicion that just occurred. "The dog that barks when the wind changes direction didn't even wake up when you were yelling."

"No." He dropped on the loveseat as the enormity of what happened crystallized. "My God, that fiend has her. Sebastian must be drugged."

"Stay right there. We're coming over. Call the police too."

CLINT'S THREAT TO shoot her had her stumbling over a tree root. No, she didn't want to die like one of those stupid women in the horror movies always falling and screaming. A large glossy holly bush squatted slightly off the path. As a kid, they had a similar bush in their yard. Memories of crouching inside the shell the bush made with its pointy leaves returned. She hid inside of it whenever she was angry with her mother, knowing her mother would eventually panic, calling and calling for her.

She limped off the path toward the bush. Once she reached it, she could hear the sound of Clint's boots landing heavily on the dead leaves. No time to dither about how to insert herself into the greenery.

A stumble sent her into the bush. Not as roomy as her childhood bush, but she pulled her feet and hands out of sight just as Clint entered the area. His footsteps slowed and stopped.

The racing of her heart filled her ears. Surely Clint heard it. That's why he stopped. Perhaps a tiny patch of color showed through the holly leaves. She could hear breathing, not sure if it was his or hers.

"Tonya. Come here. I'll forgive you." The shouted words sounded less than forgiving. "I care about you." If he was trying for sincerity, he failed. The words sounded more like *I think you're a stupid cow who will come when I call, because it will make killing you so much less work.*

A hand over her mouth muffled her breath while she kept her eyes squeezed shut. Not taking chances peering through the greenery where a tiny glimmer of white among the leaves would assure him the bush needed investigating. Her thighs protested her crouched position while the shard of glass between her toes made itself known. To think, yesterday losing her job consumed her thoughts. However, some worry about Clint had crowded in there, too.

The footfalls sounded again, only slower as if he was loathe to leave the area, as if he knew she was nearby. Then they stopped. The man probably stood half-hidden by a tree, waiting for her to break out of her hidey hole and dash back to the car, the cabin, or civilization, in general. Yeah, a trap, he'd set one, assuming she'd be foolish enough to fall for it.

Nope. Think again. Your mistake is in thinking you know me. You don't. She opened her eyes and lowered her hands the better to wait. Her thigh muscles burned due to holding the position. She shifted her weight silently, leaning against the trunk of the holly. A tiny quiver went through the bush. Was Clint looking in this direction? Did he see the bush move?

A tickling sensation of a bug crawling up her leg had her twitching. Her fingers moved slowly, trying to find the offending insect while she held her breath. The urge to squeal and thrash about similar to a hooked fish pushed at her. It might as well get in line with all her other responses, including her desire to scream out the injustice of her situation.

Her fingers found the bug and brushed if off her leg. Unfortunately, he returned. She chose not to brush it off the second time. As a visitor in the bush, she could be irritating the bug. If only she knew what time it was. Too bad she couldn't take a snooze while she waited for Clint to leave. She hadn't gotten much sleep the night before with running outside to check the perimeter, then Will's nutzo client calling from jail, and then there was the kidnapping and escape. She yawned, feeling tired. Maybe a catnap, that's all.

The smell of wood smoke woke her. Someone must have a fire going in his fireplace, the right time of year for it. She opened her eyes to an interwoven pattern of holly leaves with the sun streaming through the open spaces. She blinked, trying to clear her focus. Where was she? The bottom half of her body was numb while her hands clamped around cramped limbs. Her situation came back with a crash, rather like on oversized monster mashing into a house.

Clint was waiting outside in the woods. How long had she slept? The sun shone directly down, indicating noon. If she ran into the woods in the morning, surely Clint didn't wait around for her to come out. The psychopath rushed back to the city to lure some unsuspecting woman into being his alibi. Now she'd find her way back to the city or at least a telephone. A bird flew into the bush, startling her and causing her to fall backward. The outraged bird flapped around her, screeching.

She flung her head side to side, avoiding the beak and talons of the bird. A broken branch served as an impromptu sword. Tonya brandished it, keeping the bird at bay long enough to roll to all fours. The needle-like sensation wrapped around her legs and feet as she stood. The bird still fluttered about, making her think it had a nest somewhere.

"Stop it. I'm not going to hurt you. What is it with you?"

The clearly agitated bird continued squawking and flying in a circle around her. As annoying as it was, she didn't want to hurt it. A rustling near her feet revealed a rabbit who hopped over to a burrow opening and disappeared inside. Limbs breaking heralded the arrival of two does leaping through the undergrowth. The smell of wood smoke, coupled with the scent of burning leaves, grew stronger. Guess more than one person decided to burn leaves today.

A backward glance revealed black smoke filling the sky, along with flames dancing along tree trunks. A forest fire. The moving flames transfixed her. What were the possibilities a fire would occur on the same day she escaped in the woods? The fire blocked her access to the cabin, road, and freedom. Eventually, someone would call the fire in, but by that time, Clint would be gone.

A fire explained the erratic wildlife behavior. No wonder the deer ran and the bird acted crazy. Ignoring the pain in her cramped limbs, she limped toward the main path. Though she didn't know where it went, at least it wasn't on fire, yet.

The heat of the fire wafted toward her, warming her chilled skin and loosening up her muscles, allowing for an easy lope. Birds flew in a dark cloud heading up out of the woods and the smoke. The acrid odor hung in the air, reminding her of the moving wall of death behind her. A few blood-curdling shrieks signaled some of the animals didn't make it.

"Lousy, vicious bastard. Karma needs to catch up to him." The forest darkened with the approaching fire, turning the woods into a twilight murkiness. The smoke moved in front of the fire, sucking up the oxygen.

Tonya used the collar of her nightshirt as a mask, pulling it over her mouth and nose. Fear and heat dried her mouth out, making saliva hard to come by, but she managed to wet her T-shirt by sucking on it and turning it into a filter.

Deer ran past her, one doe even bumped into her, but she didn't fall like one of those too stupid to live heroines from the horror movies. A deer turned and looked back at her. Its streamlined head morphed into Clint's face. He smirked at her before bounding away.

No, couldn't be, imagining things.

A headache started at the back of her head, working its way to her sinuses. Great. Might as well have a headache, since everything else on her hurt. A sense of fatigue dropped over her, rather like the proverbial wet blanket, only it wasn't wet, just heavy. Breathing became a challenge. A mossy area off the side of the path beckoned. Soft, cuddly—a great place to curl up and sleep. Tempting.

The shrill blast of sirens broke through her lethargy. Hard to pinpoint the direction, they sounded almost as if they were all around her. Weird. Her mind, befuddled by the smoke, played tricks on her. Hallucinations. Here came one now, running down the path in yellow fire gear, carrying an ax. Instead of disappearing as he drew closer, he spoke, "Ma'am, Ma'am, is there anyone else trapped in the fire?"

Her stomach chose that moment to rebel. Instead of answering, she vomited on the hallucination's boots. Disgusting, but at least she didn't have to worry about the embarrassment since he didn't exist.

The figment of her imagination grabbed her hand with a gloved one and steered her in the direction she intended, and then spoke into a radio. "Jones, smoke inhalation victim."

Two more yellow-jacketed firefighters jogged past her with a nod. A woman in a paramedic uniform appeared ahead. Two ground-eating steps brought her to Tonya's side. "I got her. Did she tell you if anyone else was in the forest?" The firefighter looked down at his boots. "Not exactly."

"Sorry." Tonya managed to push out the word through her smoke-roughened throat. "My kidnapper, Clint, might be in there, but he probably left, especially when he heard the sirens."

The medic wrapped an arm around her waist, helping her walk. Everything spun around her, making the tall trees into a kaleidoscope and the path into an impossible to follow curvy ribbon. The drifting smoke made it harder to distinguish anything.

No matter how much she squinted, she couldn't bring anything into focus. A voice spoke close to her, the paramedic. She remembered her vaguely.

"Lack of oxygen is messing with your vision. Trust me to guide you, and you can close your eyes. I'll get you to the ambulance."

Trust her. She made it sound so easy. What if the paramedic turned around and led her back into the forest? The possibility stopped her. The soothing voice came again, speaking directly into her ear.

"No, you can't stop. You need to keep going before you lose consciousness. Once we get to the clearing, you can lay down, sleep all you want."

Sleep sounded wonderful. First, she had to trust the woman. Why would a total stranger care about her? Trust someone she didn't know? She didn't even trust her best friend, Lynne, to tell her about the stalking until recently and only because Will insisted on it as a safety measure. Trusting, she didn't do. Too many people betrayed her trust over the years, making her hesitant to take chances, certain she'd fall.

Even when she didn't trust, bad things still happened. Her eyes fluttered shut, allowing the helpful medic to steer her like a little red wagon with a stuck wheel. Even with her eyes shut, the flashing lights of the ambulance penetrated.

Half a dozen emergency vehicles crowded the neighborhood street. Red, white, and blue lights flashed in the increasingly smoke-darkened air. A few people stood in front of their modest ranch homes, casting worried glances at the woods.

Comments flew at her as the medic steered her in the direction of the ambulance. Another medic rushed up, rattling a gurney behind her.

"Here, get her on the gurney before she passes out."

Why did everyone think she would... suddenly everything went black.

Chapter Seventeen

THE SOUND OF voices asking questions penetrated her mental fog. A slight hiss reminiscent of a balloon leaking air filtered into the mix. The voice of the woman who walked her through the woods spoke with a man.

"Diane, do you think that's the woman everyone is looking for?"

"Hard to say, but we need to get her to the hospital. We need to know if she has any family in case they need to be notified."

Another male voice entered the conversation. "Lock her in, we're cleared to go."

"Will do." The vehicle dipped slightly as the two scampered in and shut the door behind them. Tonya kept her eyes closed, hoping to find out what was happening to her. She smelled like a cross between a campfire and a spent charcoal grill. Her throat and eyes itched.

Diane, as she now identified her medic, spoke while adjusting something on Tonya's face. "Oxygen is flowing well. Should be coherent soon."

A growl of an engine, along with a lurch as it regained the road, signaled their departure. If that wasn't enough, the strident wail of the siren accompanied their exodus. Why couldn't they turn it off? It hurt her ears. Besides, she wasn't that bad—some scratches, a piece of glass in her foot.

"Why would someone be in the middle of a forest fire in a night shirt?"

"She told me she'd been kidnapped."

"It would make sense, especially since the APB concerned a woman abducted from her home. My girlfriend, Lesley, is a police dispatcher. She told me it was a high priority case. The chief of police and the mayor demanded the woman be found. Glad we found her."

"Yeah. Me, too. Do you think there's a reward?"

Tonya stiffened up, thinking her saviors were mercenary-minded. The man chimed in with a laugh as he wrapped a cuff around her wrist. "You know first responders don't get rewards. It's what we do."

"Joe, you know me better than that. I was just wondering if she were so important someone might offer real money to find her."

"Yeah, I know you. Just messing with you. You call it in."

The crackling noise sounded. "Inbound, unknown female, forest fire inhalation victim. Oxygen currently administered. Pulse high, but to be expected. Unconscious. ETA 1:15pm."

That answered what time it was. The gurney shifted as the driver took a curb on two wheels she bet. A last blast of the horn meant people failed to go to their right, allowing the emergency vehicle through. A bump, then a drop, had the paramedics grumbling.

"Wish Hector wouldn't run over those curbs."

"That's what the straps are for. Grab one. Hector wouldn't have to do that if people paid attention, got off their cell phones, and turned their radios down to a reasonable level."

Yeah, she'd had similar thoughts before, but never thought she'd be the one in the ambulance hurtling to the hospital. She opened one eye a tiny bit.

"She's coming to." Diane acknowledged the obvious, unaware she'd been listening the entire time. The female medic hovered over the gurney, her face only inches from Tonya's. "Do you know where you are?"

"Ambulance." She chose not to elaborate since even one choked out word hurt terribly.

Instead of talking to her, she spoke to the medic behind her.

"Alert." She turned back to Tonya and smiled. "Can you tell us who you are?"

Why wouldn't she be able to tell them who she was? Of course, amnesia. That made sense or if she were some criminal on the lam, then she'd have to come up with an entirely new identity. Luckily, neither one applied. "Tonya Smiley."

Joe peered around Diane. "You're her. The woman they're searching for. I need to call it in." She nodded, not wanting to talk again.

His words drifted in and out, "Found" and "Hospital," then she drifted in a gray misty land: a mysterious place endowed with the general feeling of comfort and safety. She drifted through the mist as if floating in a pool. No pain, no discomfort, no worries, very pleasant, until the ambulance's stopping brought her back to reality—people slamming doors open, yelling about IVs. The last time she had so many hands on her was at a concert with festival seating.

The white glare of the hospital lights made her blink. The male medic and a nurse strolled beside her gurney, exchanging medical info while pushing the gurney through a series of doors. Part of her wanted to go home, but another part enjoyed the process of not running, hiding, or escaping. Yep, lying underneath the blanket ruled compared to her previous hours.

"Tonya." Hearing Lynne's voice, Tonya half sat up, trying to locate her friend. A burly hospital guard stood near her, half-blocking Lynne's way and pointing to the chairs in the distance. Two men moved toward Lynne and escorted her back to the lobby. Marc's height and bald head were easily identifiable. Will? How would he even know about the kidnapping? She craned her neck for a better look at the man. He came back and didn't go to his house just because she acted the bitch when he left to help his crazy client.

Hmm, it bore thinking about. She flopped back on the gurney as it turned the corner and a corridor obstructed her view of the waiting area. A hand patted her shoulder as the nurse leaned in her direction. "Just take it easy, sweetie. You've been through a great deal. You'll be safe at home in no time."

Safe at home. Those words didn't mean the same thing to her as they used to, since Clint abducted her from the house. Despite Will's efforts to make it into a fortress, he still waltzed in due to their inattention. What would prevent it from happening in the future?

A shiver coursed through her body.

"Hurry, I think she's going into shock." The nurse yelled at someone nearby. An electronic beep, then a warmed blanket covered the one already on top of her. The heat seeping through the covers relaxed her muscles, but offered no comfort to her mind while they transferred her from the gurney.

A woman with a nametag that read Sawyer with doctor underneath approached with a somber expression and a raised pen over a clipboard. "Heard you had some problems. Since you're coherent, could you tell me what happened?"

Tonya's gaze traveled around the room, counting the personnel crowded into the small area. A woman in a headscarf fiddled with her IV. Another person near her feet attached something to her ankle that had the feel of a sticky hand toy found in trinket dispensers. Another man had his back to her, looking at a monitor. No reason everyone had to hear her story. She'd rather talk about if Sawyer were the doctor's first or last name. Then a woman in a red smock stuck her head in.

"The police want to question her."

The doctor sighed heavily before speaking. "If it's my ex, let him wait."

A man in a tweed sports jacket and a feathered hairstyle straight from the seventies appeared, even before Ms. Red Smock could turn and deliver the message.

He grinned in her direction or rather the doctor's. "Figured you say that, Elaine. That's why I didn't bother waiting."

"Yeah, I should have expected the same bombastic behavior from you. Tom, give us a chance to clean her up at least. Check the vitals. The usual."

The man strode into the already crowded room, leading with his chest—a short man trying to intimidate others with his manner, since he couldn't with his size.

Tonya watched the man puff up like a bantam rooster. She knew his type wouldn't let the comment pass. The nurse turned from the keyboard and looked up expectantly, obviously expecting fireworks, too.

The detective's scowl made him look more bulldoggish than menacing. "Every second wasted gives us less time to track the perpetrator."

She didn't have an issue with talking, especially if it helped run Clint down.

The technician fiddling with the blood pressure cuff stopped and glanced at the doctor. The physician's tight jaw lessened as she opened her mouth. The sounds of running and shouting outside the room masked whatever would have been her response.

A gasping Will made it to the doorway with a uniformed guard behind him. The sizeable guard placed a beefy hand on Will's shoulder. "Sir, you have to come with me. You're not allowed back here."

Will's eyes whipped around the room until he met hers. For a second, their eyes connected, enabling a silent communication amidst the emergency room chaos. A reassurance settled over Tonya that everything would be all right. The guard jiggled his hand, moving Will backwards a fraction. Aware of this technique, Will braced himself in the doorframe with both hands.

"Give me a second and I'll go back to the waiting area."

The guard dropped his hand. He crossed his arms and tapped a leather-shod foot as he waited.

"Tonya," he said the word in a gentle tone, unlike his earlier manner. "When I returned to the house and discovered Sebastian drugged and you gone, my heart stopped for a second. I wasn't sure it would ever start again."

A feminine sigh sounded, maybe more than one.

Will's eyes stayed on her, his expression morphed from loving to grim with his jaw taking on tightness and his brows lowered as he spoke. "I knew despite my efforts, Clint had gotten to you."

Tom, who had leaned against a wall and crossed his ankles, acting bored at the display of emotions, interrupted. "Who's this Clint?" He directed the question at Will and pushed off the wall.

"Who are you?" Suspicion flavored the question, along with a certain amount of gruffness.

Despite her exhaustion, Tonya leaned forward in an effort to watch the unfolding drama. The hospital employees kept moving, making it difficult for her to get a clear view. Damn it, didn't they realize this was the first man ever to stand up for her? No way she wanted to miss this.

Tom squared his shoulders, ready to go into his tough cop impression. "Detective Tom…"

Before he could finish, Will interrupted. "The police, huh. Tonya filed a report about being harassed, breaking and entering, even had physical evidence of threats. When she disappeared from her home in the middle of the night and her dog was drugged, what did the police do?"

"Hey now!" The detective held up a hand as if it would stop the words.

"Nothing! They told me maybe Tonya decided to go out for a coffee in the middle of the night without her car, her purse, or even her phone. One female police officer suggested she did it to punish me for going to bail out a client. No one wanted to do anything."

Tom bristled, taking the brunt of the accusation. His hands hung loose at his side, but they twitched as if wanting to ball into fists. "Standard procedure," he muttered the words. "Ms. Smiley is an adult. Adults can come and go as they please."

With narrowed eyes, Will glared at the detective as he spoke. "Adults can also be threatened, assaulted, kidnapped, and even murdered. There was reason to believe foul play was involved. Nothing happened until I went to the chief of police."

"Oh."

A look of understanding crossed Tom's face. His right hand rubbed his beard-shadowed face. "You're the one. Pulled some fancy strings, didn't you? What are you, some hot shot lawyer or something?"

Tonya gave the detective a baleful look. Not too hard to figure out why the man was divorced. The difficulty lay in why Sawyer married him in the first place. Tired of his manner, Tonya answered his question.

"Yeah, he is. One of the best. Why aren't you out there arresting Clint Fairweather, rogue private eye and sociopath?"

The detective pulled out a small tablet and pen. "Is that his real name?"

Good question. She always assumed it was his name, but then she assumed a great deal about Clint. "It was what was printed on his private investigator's license. That makes it real, doesn't it?"

The detective's mouth twisted to one side as he wrote the name. "Should. Of course, it could be false identification. Hard to say for sure. Do you know where he lives?"

"I know where he used to live. Can't say he's still there, though. 3122 Bancroft Boulevard."

Will raised an eyebrow as she recited the address. It wasn't as if she wanted to visit him, but apparently, it resided in long-term memory along with the names of her primary teachers and her personal nemesis, Leslie Hall. It didn't mean she wanted to see any of them.

Tom scribbled furiously, and then looked up with a sly expression. "What's the connection between the two of you? Seems like you know a great deal about your kidnapper."

A staffer swiped her arm with antiseptic, leaving behind a burn on all the open cuts and scratches that stung. "We dated."

"Ahh." He managed to pack half a dozen sleazy innuendos into the tiny word.

Will made a low sound in his throat, but the doctor had finally had enough.

"Burton," she directed her words to the guard. "Can you see the detective out?" It served more as a directive than a question. Will dropped his arms and stepped out of the doorway allowing the guard to pass. Once the detective and guard disappeared, Will reappeared in the doorway.

"Could I give her a kiss on the forehead before I leave?"

"You're still here?" Her gruff manner didn't dissuade the man. She gave a short nod. Not risking a possible retraction, he carefully picked his way around equipment and people.

Tonya's eyes devoured him. He wore the same clothes he'd shrugged on when he left the house, more rumpled, the shirt misbuttoned, and coffee stains on the front. His hair stood up in places, most likely from his habit of running his hands through his hair. His bloodshot eyes and weary gait probably made most of the staffers doubt her hotshot lawyer claim, but he was the hottest thing she'd ever seen. He leaned over her and took her IV free hand, holding it gently. His lips touched her forehead before he whispered. "I love you."

"I love you, too. Sorry, I—"

His finger pressed against her lips before she said any more. He shook his head, stilling the apology.

"I was the dumb ass. I almost lost you. I'd never be able to forgive myself if anything happened to you."

Another sigh sounded near her and this time, it wasn't her. "You can't get rid of me that easily. Could you go check on Sebastian for me?"

"I could, but I won't. Marc's already left for dog duty. I'm staying right here by your side. When I leave, bad things happen." He squeezed her hand as if to confirm. She squeezed his back, wondering how she could have ever doubted him.

"Okay, kids," the doctor called, despite the fact she could only be a few years older than the two of them. "Time to break it up. Sooner I get my job done, the sooner you two can be swapping spit."

Swapping spit. Talk about unromantic. A glance at the doctor revealed a little glassy-eyed-ness, showing she wasn't as tough as she pretended.

Will smiled, touching her nose with his index finger before he turned and left. The nurse at the keyboard glanced after him. "I wish I had a man who loved me like that."

"Back to work." The doctor fixed everyone with a look that let them know the sideshow was over. "No use longing for stuff that isn't going to happen. Men like that are rare."

Chapter Eighteen

T HE HOSPITAL INSISTED on keeping her for observation. All she had was several abrasions, bruising, and one stitch worthy cut. There was some talk about possible infection and delayed shock. In the end, Will surprised her by taking the hospital's side.

He sat beside her bed in a wood and vinyl straight back chair. A television game show droned on in the background. She tracked the progress of a squeaky cart in the hallway. Whatever it was, it headed away from her room.

"I know you don't want to stay, but you're better off here." His hand slipped through the bed rail, tangling his fingers with hers.

Her lips twisted together as she considered framing her reply without sounding like a whiny kid. "It's not home. There's no Sebastian."

"Even if you were home, Sebastian would still be at the veterinarian for observation."

Whatever Clint slipped her pooch almost did him in. Her top teeth came down on her bottom lip, worrying it. What a nut case. Her hand tightened on Will's. The men were night and day from each other. "It stinks here, antiseptic, bleach, and hopelessness."

"What does hopelessness smell like?" The corner of his mouth tipped up as if he recognized her excuse for what it was.

"Take a deep breath. That's it. Besides, I want to go home and be in my own bed with you beside me."

"Aha, now we get down to the real issue." He winked at her, reminding her of their first meeting not so long ago.

A throat clearing announced visitors. Marc and Lynne, armed with flowers and helium balloons, entered the room.

Lynne called out, "Hey, you lovebirds, sorry to interrupt. We thought you might like a dog update."

Tonya dropped Will's hand and pushed her slumping body upright. "Look who's here. Yes, I do. What do you have for me?"

Will nodded in her direction. "Did you hear that, Marc? How fast she threw me over for a dog?"

Marc nodded. "Yeah, but she's known Sebastian longer. Stick around and maybe you'll get the same treatment eventually."

Tonya listened to them while Lynne presented the flowers, balloons, and even pulled a stuffed puggle from a bag hanging from her arm. "It's adorable. Give it to me." She hugged the stuffed animal, wishing it were her own living pup. Placing it on the bed beside her, she grinned back at Lynne. "I'll be the envy of all the kids in the pediatric ward. Balloons and a stuffed animal. How's my dog?"

Marc pointed in Lynne's direction. "You owe me five."

Tonya's attention flickered between her two friends. "She owes you five, why?"

Lynne laughed before explaining. "I bet him your first words would be about Sebastian. Instead, you said, Look who's here."

Did she say that? Guess she did. "Whoa, I would have taken that bet, too. The kidnapping rattled me."

Lynne placed her free hand over her heart. "It rattled me, too. I just want the police to catch that fool."

"Not as much as I do!" Will shot up and strode to the window. Marc pulled out his cell phone and started a video of Sebastian. The dog kept looking away from the camera, even to the point of turning all the way around, presenting his butt. Lynne crooned in the background about saying hello to Momma. Sebastian gave a familiar woof.

She clapped her hands together in front of her. "He's okay. I was so worried."

Face wiped blank, except for a telltale twitch near the mouth, Will faced the group, slapping Marc on the back. "You did well."

They discussed the possibility of Clint returning to her house and agreed the hospital was the best place to be. Could they have convinced the hospital to keep her? Nah, she doubted it.

"Marc and I wanted you with us." Lynne volunteered, patting her friend's blanket covered feet as if she were a cat. The offer didn't tempt her. Friends remained good friends if you didn't impose on them. Babysitting her dog, and covering for her at work without actually mentioning kidnapping exceeded the bounds of ordinary friendship. Her only hope of staying employed rested on the many who had already jumped ship. Still, even filling in the gaps wouldn't hold up against having a dangerous stalker.

"Oh no, she's staying at my house," Will asserted, moving his thumb back toward his chest. "Not safe at her house."

The three of them argued back and forth across her prone body as if she didn't have a voice in the discussion. At first, it irritated her. Did anyone ask her what she wanted to do? Everyone was too busy saying what was best for her. Her skin flushed as she listened to each one insisting why their home would be the best spot.

"Marc and I would serve as a double warning system since there are two of us," Lynne insisted, and then folded her arms. Her usual sign that she'd tabled the discussion.

Will, unaware of her body language message, continued to argue his point, even leaning across her bed. His index finger went up and stabbed the air as he spoke. "Two guard dogs, huh? More like two lovebirds snug in bed, too into each other to detect Clint's sneaky entrance. I, on the other hand, would be in bed with Tonya with my arms firmly around her."

Their attitude, and their insistence that Clint would be back for a second act, shattered the fragile calm she'd cobbled together. Her stomach rolled as she listened to Will insist Clint could get past ordinary locks as if he were a ninja or a ghost.

"Enough!" The shout silenced all three of them. In the doorway stood her nurse with her fisted hands on her hips and an expression even the most dimwitted knew not to cross. "Get out of here. All you're doing is upsetting my patient. She's been through enough." She made shooing motions with her hands.

"Bye." Lynne grabbed Marc's arm and settled for a wave as they hustled out the door. Will glanced at the nurse, then back at her.

The nurse wasn't having any of it. "You too, buddy."

Indecision flickered across his face before he bent and kissed her. "Goodbye for now." His unspoken message was that he wouldn't be scared off for long. The woman stared him down until he walked out of the room. Her hand reached for the curtain and pulled it around the bed.

Chart in hand, she approached the monitor measuring Tonya's heart rate. "I'm Doris, the second shift nurse. Your heartbeat is rapid— not surprising with those fools arguing over you."

A head swivel allowed her to see the red line going up and down faster than previously. Tonya felt obliged to defend her friends, but before she could, Doris did it for her.

"Acting the fools out of love, fear, and guilt." She patted her shoulder, and then inspected the saline drip. "Gonna need a new bag. You were close to dehydration, especially with the smoke inhalation. Surprised the doctor didn't put you on oxygen. Still might."

"Would that delay my leaving?" She wasn't looking forward to spending a night in the hospital. Plenty of thrillers had people murdered in hospitals, especially those with an IV unit.

"No, shouldn't. Have you voided your bowels yet?" Her head bent over the chart missed Tonya's crinkled nose at the question. Great Aunt Matilda would always ask her if she had a BM as if that were the highlight of the day. She needed to get home where people did not ask her personal questions involving elimination processes.

"Um, no, but I haven't eaten in forever. I'm not even sure what time it is now, but it may have been a day since I've had anything to eat." Her stomach growled as if realizing its empty state.

"Goodness. We need to do something about that. Not sure if you'll get much now with the kitchen between meals, but they should have at least broth and gelatin." Doris held Tonya's scratched arms up to the light, examining them and ignored her grimace at the mention of broth.

Another reason for her to go home with a stop by a local fast food place. Something being pushed across the floor stopped somewhere outside of the curtain. So far, she'd been poked, prodded, stitched, X-rayed, and blood taken in an effort to determine how she was. All they had to do was ask. Who knew what machine rested on the other side of the thin fabric?

"Nurse Humferee, you in there? Brought the sleeping chair. I'll just leave it." Footsteps started toward the door, but Doris grabbed the curtain, swinging it open and making the rings on the rod screech in protest.

"Leroy, get back here and put the chair where it belongs."

A young man, slight in stature, stopped and pivoted at her words. His hair stuck up at the top, which could have been the style or his reaction to being caught sneaking out. He turned slowly, red faced, mouth slightly open, and walked back to the chair, shoving it in the corner before he left. Doris eyed him like a hawk as he sauntered by, trying not to make eye contact with anyone.

"Leroy." Her face puckered at the name. "Boy tries to get away with as little as possible."

"Why don't you just fire him? It's obvious he doesn't like to be here." Besides, she didn't need a sleeping chair in the first place. The boxy avocado green unit resembled a lounge chair, but she definitely could do without the sullen Leroy returning.

"Oh him, he's doing court-ordered community service. He doesn't get paid."

Oh yay, felon in training coming in and out of my room. Now, why was the hospital safer than her home? Open doors allowed people in and out privileges. The idea of spending the night here, while never desirous, just seem incredibly stupid. Sure, Clint knew where her house was, but he knew where the hospital was, too. Since he had a police scanner, he'd know she'd made it out.

Great. Here she was a sitting duck. Doris chased away her friends who might have driven her out of the county or at least somewhere moderately safer. A visit to her mother in sunny Florida would be unexpected, considering the issues between the two of them. Nope, Clint would expect that. She could call a cab, but wait, she didn't have her purse. How would she pay the cabbie? Better yet, how would she get an airline ticket? Definitely needed her credit cards.

Doris plumped a pillow and shoved it behind Tonya's back without asking. "There you go. You might want to comb your hair." She gestured to a bright blue fine-tooth comb on the bedside table. "Want to look your best before your fiancé comes back."

I have a fiancé. What if it was Clint? It sounded like something he would do. "Um, what makes you think he's coming?"

Doris rested the back of her hand on Tonya's forehead. "No temperature. You must have taken a hit to the head. How could you forget such a handsome man? He was just here, arguing with your other friends. Guilt is eating him up because he didn't protect you better. Don't go too hard on him. Most husbands don't use the sleeping chairs. Instead, they go home to their own beds."

Aha, not Clint. A deep sigh escaped her lips.

"Yeah, I'd sigh, too, if I had such a fine man to call my own. You might want to do something about that hair." Doris flipped the mirror embedded in the tray table. A woman with a swollen lip, dried blood on her face, red eyes, and crazy hair stared back at her. Will kissed that. He must love her.

"Yuk. I'll need something more powerful than this comb." She started at the ends, working on an inch at a time. Doris returned with a brush still in a package, making her suspect she bought it at the gift shop.

"You shouldn't have."

Doris flashed a grin, and then shrugged her shoulders. "As hard as it is to believe, I was in love once."

The no nonsense nurse once becoming soft and gooey at a certain man's voice was a little hard to believe. Tonya knew better than to inquire because she'd bet the romance did not end up happily ever after. The nurse swung out of the room, leaving a void behind her that the chatter from the television didn't fill.

The walls were a gray green color never found in nature. Cheap impressionistic landscape scenes decorated the walls. The muted images, which should have been vaguely dreamlike, resembled a nightmare with one blot of color fleeing from a bigger, darker blob of color. Not a pleasant observation, considering people died in hospitals. Sometimes on their own, but usually not for the reason they came in.

Morbid. She needed to think of something else. Why did Will identify himself as her fiancé? Most men tended to be commitment phobic. As a divorce lawyer, Will should be allergic to any commitment. He saw and heard too much to believe two people could live together in harmony. Picking up the remote, she surfed through the cooking channel, house flippers, some scurrilous talk show about granny strippers, before catching a news update. A snapshot, sometime early in her career blossomed on the screen as the words flowed underneath about a missing local woman found alive.

Alive was good, but everything was supposed to be hush hush. Hard to convince her boss she had a loose crown when the news insisted firefighters had rescued her. Never mind the horror of facing down death, outsmarting Clint, and eventually escaping.

Her lips puckered as she considered the possibility of her nemesis catching the news. With an ego the size of Texas, he'd surf all media sources for a hint of his actions. Smart criminals used the news to monitor the police's next actions, according to Clint. Makes sense that he'd be waiting for a tidbit. Did they say where she was?

The air became trapped somewhere deep in her lungs. Not allowing her to exhale or inhale. Her hand splayed across her chest as she felt the pressure building. Not breathing. How could that be, breathing was an automatic reflex. You didn't think about it to make it happen. Panic wrapped around her, squeezing out any residual joy left from her recent rescue. What if Clint lurked somewhere in the hospital and tampered with her IV bag. Instead of saline, a nefarious substance dripped into her veins, shutting down all her systems, starting with her lungs.

Doris walked in holding a vase of yellow roses partially blocking her face. The nurse strolled to a nearby table and moved items around, clearing a place for the vase. Didn't she notice her patient's inability to breathe? Was she in on it? Tonya flung one arm wide, knocking over a plastic water pitcher and drenching herself in the process. The unexpected cold splash had air whooshing out of her lungs.

She could breathe. Her breath made soft, panting sounds as she breathed in and out lightly. Doris hummed as she arranged the cut flowers, unaware of the drama unfolding beside her. Just as well, she could breathe. Fear had caught her breath and held it. If she hadn't knocked over her water, she'd have passed out. Not a big deal, but embarrassing all the same.

"Interesting roses," Doris commented, startling Tonya at her closeness. "They have red edges. Look."

A long-stemmed rose waved in front of her as Doris held it out for inspection. The sunny flower did sport delicate red trim. Unusual. "You're right." Not the best comment, but small talk never was her forte, especially after she scared herself half to death.

The rose twirled once between the nurse's fingers before she shoved it in the vase. "Yep, the man's stuck on you. Yellow roses, I know mean friendship. Never saw any like this. Special roses. Must have cost a pretty penny."

"He could have picked them up at the grocery store." She offered the excuse, knowing it painted Will in a bland color, as opposed to the vivid hues of a love-struck suitor. Not fair considering everything. The man had jumped into the chaos theme park called her life and started offering solutions immediately, from job searches to security. Most men, or at the least the good ones, were natural problem solvers. Will was no exception.

Images of him fixing her car, making dinner, and later his eyes dark as he balanced himself over her while he stroked her to a screaming climax had her lips tipping upward.

A white envelope fluttered to her bed tray stand as Doris dropped it. "I imagine you want to read that in private. A florist delivered the flowers, which makes them pricey. Not the hospital florist, either."

"Oh." There she went again with the witty small talk. Her fingers were already reaching for the envelope as Doris slowly walked from the room. Was the woman doing some slow-motion act determined to torment her or was it her perception? Her top teeth worried her bottom lip until the woman left the room.

She ripped into the small envelope, cutting the space between her forefinger and index finger in the process. "Ow!" The small card dropped to the table as she brought her hand up to her mouth to suck on the wounded area. "Paper cuts are the worst."

Her fingers separated into a V, exposing the injury beaded up with blood. The handwriting on the card caught her eye. Long, sloping letters that bore no resemblance to Will's efficient upright script. A tissue clamped between her two fingers staunched the flow. Using her uninjured left hand, she picked up the card, which had balloons and noise makers stamped in the corner with the small printed word, congratulations. The greeting puzzled her, more suited to a birth, birthday, or even a wedding.

The cursive resembled dominos falling down with the last word almost flattened by the other letters. The sender's name ended up being a short scribble almost off the card. Indecipherable most of it. The word *Eyes* stood out near the top of the message. The first word she couldn't really make out. She squinted, bringing the card in closer, then out as if that would focus the card. It didn't. Damn. Why bother with a card when she couldn't read the message?

Maybe she could ask Will what he wrote. She turned the card over hoping for some more info. Clearly typed was the delivery info. Rush delivery today before five pm. Not sure why it had to be before five, but could be the florist was only open that long.

An aide walked into the room, threw a smile at her, checked a panel on her wall, and pivoted to leave.

"Wait," Tonya called, a little chagrined at what she was about to do. "Could you help me?"

The woman turned back to her, smoothing out a look of irritation that flickered across her face. "Yes, what do you need?"

Tonya held out the card. "I received these beautiful flowers, and I can't read the card."

The woman's eyebrows went up at her words. Tonya hurried to correct her wrong assumption. "I mean I can read. English. The handwriting is too bad for me to decipher." A hopeful smile graced her face as she held out the card.

The woman grasped the offered card with a grin. "Piece of cake. I read the doctors' and nurses' handwriting all the time. Don't go thinking the nurses have great handwriting. It's part of the reason everything is typed in now. Still, I have skills. Name's Flora."

"Thank you, Flora." The aide moved closer to the light as she held the card up. Her lips pulled down in a frown as she concentrated.

"I have to tell you this is some bad handwriting as if someone was trying to do three or four things at once. It looks to me like it reads *my eyes are on you.* It could be I have eyes for you, which makes more sense."

The first message had a threatening quality, although Will had done an excellent job watching out for her so far. She preferred the second message, which was more old school romance, which sounded like the man. A warm, soft feeling rushed through her. If she were with Lynne or even alone, she'd "aw" about the note, but not yet while Flora still stared intently at the note.

"Is there more?"

The aide shrugged her shoulders as she straightened her neck. "Not really. Trying to make out the signature. All I can get is CL and then it is a line. Ya know when someone knows their name and doesn't bother writing the rest."

CL, the two letters froze the blood in her veins. Flora continued talking, unaware that danger lurked nearby, waiting. "Yeah, when I first started here, about twelve years ago or more, there was a big screw-up because a nurse couldn't read a doctor's handwriting. Gave a baby the wrong amount of medicine. Thought it said 100 cc, instead of 10 cc. Didn't ask anyone because the doctor was a huge prick." She adjusted the blinds before glancing back at Tonya.

"Mercy. You look about ready to upchuck. The baby ended up being okay, although the nurse got canned." The aide glanced at the door. "I shouldn't have mentioned it. Nothing like that will happen now. You'll be fine. Really."

The talkative woman grew silent and hustled out of the room after her vague reassurance, aware she'd said something to upset her. The open door mocked her, allowing people to enter her room at will. Not safe. Another breaking news banner scrolled under the television show banner. Wasn't there a privacy law that withheld the names of the victim? Might as well have flashing letters announcing her location similar to the closeout sales ad.

Had to leave. Escape. The flimsy hospital gown wouldn't work for clothes. She needed something else. In all the movies, both heroes and villains ducked into unlocked linen closets and donned surgical scrubs complete with hats and masks. The idea had possibilities, except for being fiction. Too many weirdos walking around who might take advantage of free scrubs. Yep, the last thing a hospital needed was someone playing out his or her personal fantasy of being a surgeon.

Still, she had to try. Voices in the distance discussed upcoming weekend plans, probably the nurses. It allowed her to pinpoint their location.

"Louisa had her break already. How about you?"

Tonya couldn't identify the voice, but break meant one less person patrolling the halls; one less pair of eyes surveying the hall. A tiny break in the routine, which would facilitate her exit. She kicked at the tight blanket that bound her lower body to the bed. Feet free, she slipped them over the side of the bed. They dangled in the air as she pushed the bed table out of the way with a small nudge. The table resisted with a slight squeal, causing a wince, certain everyone in the corridor heard it. Her eyes closed, and she tried to manufacture an excuse for the noise, but no one came.

Thank goodness for inattentive staff or maybe the noise wasn't too loud. Her feet touched the cold tile floor. A tug on her left hand moved the IV needle sending a shaft of pain up her arm.

"Damn," she whispered the curse under her breath. The needle had to go. It went in easily enough. It made sense that it could come out, too, though she had no experience pulling out needles. Would blood gush out of her hand? Other wires trailed from her gown, too. What were they? Her fingers followed the one closest to her neck. It ended in a patch between her breasts. She peeled the sticky patch off slowly. The adhesive tugged a little, but no worse than duct tape. The one on her back, she jerked.

"Ow." She winced, aware her yelp could trigger unwanted attention. Had to hurry, good chance someone would notice the monitor suddenly wasn't monitoring. Three more patches to go, the slight hum of the monitor morphed into a telltale shriek, the staple of medical dramas. Almost done, then she could run.

The electronic shriek grew louder, birthing a desire to yank it out of the wall. No time. Yelling accompanied running feet slapping.

"Code Blue! Get the cart!"

"What room?"

A disturbance, exactly what Clint would do to enter the room unnoticed. Adrenaline flooded her body, priming for flight just as a form blocked her exit. Her heart stopped for a second as she examined the backlit silhouette. Her failure to outthink Clint spelled her demise. Her hand stilled on the IV needle she'd gripped, but hadn't pulled out.

Uncertainly winked in and out at the edge of her mind. Not right, something wasn't right. Clint stepped into the room and put his hands on his hips, not an action she expected, and morphed into Doris. What? Other personnel surged in behind the figure including two pushing a cart with knobs, paddles, and electronic gadgetry. They all just stood and stared at her before Doris gave a resigned huff.

"Another runner. I'll deal with this." The nurse motioned for the others to leave. A few muttered complaints floated behind them.

"Pushing that cart and running takes a few years off my life every time. I'll need the cart soon."

"Diva."

Wait a minute. She wasn't a diva. Exactly the opposite, she'd prefer no attention. Unwanted news coverage placed her in the position of trying to escape from her hospital room. Feet on the floor, she took an involuntary step toward the door. Doris blocked her before the still attached IV made itself known. The woman could move.

"What exactly are you doing?" Doris demanded, angling her chin, and placed her balled fists back on her hips. Her stance broadcasted she didn't tolerate fools or liars. Both authority and intimidation existed in the short question.

Tonya backed up until her hips hit the bed. No excuse would satisfy the woman. Not that she could think of any decent ones in her befuddled state. Not that she'd ever excelled at bluffing or lying. "I was trying to escape before Clint finds me."

"Clint?" The nurse's eyebrows met in confusion. "Who's Clint?"

"My kidnapper." She bit out the words, realizing every extra second she spent in the hospital gave him time. Even now, he could be on the premises. Doris's confused expression melted into concern.

"No wonder you were sneaking out of here like some character in a bad movie." Her hands reached out, gently tucking Tonya back in the bed. "Now, some patients just want to leave because they're too stubborn to accept medical care. A few just want a smoke. Hard as it may be to believe, some try to escape my own version of TLC."

The comment made Tonya laugh. The husky raspy sound strained her throat, a reminder of the smoke inhalation and her narrow escape.

"Don't worry." Doris picked up the leads hanging from the monitor and looked at them. "Not sure you need these. You've already proved you're capable of moving around. I'll contact Dr. Lenin. Might be able to talk him out of reattaching them." She winked.

Most nurses would never question a doctor, but she had the feeling not only would this nurse question the doctor, but also would have some doctors agreeing in a matter of minutes. Thank goodness for the pit bull of nurses. However, she'd heard the breed could be unusually caring and gentle. Not too unlike Doris.

With a final twitch of her pillows, the nurse left. A scent cloud of rubbing alcohol and another unidentified medicinal product lingered in her wake. Sniffing the air, she picked up bitterness, a slight tang of iodine, and a chemical base. Hard to say what it was. The volume on the television jumped, blasting out another news bulletin about her rescue.

No chance for everyone at work, missing the annoying bulletins interrupting their shows. Kiss her job goodbye. Doubt they'd even let her return to work for the required two weeks before moving on. All they'd see is a woman who came with her own personal stalker. Even if the police caught him, she'd be the type to attract dangerous men who showed up at work with enough ammunition for a massacre. That meant Clint won in the end.

"Damn it!" She smacked her fist into her cupped hand. No matter what she did, the man still got what he wanted. Well, mostly. He probably didn't want the police on his trail.

"Not the reception I expected, considering I faced derision from my fellow males in the elevator for carrying a purse." Will walked toward her with a fast food bag in one hand, her purse over his shoulder and a flowered duffle bag.

The sight of him lifted her spirits considerably until she remembered how she looked. "Don't look at me. My hair's a mess."

"It is. That tends to happen when you're diving into a thorn bush and running from a maniac. Tell you what. I am actually an expert on detangling hair. You eat, and I'll detangle." Will placed the bag and purse on the chair and opened the fast food sack, releasing fry scented air out.

"Yum, my favorite." She reached for a battered fry. The cheeseburger combo and vanilla shake tasted like paradise. Almost anything even slightly palatable would have been heavenly. Will very carefully worked the tangles out of her hair and soon the brush went from her crown to her ends without stopping.

Tonya leaned back, savoring the sensation of his brushing her hair. "You don't have any little sisters. Where does your detangling experience come from?" As soon as she asked, dread crept up her back, wrapping around her neck. Of course, he'd mention a previous girlfriend whom he'd spent hours brushing her hair. Even though it would be a former love, jealousy still made an appearance. A shampoo model with luxuriant locks wearing a towel and little else crowded into her imagination. A bare-chested Will pulled the brush through the woman's hair as the sound of falling water and violins filled the air. Will's lips moved. What was he saying to the woman?

"Fishing line. You think hair is bad, try untangling fishing line. No treat. It takes patience." His matter of fact words charmed her. Turning at the waist, she hugged him. "That's why I love you. You're so unique."

His arms wrapped tight around her. His voice husky with repressed laughter asked, "Unique as in totally weird. It's what your aunt calls you when you act the fool, but being related prohibits her from commenting on it in public."

"No, I'm glad you're you. How did you wrangle a sleeping chair?" She rested her head on his shoulder, enjoying the scent of him, a hint of soap and deodorant. "Hey, you showered." Her voice held a slight accusation.

"Five-minute shower, that's all. I'd be happy to give you a sponge bath." He wiggled his eyebrows.

"No, thanks. Maybe another time in a not so public setting. I think I might have a shower or something. Haven't been out of the bed, but I could walk to the bathroom." She started to swing her legs over the side, but Will stopped her.

"Wait, you're still hooked up to the IV. We have to carefully walk it with you." He slid off the bed and moved to where the IV bag hung from a rod. He unhooked it and held it up. "Now we can go."

Her legs threatened to buckle underneath her. She sat back down. "Can't believe I'm still so weak."

Nurse Doris poked her head in. "What are you doing to my patient? Hopefully, not staging another escape attempt?"

Will didn't melt under the woman's bombastic manner as everyone else did. "Escape attempt?"

Tonya shrugged under his questioning gaze. It sounded so stupid now, but it felt anything but stupid then.

The long look and the slight angling of the head announced Will expected details later. He smiled at Doris, who eyed him the way she would a copperhead. It was his best. The one that caused her to melt into a puddle of longing. Doris merely sniffed, unfazed.

He wrapped an arm around her waist and helped her up, while continuing to hold the IV bag up with his other hand. "I'm taking her to the bathroom. She'd like to clean up, but the IV bag is presenting issues."

"You know I could order you a sponge bath." The nurse commented as she stepped into the room.

Tonya shook her head emphatically, hating her weakness and having to depend on others. It made her feel like an infant, not something she cared for.

Will chimed in as Doris cradled Tonya's hand with the IV in it. "She turned my offer of a sponge bath down, too. Don't feel too bad."

"Bet that really chafed." Doris released the line attached to the shunt. "Keep that hand out of the water. I could call an aide to help."

Tonya shook her head. Enough with the nakedness already. The only person she didn't mind seeing her naked was Will, but only if cleaned up and smelling good.

"Figured that'd be your attitude. Knowing you, aided and abetted by your sweetie here, you'll do what you want anyhow. Get cleaned up. Then I'll be back to put the leads back on since it's what Dr. Lenin wants. I'll give you ten minutes, no more."

Her rubber soled shoes squeaked as she left. Will escorted her into the tiny bathroom and positioned her on the closed toilet, before shutting the door. Ceramic tile lined the floors, and the walls were white, as were the sink and toilet. A small shower stall squatted to the side, covered by a white curtain. The motion control light flickered on as the two of them entered, flooding the room with light bright enough for surgery. A utilitarian mirror hung over the sink, but she had no desire to use it.

"Talk about a barracuda. Your nurse would make a formidable opponent in the courtroom," Will commented as he pulled back the shower curtain, examining the tiny tiled unit. A white shower chair cramped the area.

A need to defend the woman asserted itself. "She's not so bad. Just trying to do her job and all."

Water shot out of the showerhead as Will adjusted the knobs. "Hmm, sounds like she has a defender in you."

"Well, maybe." She raised her eyebrows as he unbuttoned his shirt and hung it on the back of the door. He slipped off his loafers, tucking them and his socks under the sink. His hand was on his belt before she finally asked. "Stripping to lift my spirits?"

"Is it working?" His hand hesitated on his fly.

"I'm not sure. Keep going." Tonya giggled as his face crinkled into a mock shocked expression. He stepped out of his pants, hanging them up on the door hook, too. Attired only in his boxers, he gathered up the sample-sized toiletries and placed them into the shower stall, turning his back to her again, displaying the evocative tattoo.

"Will, this might sound crazy, but were you ever an exotic dancer?"

He winked. "I wondered when you would put the dots together. Yeah, after my mother died. A buddy of mine asked me to go along with him to an audition. Moral support. Apparently, they tried to keep a bunch of nationalities, and they just lost their ordinary white guy."

"You're far from ordinary. No desire to continue?" It had to be most men's dreams to have so many women in a sexual frenzy.

"Nope. Needed the money for college. Did two summers with a touring group and eventually they offered me a regular position. I passed the bar and didn't need it."

Her eyes slid over his toned torso, recognizing that hundreds of women wanted to be exactly where she was. Her hand went up to her lips as she considered she really did land a very hot lawyer. Obviously, that made her something special. Her lips tipped up as he approached her brandishing a shower cap.

"For your hand." The thin shower cap wrapped around her wrist twice served as a barrier. "Now my dear, we'll have to dispense with this beautiful gown you're wearing."

She snorted her agreement as he reached behind her, untying the top tie. His warm fingers brushed against her skin. Her eyes remained on his, assuring herself that this was Will touching her, not Clint. Still a thrill of fear shot through her. It dropped off as she watched his lips move. No sound, but he had to be saying something important. The water sounds bouncing off the wall were louder since he'd pushed the curtain aside. A mist landed on her skin, cooling as it evaporated.

The discarded gown landed in the sink bowl with a flutter. Her shower cap covered hand slipped down to cover her nether regions while her other arm banded across her breasts. Instead of commenting on her actions, Will slid one arm under her knees and another behind her back and moved her to the chair. He spun the chair around, backing her into the shower. The warm water pelted her back and head, relaxing her.

The open shower curtain allowed the water to splatter the floor as Will stood in his boxers with a bewildered expression on his face. "I can keep my boxers on if you want."

She appreciated the offer, but shook her head no. "I want the full Monty. Nothing happened with Clint. No worries. I am more worried about your going commando." The chair turned as Will entered, turning her face into the spray and eliminating ogling chances.

The water saturated her hair, plastering it to her skin. The tight spot, heat, and knowing Will had her back controlled her anxiety. Her backbone slumped against the plastic chair as Will shampooed her hair, working his fingers deep into the strands, massaging her scalp. Reminded her of the time she and Lynne splurged on an expensive salon. Of course, they didn't have any gorgeous men shampooing them naked. Probably would have had to charge more than the hundred dollars they spent for a cut and style.

Both women agreed a hundred dollars was too much for a haircut, but treated as if special was priceless. Like right now. Even the plastic chair she associated with being elderly and infirm had positive points, though she'd never thought of sitting in the shower. It would make shaving her legs much easier. Will dropped his head, resting it on her shoulder and spoke. "You know I'll never let anything bad happen to you again."

The words slipped over her as warm and gentle as the spray. That didn't stop bad things. Still, she had to give him credit: without him, no one would have been looking for her. In the end, knowing she had started something great with him gave her the determination to escape. Would she have given up if she felt nothing good existed outside the cabin walls? No, of course not. She had to be around for Sebastian. Her fingers plunged into her sudsy hair, scratching as if she could loosen that dark moment and rinse it away with the lather.

A loud knock penetrated the steamy bathroom. "Ten minutes is up. You're not at a resort. Doctor is on his way."

Will's head still rested on her shoulder as he asked, "Still think she's a sweetheart?"

Before she could answer, Doris did.

"I heard that."

"Almost done," Will answered for both of them. His hand sluiced down her hair, stripping off the lather. When done, he glopped on conditioner, smoothing it over her head and down to her roots. His actions made her resemble the hair product all smooth, liquid, and pooling onto the shower floor.

The cooling water broke the sensual stupor. "Almost out of hot water. We need to hurry." Never a fan of cold water, she avoided it when she could.

"On it." His hands lifted her hair to the spray. "No wash cloth and one stingy towel. I'll have to use my hands to wash you."

His soapy hands all over her body reminded her of their first shower. "I guess I can tolerate it."

"Tolerate it?" His voice swung up in feigned outrage. "You'll do more than tolerate it."

Before she could think of a teasing comeback, Doris cracked the door. "You two hurry up. Think of me as a killjoy, but I've bent the rules allowing you two your personal clean up time. I want to last long enough for a pension."

Her words sped up the process as Will lathered up his hands and ran them over her body, not even lingering in any choice spots. Sad. The pelting water grew gradually colder, causing her to shiver. Blocking the spray with his body, Will twisted off the knobs.

Using the rough towel, which was none too white, he rubbed down her torso and then blotted her hair. He picked up the dirty gown and then let it drop to the floor.

Slipping his boxers on his still wet hips, he cracked the door. "Um, could you get me the new pajamas out of the flowered duffle?"

A cellophane-wrapped pair of flowered pajamas came through the crack. A tear opened the package, spilling out a soft peach fabric lavished with peony blossoms. Will knelt on the floor, lifting each foot and guiding it through the pajama leg. She stood in his loose embrace as he pulled up the bottoms and threaded her arms through the top. Anyone else dressing her would make her feel ridiculous, but somehow his actions cherished her.

"Can you stand up by yourself while I put on some clothes?" He placed her hands on the sink for support.

"Yes, of course." What else could she say? Why did she even think her shaky body would have carried her out of the hospital? Adrenaline would have kept her moving for a while, but the aftereffects of kidnapping and escape still showed in her unsteady balance and trembling limbs.

Without bothering to use the now wet towel, Will shimmied into his jeans and slid on his shirt. Shirt open and tails flapping, he pushed the chair back into the shower giving them more space to walk.

He wrapped one arm around her and tilted her chin up with his index finger. "You're the most beautiful thing I've ever seen." He dropped a kiss on her wet hair, then a brief one on her nose, and finally, her lips. Her shower capped hand reached for his neck, crinkling as it found purchase.

Rocking up to her tiptoes, she returned his kiss with an ardor that challenged her precarious balance. A loud throat clearing alerted her to the nearness of her personal watchdog nurse. It didn't stop her from whispering, "I love you, Will Robinson."

"Will Robinson, what type of pet name is that?" Doris grumbled from the other side of the ajar door.

Will cut his eyes to the door and grinned. "It's the name of a man who loves Tonya Smiley more than life itself. My life would be nothing without her."

The words started a chain reaction, cracking emotional dams she'd thought hardened over the years. Tightening her embrace, she rested her head against his. The tears ran down her face and dripped onto his shirt.

"Come on, move it outside. I can at least hook up the leads before any pop-in appearances by the good doctor. You're a celebrity of sorts, which means he'll come by more often, hoping for a picture op."

The idea inspired a desire to stay hidden in the steamy room, but Will opened the door all the way, turning sideways to allow his arm to stay around her as she exited. Doris eyed them both with a suspicious stare.

"If I weren't such an old battle ax, I might be touched by the picture the two of you make," she declared, giving a small sniff as she refitted the sticky patches with new ones. She waited until Will had lifted Tonya up on the bed before she busied herself hooking everything back in place. "Don't think too much harm was done letting you get clean." She nodded in Will's direction. "Might want to finish getting dressed, don't want anyone to get the wrong idea."

Will's fingers flew over the buttons, covering the swath of bare skin exposed. "Yeah, can't let anyone think people might care about one another. Can't have that."

The monitors flicked to life and started the monotonous hum once the wires were reattached. The nurse cuffed Tonya's shoulder. "Watch out. You got a smart ass on your hands. Keeps life interesting." She pivoted and walked out fast, without even waiting for a reply.

"I think she must have had a smart ass in her life, too. Sometime, but apparently not now." Tonya felt sorry for the outspoken nurse who accidentally revealed her softer side.

"Yeah. You're right. I'll put on my shoes, get the hair dryer, and dry your hair." Before he could dart to the bathroom, a lab coated man strolled in carrying a tablet. "Tonya Smiley. Hi, I'm..."

Will finished the introduction, "Declan Winters. As I live and breathe. You wearing that lab coat in an official capacity?" Will queried with a broad smile.

The man's mouth dropped open as his gaze flickered between Tonya and Will. "What are the odds of running into you? I'm a surgical resident at the hospital, but I'm doing follow-ups for Dr.

Lenin." Declan's teeth flashed white against his dark beard.

He continued. "The fact I'm here instead of Dr. Lenin is good news. Besides mild dehydration, some smoke inhalation, lacerations and abrasions, you're in good condition."

Tonya directed a hopeful look at Will as the doctor kept talking.

"We're going to keep you the night for observation purposes."

A heavy sigh accompanied her collapse back into the plumped pillows.

"Come on, it's not that bad." Declan flashed his smile again and gestured to Will. "You have one of the hottest dancers from Machismo at your beck and call." He lifted his eyebrows inquiringly at Will.

"Yeah, she knows."

Even though the news wasn't what she wanted to hear, it could be worse. The relationship between the two men intrigued her enough to put her disappointment behind her. "How do you two know each other? Did you go to school together?"

As soon as the words were out of her mouth, she realized a future lawyer and doctor would not be attending the same classes.

Both men glanced at each other and laughed. Will grinned, then explained. "You could say we went to the bump and grind school together. Declan used to come out on stage with a lab coat and a stethoscope. He billed himself as Dr. Feel Good."

The image resulted in her giving the bearded man a thorough look. She didn't remember him. Obviously, the man left no lasting impression. "Did Will have some lawyer routine, then?"

The man snorted and shook his head slowly. "Not a whole lot you can do to make a lawyer sexy. Even tried calling himself esquire, but that didn't work. He was the vacation fling guy. The one-night stand women can't forget, especially with that memorable hip swivel of his."

Ah yes, she remembered the hip swivel very well since it had been less than twenty-four hours since she saw it.

The doctor chatted for a few minutes with Will, disclosing he was new in town and never had a chance to meet anyone since he worked long hours. She mused if any of the nurses knew their newest resident had an exotic dancing background.

AN HOUR LATER, hair dry, and eyes half-closed, she mused on why she'd never met anyone like Will before.

You weren't ready.

Her eyes snapped open. Hadn't she done her failed relationship time? Surely that should have made her more than ready. Soft snores came from the right side of her bed where Will dozed. The chair sat in its unfolded state with Will's long legs splayed out in front of him and his head at an odd angle. Who else? Her eyes made a cautious survey of the room, expecting someone, but seeing no one. Weird. Where did the voice come from? Maybe she imagined it. Could be her subconscious trying to communicate with her.

Wasn't ready. That could be true. Too many movies extolled the virtues of the bad boys, and she believed them all. Her nose crinkled as if she smelled something rotten. Not necessarily all bad boys, just not great men, and one total sociopath. Her eyes lingered on Will affectionately as his lips moved in his sleep. The one syllable word wasn't too hard to make out. Run. Her shallow sense of comfort vanished as he repeated the word. Must be dreaming, that's all it was.

She was uncomfortable with Will's silent plea to run. It didn't mean it involved her. A lion could exist in his dream world. The description sounded too much like Clint. The flowers, she forgot to tell Will about the flowers. A man in scrubs walked past her door. The brief view showed what she assumed was a man in surgical scrubs complete with a hat and booties. Not sure if he had the mask on or not. The perfect disguise in a hospital.

"Will," she hissed the words, afraid she might be overheard. His snoring continued unabated. "Will, wake up," she raised the volume a notch, but he slept on, tuckered out from searching for her all night. He needed to be awake instead of him telling her to run. It might be up to her to warn him.

Leaning over the metal rail, she managed to reach his head. Stiffening her fingers, she poked him. "Will, Will, wake up now."

"What?" He opened his eyes, blinking twice before sitting up straight. "What's happening?" he asked as his head swiveled to take in the entire room. Feet on the ground, he tensed as if ready to spring forward and attack. Of course, nothing threatened.

The sense of unease vanished as soon as Will woke. Still, there was the cryptic message with the flowers. Grabbing a tissue, she picked up the card and held it out to Will. "I think Clint sent me flowers."

He took the proffered card, not using the tissue, fingerprinting it. "Clint did not send you flowers. I did." He gestured to the roses in the vase by the bed. "Picked out the yellow with red edges because it signifies falling in love. Had to call three florists before I found the right color."

He turned the card around, squinting as he looked at the message. "This is illegible."

"I couldn't read it, either. Flora, the aide, read it to me. Thought it said something about the eyes and the signature had the first two letters CL."

Relief swept over her as she slumped against the pillows. Not Clint. Still, the card and its message. Weird.

Will kept turning the card over. "I knew that girl wasn't paying any attention to me when I called. I guess I'm lucky the roses even made it to you. I wanted her to write *my eyes adored you*. It's from an old song by Frankie Valli. It's about a guy having a crush on a woman he never touched."

Her lips tipped up. His words made her fear ridiculous. Thank goodness she didn't escape in her drafty hospital gown. "Well, that doesn't sound like you and me. A whole lot of touching is going on."

"Yeah, I know. I just wanted you to realize I was crazy about you, especially since you were angry with me about bailing my client out."

"Not angry. It's over. I'd probably steal Sebastian back if anyone took him." The woman who resorted to stealing her own dog wasn't the idiot she'd considered her.

Will held up the card. "The signature is weird. It's hard to know what she meant to write—someone's name that started with Cl."

"Clint, Clarence, Claude, not a lot of male names." She reviewed the names. "Could be a girl's name like Clarisse, Claire, Claudine, Claribel."

His brows furrowed, then went up at one name. "That's it. I remember someone in the background calling her Claire. She signed her name. Seriously, how incompetent can a florist's help be?" He gestured with the card. "I have a good mind to call up the florist."

"Forget about it. As long as it isn't from Clint, I'm good." At Will's open mouth, she added, "I'm glad they're from you and the meaning, too. I'm falling for you, too, but you already know that."

Their fingers tangled through the slats in the bed rail. "I know that. You won't ever have to worry about Clint anymore."

The sense of finality that came with the words made her wonder. "Why?"

A slender woman stood at the door, looking around furtively. Her navy cardigan and slacks made her look out of place at the hospital, especially since it was past visiting hours. She darted into the room and flashed a forced smile at the two of them.

"Hi, I'm Dara. How do you feel about the fact your attacker perished in the forest fire he may have started?" She held up her cell phone in Tonya's direction. A red glowing button indicated it was recording.

Clint was dead. As bad as he was, she wouldn't have wished death on him. She'd never have to worry about him again. Not ever getting involved with anyone else like him again. Nope, her time and affection belonged to Will.

He stood and glared at the woman. "Leave. You don't have permission to be here. I'm Ms. Smiley's lawyer."

On the word lawyer, the woman scampered out of the room. Smart. Was she with a media outlet or just curious? How did she know so much?

Will walked to the door, and she could hear him alerting someone about the woman. Still visible in the open doorway, his hand covered his face in a gesture already familiar to her. Yep, something difficult that he didn't want to say.

"You knew Clint was dead?" The question formed before she even considered the implications.

He dropped into the chair with an exhausted sigh. "I thought he was dead, but didn't have confirmation yet."

"How?" She wasn't sure if she wanted to know, but she had to know. Would it change the way she felt about Will?

His hands rested on his knees as he angled his body in her direction. "When I drove back to your house, I came in through the garage expecting you to be asleep, but you weren't in bed. I searched the house. No you, but your car, purse, keys, and cell phone were there. I suspected foul play. Called Lynne and Marc immediately. Marc noticed that Sebastian was still sleeping as opposed to barking.

"Then I called in every favor I had along with a few of my boss's, especially when the police initially insisted you went off in a huff. I gave them Clint's name. They traced his car. He ran a red light at one time, which gave us the time and direction he was heading. I followed in my car, against instructions and pulled up at the cabin, right behind the black and whites."

No wonder the man looked exhausted. He micromanaged every step of the search. "Not sure why Clint was there, but he was at the edge of the fire, waiting."

"He started it to smoke me out. He knew I was in the woods. That's why I ran the other way." Her blood chilled at the cold-bloodedness of it all. He had no issues with killing her, but Clint never claimed he loved her.

"The fire consumed everything in its path with a loud, crackling of the underbrush and sending trees plummeting to the ground. Could be he didn't hear the cars, but when an officer yelled, he ran straight into the fire. I heard him scream. I chose not to tell you because I thought you'd find out eventually. You didn't need anything else to worry about."

It all made sense. Will wasn't a bloodthirsty person; Clint was. It embarrassed her that she'd even considered it. "You didn't yell, run?"

His hand reached for hers. "Do you believe all the bad things you hear about lawyers? I would have shouted *stay*. I'd want to see him behind bars. Dying was not punishment enough for what he did to you.

Death worked for her. The man would never have the opportunity to stalk, harass, or threaten another woman. "He's gone. That's all that matters. We're alive. I need to look forward to the future."

"I hope I'm a part of that future." His expression looked almost dubious.

"You have to ask. No way am I letting loose of a man who gives excellent scalp and foot massages." She winked at him, remembering the first time he winked at her. Her heartbeat tripped over itself. Her life had finally shifted toward the good. Make that the very good.

THE END

Ready for the second book in The Men of Machismo Series?
Dangerous Reg Chapter One

ON A TUESDAY afternoon, the library resembled a morgue, minus the stiffs. Darcy pushed the fiction cart toward the book stacks. Her eyes flickered over the spines of the recently returned books. The usual collection of well-worn cozy mysteries and romances featured billionaires and Navy seals. The occasional author managed to combine both. Perhaps, that was her problem, no billionaires or hot military men in the stories she penned. So far, no agents begging to represent her.

The low sound of voices punctured her absorption in her non-existent writing career.

"It has to be now."

The urgency in the man's voice had her abandoning her cart. Her soft-soled shoes allowed her to move down the aisle without a squeak or a telltale footfall. It could be nothing, but it might also be a bit of conversation she could include in her next literary effort. If her granny were still alive, she'd mention *that eavesdroppers never heard anything good about themselves.*

"You owe me."

The gruff reply had her peering around shelved books to see who was talking. Monrovia wasn't exactly a huge town, so she should be able to recognize the men. The first voice sounded somewhat familiar, but she couldn't quite place it. The second one she didn't know. All that meant was he'd never be in the library, taught at the local school, or was a relation.

The first man's voice grew shriller. "I had nothing to do with you getting nabbed. You can't blame that on me."

Darcy tiptoed closer, trying to see who was speaking. An expanse of black broadcloth material came into view. She blinked. My goodness, she didn't realize how close she was. Her initial impression of the men speaking in normal voices must have been a mistake due to the absolute silence in the building.

"Don't believe it for a second. I figured you took off with the emeralds and left me pay the price for the heist you engineered."

Darcy gasped. *Emeralds.* Heist. It sounded like a movie of the week. Footsteps signaled one of the men had sidled to one side. Her position, peering through an open place on the shelf, allowed her to only see the back of one of the speakers, but she could still hear.

"No, never. I had second thoughts about the whole deal, which is the reason I changed careers."

"Ha! I know you're sitting on them until you can move them. I expect my share. The way I figure it, you owe me more for my time spent in the pen. Cross me again and you're a dead man!"

The vehemence underlying the words had her stumbling backwards and knocking a paperback thriller over.

"What was that?"

Darcy hit the floor. Her body trembled as she crawled down the aisle as if she were under fire, stirring up dust as she went. The men were still talking as opposed to hunting for her. Her breath sounded loud in her ears as she reached the end of the aisle where the summer reading program boxes provided a welcome shield.

Her small size allowed her to work her way into the center of the boxes. She grabbed one box and pulled it in place as footsteps passed her. Her heart managed to dislodge itself from its normal location and work its way up into her throat. *Thank goodness, no one saw me.*

Curiosity got the better of her, causing her to push the box aside an inch to see the black suit and the back of a balding head. Her head jerked back. She had the same view at church the previous Sunday.

A heavier footfall had her shrinking back against a box as a bald man with a mangled face that indicated a history of fighting came closer. His dark eyes stared straight at the boxes causing her to hold her breath. It felt like he could see right inside the dark cave the stacked boxes made. Thank goodness, she'd been slow to move the boxes to the basement as asked. Sweat beaded her upper lip as she peered through a crack, waiting for the man to move on. He hesitated and surveyed the area.

Baldy, as she nicknamed him in her head, turned all the way around in search of witnesses. Darcy's cheeks puffed out, and her face flushed as she struggled to hold her breath. It had never been her strong point, which is why she eeked out a C in swimming. Finally, the man moved on, allowing her to breathe again.

Would he remember her at the circulation desk? Worse, would he notice she wasn't at the desk on his way out? That wouldn't necessarily mean she'd eavesdropped on them. She could have been in the backroom or the bathroom. Technically, she'd been the only one on duty since her boss, Leticia Blankenship, took off for lunch.

Darcy waited in dark, hot space waiting for the men to leave the place. Her luminous watch face counted off five minutes, managing to stretch it into hours. Surely, enough time passed to safely exit her hiding place. She pushed the box aside and crawled out. A pair of no-nonsense Oxfords met her initial glance. Her eyes continued up past the orthopedic hose and the wool pleated skirt past the peter pan blouse, to the lips pulled down in a disapproving expression. Leticia tsked as she crawled out of her cardboard sanctuary.

Darcy stood dusting off her dress to no avail. This morning she had second thoughts about the wispy white dress as work wear. She'd considered spaghetti sauce as an issue, not blood, possibly hers. The woman glared at her through her half-moon glasses. "Give her a chance, your mother pleaded. She's a great reader. Bound to be able to recommend books."

It had been no secret that Leticia Blankenship did not appreciate her creative turn of a phrase, especially when caught turning said phrase at work. The fact she had time to write demonstrated the lack of actual duties, which meant her measly job could end. All Leticia needed was someone to spot her during her lunch hour and operate the circulation counter when she held book talks. While the pay wasn't extravagant, even the laugh-worthy amount kept her in Ramen noodles and Sylvester, her kitty, in cat food. Well, this job and her second part-time job waiting tables at the local bar and grill did.

"You won't believe what happened when you were gone." She held her hands up knowing she had a legitimate reason for crawling out from the summer reading boxes cave like a toddler.

The woman crossed her arms and sniffed. "This I have to hear." She held up her index finger and wagged it. "No more of your far-fetched lies that you refer to as stories, either."

Darcy pressed her hand against her chest. How could a woman who worked in a library have such a hatred for fiction? "Two men were talking about stolen emeralds in the D-H fiction section. Our library is an assignation spot for felons. You won't believe who one of them is?"

Before she could continue, Leticia's hand flew up, palm out, in a stop fashion. "No more. I'm tired of your Elven visitors at the local tulip festival."

"Wait, he could have been an elf. Tall, slender, long blonde hair, and pointed ears."

Leticia's frown deepened. "I'm tired of this. Elves. Aliens. Now, felons planning emerald heists in our library."

Not only did the woman not welcome an observant eye and an open mind, she was a bad listener, too. "They already had the heist. They were arguing about the emeralds, and one of them was my—"

"No more. I refuse to listen to your nonsense." She pivoted on her heel and marched down the aisle.

The angular frame, the pursed mouth, the crabby attitude reminded Darcy of another literary character, Leticia wouldn't appreciate the comparison. Might as well get back to work.

She slid into her chair at the circulation desk, grateful the high desk hid most of the dirt-smeared dress, but not enough. The squeak-squeak of the shelving cart came closer, which meant Leticia would have another run at her.

The woman rounded the desk and shook her head. "Go home. You're a mess. Don't waste your time calling the county law enforcement agency. I already warned the sheriff, Donald, my cousin, you might."

Darcy reached for her purse wondering at what cost this unexpected short shift came. "I'll be back tomorrow at nine."

"Let me think about that. I'll have to consider how long your mama and I have been friends. I don't understand why you can't be more like your brother, William."

Ah yes, the golden child, William, who never did anything wrong. Despite being named Fitz William after her mother's favorite Jane Austen hero, it didn't seem to taint him the way Darcy did her. Of course, William lost the Fitz immediately since her father read somewhere it referred to illegitimacy. Her father, a man of firm opinions, didn't want anyone calling his son illegitimate.

Darcy's name, on the other hand, caused her no end of frustration, telling teachers and playmates that her first name wasn't her last name. It didn't help that the family's last name was Darlington. It made her sound as if she were part of a bizarre tongue twister.

"You're not the first person to ask me that." She shrugged, not wanting to elaborate. Most of the time, she liked her twin, William, like everyone else. The man with his helpful attitude was hard not to like. Only when people wanted to know why they were so different, implying Darcy wasn't quite right, did she resent William the tiniest little bit. It would be helpful if the man would do something reprehensible for a change and take the heat off her.

She shouldered her bag and waved goodbye to her boss. At least she hoped she was her boss and not her former one. Her rust-dotted car rested next to the curb. She'd love something newer and sportier, but that would have to wait until she became a famous author. At this rate, it wouldn't be in her lifetime.

A navy muscle car slowed as it came to a stop sign at the end of the road. It allowed Darcy a chance to check out the occupant, a man with strong features and a short haircut. Possibly a Navy Seal, a billionaire, or a billionaire former Navy Seal. Whoever he was she knew he didn't live around here.

Her second job at Sweaty's, which she thought was a terrible name for a sports bar, gave her the opportunity at one time or another to wait on the pick of the town's bachelors accompanied by their dates. It would be hard to forget that profile. The man turned and smiled at her. What had started as a mediocre day, and then took an abrupt turn south, showed signs of improvement. Her hand went up, and she waved her fingers in a flirty wave.

Ronny Benson rolled up behind the man in his jacked-up truck and slammed on his horn.

Darcy cringed at Dixie being played at ear-blasting decibels. The unknown handsome man drove away. Figures. Whenever she was within spitting distance of anything good, Fate bitch slapped her.

"Hey, sweet cheeks, wha' cha doing?" Ronny leaned out the window of this truck reminding her that she'd been so desperate she went out with him once. Even though it had been several years ago, that one date created a belief in Ronny that they had an on and off relationship. It had been off for about as long as she could remember, but Ronny remained hopeful.

"I'm leaving one job to go to another." She opened her car door, releasing a wave of heat.

Ronny stared down at her from his high perch with a wide grin. Darcy grabbed the back of her dress, pulling the bodice back to prevent the man from peeking at her breasts. The truck kept her from pulling out. Apparently, Ronny hadn't finished his run at her.

"You wouldn't have to work if you were my gal. I got a brand-new double wide."

The broken driver's side window that wouldn't roll down and the sweltering interior temperature forced her to crack open the car door as she spoke. Ronny would see it as a sign that she might be caving into his dubious charms. A twist of her wrist had the engine running and, in a few minutes, it would be safe to turn the air conditioner on.

"Yes, I heard all about it. Even the Jacuzzi in the master bath but I have to get to work. I'd appreciate it if you could move your truck."

He gave her a two-finger salute, but refused to take the hint. With any luck, she wouldn't see him at Sweaty's. It was even harder to give Ronny the brush-off in public. Too many people thought they were an item. She wasn't sure if it was his numerous appearances at Sweaty's when she was working or possibly the rumors, he spread that they'd done the nasty. In a small town like Monrovia that equaled putting a bumper sticker across her body, declaring her property of Ronny Benson.

"Ah, you're keeping tabs on me." His eyebrows lifted as his smile stretched revealing his gold tooth.

As much as it pained her, Darcy needed an explanation for her knowledge. "Why a man like you isn't married in a town with few eligible men confounds me. People talk." She knew exactly why he wasn't married. His bullying behavior that pinned her into her parking place said it all. If she wanted to leave before Christmas, then that meant applying a little sugar. Her father grumbled she hadn't learned anything at college, but she did learn to maneuver around muscle-headed football players and lecherous professors. It never involved in giving anything up, but convincing the problem male that there might to be the tiniest possibility. Men would do backflips if there were even a scent of action.

"Who?" Ronny eyebrows met as he tried to work out the mystery of who might be spreading his news.

"I'm not telling until you let me out." Time to bring out the big guns. "Sweet Cheeks." Her eyes checked the back mirror to make sure no one heard her. A black and white terrier watered a nearby tree, but he wouldn't be repeating anything.

"All right." He threw the truck in reverse so fast that the gears ground. Darcy shot out of her space and ran the stop sign. Her small, compact tires squealed as she made the turn too fast.

A lack of brains figured prominently into why Ronny and she would never be an item. That, paired with his desire to emulate the old television characters, *The Dukes of Hazards*, kept most women far, far away. Honestly, he wasn't bad looking. He was on the right side of forty and employed. Her mother accused her of being too fussy, but she didn't think so.

A couple hard right turns lost Ronny. Although, there wasn't too many places she could hide from the man if he wanted to follow her. He knew where she worked and lived. Ronny might be over the top whenever they met in public, but he never stalked her. His truck roaring up on the short street beside the library struck her as odd. Her nose wrinkled when she considered she didn't even know if Ronny read. She'd never seen him in the library.

The quandary of a smitten Ronny faded away as she turned into the apartment complex. A dented sedan indicated Lorna, her next-door neighbor, was home. The bright red pickup truck parked beside her car meant she had company.

In Darcy's designated parking place was Ruby's vintage VW bug convertible. In between humorous and sometimes offensive bumper stickers, a spot of blue showed. Ruby, her sometime friend, joked once that the adhesive strips were the only thing that held the car together. Back when she gave her friend a house key, it was supposed to be an emergency key. Ruby's key privileges came with checking on Sylvester. The few times she had to work overtime at Sweaty's, she'd called Ruby to check on her kitty. As far as she could tell, no evidence existed to prove Ruby ever dropped by when asked.

While her friend never showed up for cat duty, she did appear whenever she was between boyfriends or road trips. *Lucky her.*

Darcy parked her car while she mentally rehearsed the speech, she'd use to get her house key back. Her apartment door swung open before she reached it. A shapely blonde attired in a peach low cut top and white short shorts that played up her tan, held up an oversized margarita glass. "Cheers. Come join the party."

Her jaw tightened as she reminded herself to get the key. Perhaps she could take it off Ruby's keyring after she passed out. "Hola, amiga." Since they had met originally in Spanish class, they both thought it would be clever to speak in Spanish as much as possible. "Que pasa?"

Ruby's shoulders went up in a shrug. "Ernie died. Heart attack. His kids blame me. They want to press charges." A sob interrupted her explanation. "I had no place else to go."

The fact Ruby's most recent elderly gentleman friend expired from trying to prove he was younger than the date on his driver's license didn't surprise her. "I was worried about the two of you trying to make a cross country trip on his touring motorcycle."

Ruby sniffed and chugged the rest of her drink. "We didn't even get past St. Louis. We were going to see this car museum after lunch. He bit into a triple bacon burger and fell out of his chair." Her fingers snapped to indicate how sudden it was.

"Was this before he ate the burger or after?" Darcy maneuvered around the woman into the apartment. Sylvester greeted her, then walked to his empty dish and meowed. "Ok, big guy, I hear you."

"It was before." Another sob absorbed whatever else said.

Personally, Darcy would have thought it would have been afterwards, but Ernie must have made a habit of devouring oversized greasy burgers. "That's too bad, but how did you get back here?" The Golden Almost Angels, senior citizen motorcycle group. stopped by the IGA for cold drinks. Ruby called her to tell her she turned in her cashier apron to follow the open road with Ernie. There hadn't been any mention of her aging vehicle.

"Bus. You know that big one that stops in front of the IGA. Mr. Oberson, the IGA owner, hadn't towed my vintage baby. I got off the bus, into my car, and came here."

Yay me! "I'm sorry about Ernie. I know you were fond of him." Ernie wasn't the first man Ruby helped to the other side. He could be dead boyfriend number three or possibly four. "Have you ever thought about men a trifle younger?"

Ruby snorted into the wad of tissues she'd grabbed from the box. "Mama always told me to go for the grateful men. That way they'd treat you well."

Darcy opened her mouth and then snapped it shut. Did she have any grateful men hanging around her? Nope, none, not a single one, although the image of the dark-haired stranger in the sports car appeared on the movie screen of her mind. No doubt the man missed the exit for the horse park or something. No reason someone like him would hang around here. Nothing to entertain an out-of-towner unless he came for the school bus double eight races. The event usually attracted several hundred people, including anxious mothers who wanted to make sure their child's bus driver wasn't a contender. Another handful of parents hoped their offspring's driver made it to the top three coveted spots. The winner received not only an oversized trophy with a dented school bus on top, but a year's supply of wings and beer at Sweaty's.

"Did you hear a word I said?"

Ruby's voice grated as Darcy popped the top of the cat food can. Sylvester's cries grew louder, perhaps afraid she might get sidetracked by her unexpected visitor. "Grateful men are better." Which summed up everything she pulled from the conversation.

"No." The woman placed a French tipped nail by her mouth while her eyes flicked upward. "Well, I mean, yes. Grateful men are always better, but I meant the part about Rhonda bringing in another roommate just because I took off."

It made sense. Rhonda rented one of the roomier town houses at the new complex across town. Her hairdresser's salary, even with tips, couldn't swing the rent alone. "Not surprised. No one knew if you'd ever come back."

Another high-pitched wail threatened to puncture her eardrums. Darcy pulled her friend out of the doorway and shut the door. No reason to wake Joel, who worked the night shift at the truck factory in the next town or Loretta, who made a habit of going out every night. Couldn't exactly call it work, all she knew was the woman could be a nasty drunk. It didn't bode well for her being all that pleasant when sober either.

The sob ended abruptly as the door clicked closed, making her question its authenticity. It wouldn't be the first-time Darcy had been played. The tequila could be putting the M in maudlin as opposed to actual sadness. The real reason behind Ruby's tears could be her failure to break free of the town once again. She shot the deadbolt with vigor. Ruby's failed attempt to escape the tenacious tentacles of small-town life could have been her story, too. The major difference lay in the fact that Ruby did go places, whereas she only thought about it and did nothing.

The townspeople condemned anyone who tried to leave. Those who successfully shook the dirt from their shoes in a sprint to freedom never knew about this attitude or even cared. The general opinion of those who returned hovered between not smart enough to realize how good they had it in Monrovia to suspicion to why they failed to make a go at it somewhere else. Perhaps, that served as her main reason for not leaving. If she couldn't make it in Monrovia, how could she survive on a much bigger playing field?

The liquor bottles in her small cabinet clinked together as Ruby searched for the fixings of a new drink. Anyone who walked in off the street and saw the collection of tequila, whiskey, and vodka containers would think she had a drinking problem, but she didn't. For reasons, she couldn't fathom the bartender Rick usually tossed the bottles, even when a couple of fingers of liquor remained. Her original intention in removing the bottles when she took out the trash was recycling, which she did. Recycling resulted in the bottles ended up in her cabinet.

Since her writing muse chose to go elsewhere, she tried to indulge in the Hemmingway method of write drunk and edit sober. Apparently, the writer never had a laptop. All she had when she woke up from her experiment were several pages of the letter L. Not one of her better ideas, she shelved it with some of the other not so great ways to jump start her career.

Ice bouncing off the bottom of a glass meant another liquor mixing triumph for her morose friend. "I'll clear off the sofa bed for you." The reminder would keep her on again and off again friend from collapsing on Darcy's bed. Ruby mumbled something indecipherable.

The few extra hours of peace she'd gained from her unceremonious ejection by her library boss vanished as she alternately fed and comforted her friend. A television movie about some girl dying from a rare disease served as a babysitter while Darcy got ready for her second job.

Sweaty's ex-wife was the one who'd come up with the idea of putting the female waitresses in black short shorts with knee high socks. Her uniform was topped off with a striped referee shirt and a silver whistle. At one time, the imaginative ex had them tuck penalty flags into the minuscule pockets of the shorts. The trailing swatches of colors had tipsy male patrons always grabbing for them. While this was an amusing game for the drinkers, it resulted in several dropped drink trays. No way could a woman manage a heavy tray with people grabbing her flag. Several men used it as an opportunity to grab her ass too, which meant she'd been felt up by half the men in town without the benefit of a combo platter dinner date.

In a town where very few secrets survived, she found it odd that most of the women regarded Sweaty's female employees as little more than hoochie mamas. The male employees got a pass because they wore black slacks. Darcy suspected they'd still get more respect even if they did don a pair of skintight shorts. Heavily pregnant Donna Lyn graduated to dark maternity pants when her shorts turned into a black strip underneath her burgeoning belly. Not what most men wanted while watching the game and throwing back brewskis with the buds. It reminded them too much of their wives.

An extra five minutes on her makeup could boost her tip potential. She swiped the eyelashes with two coats of Get Up and Be Noticed mascara before she stopped. "What are you doing?" She addressed the surprised image in the mirror. "When was the last time anyone at Sweaty's looked at my face?"

Good question and one she couldn't answer. While she didn't have the attributes Ruby packed around, she could enhance what she had. Two cold rubber cutlets shoved into her pushup bra rounded out her cleavage even though she never really liked using the things since she heard horror stories about them popping out at inopportune moments. Her fingers buttoned up the shirt as she evaluated the display of skin in the mirror.

Too much cleavage would not only validate the term hoochie mama, but wouldn't earn her the money she needed. The male patrons could look all they wanted without buying a thing. One button left undone would work. While standing, nothing showed, but that one unanchored button demonstrated promise. Any boy over twelve knew if he could get a girl to bend over, he'd get a boob flash. All Sweaty's patrons were over twelve.

Normally, Darcy avoided any provocative behavior, but today had been a day. Tomorrow, she might not have her library job, either. Then there were the felons in the library. How could they miss seeing her when she was the only employee there? All this worrying about the ethics of showing too much skin and staying employed would be a moot point if dead.

Romantic Comedy Fan?
Check out Steamy Interludes series

A sexy, younger man pursues Ashlee; she's almost decided to let him catch her.

The very last thing Ashlee expected was to meet a hot, younger guy, Nick, at her boyfriend's funeral. The tall, soft-spoken man comforted her with stories of her boyfriend since he studied under him. Grateful for Nick's help and the mutual connection they both shared with the deceased, they kept in contact.

Ashlee managed to ignore his hints for drinks and meetings, putting it down to politeness. He felt sorry for her. There was no way he could be interested in a woman at least a decade older than he was. That was until her work posse caught scent of the story and urged her to give the man a chance. Ashlee knew she had to be the most reluctant cougar in the history of womankind, but what did she have to lose?

Deidre takes a walk on the uninhibited side.

What if all your life consisted of was, work and therapy dates where middle-aged men talked about their fears in a home cooking restaurant? Maybe it would even make you long for something new, even a little wild. It did Deidre.

Call it an impulsive choice, but she finally caved into Curt, a police officer who just returned to duty after being wounded in a sting operation, who wasn't taking no for an answer. Going out with a cop fourteen years her junior was irrational according to her friends. Meeting Curt for drinks was just the beginning. What she didn't expect was the flash fire that developed between them and the possibility it could burn out of control.

Can Theo outmaneuver her high school nemesis, a persistent ex-boyfriend, and a wayward pup to win the affections of the town's newest vet?

Theo discovers her husband and sister doing the mattress dance on her 1000 count sheets. She tosses the sheets, husband, and any future romantic aspirations, but holds on to her sister, begrudgingly.

A pint-sized devil dog propels romance-phobic Theo into Dr. Brent Knight's office and arms. Unfortunately, her old high school rival, a persistent ex-boyfriend who hasn't got his head around that they're not a couple, and her own heart serve as speed bumps on the way to love.

A mysterious man gives Darla the weekend of her life. (FREE)

Darla never had time for love. Even though she worked in the perfume industry that epitomizes romance. No appropriate male ever wandered into the picture. Maybe that's why she accepted her friend's suggestion to fix her up. Desperation and a desire to make sure she even remembered how to act like a woman as opposed to a corporate warrior made her take a chance.

Too bad her arranged date fell on the eve before her meeting with some hot shot Italian nobleman she needed to sign for her company's continued success. Even more ironic, her blind date, Alex, besides being the poster child for all things delicious, had a sexy Italian accent. The accent alone should have reminded her of the need to prepare for her meeting. Instead, charmed by his old-world manners and animal magnetism, she allows him to take charge and forgets about business. Two things she's never done before.

Cinda is a practical woman with a very impractical Christmas Desire.

Cinda isn't ready to become a glorious butterfly. She's still in the caterpillar stage with her generous curves. All she really wants is for a man to appreciate who she is the way Jack did when they met at the airport. They shared a romantic day as they both waited for their flights. He kissed her goodbye and tucked his card in her suit pocket with instructions to call. It figures she'd lose his card. Luck never dealt her a romantic winning hand, but it's time to reshuffle the cards.

Six months fantasizing about Jack was enough. Raven determines not only to help her friend to become the butterfly she is, but also to give her friend a gift she'll never forget. Cinda voices her doubts about attending the masquerade ball. Raven reveals that Santa left her special gift at the ball. Her job is to retrieve it.

Marcus's name and appearance in her writing class is bogus, but his effect on Teresa is very real.

Dating's tough in small towns. The smart women gobbled up the town's eligible bachelors while Teresa obtained her degree out of state. Back home in Kentucky and teaching at the local high school, she finds herself competing for the attention of the taxidermist with a tricked-out truck and a dentist who thinks he's the reincarnation of James Dean.

A sexy stranger appears in her adult education class. The man is definitely no townie with his exotic looks and even stranger accent. It's obvious he's lying about why he's in her class, but that doesn't dampen his appeal. There was a rule against staff and students fraternizing, but she might be tempted to break it.

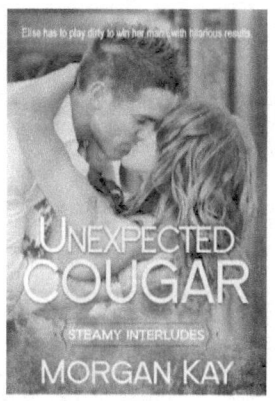

Elise has to play dirty to win her man.

A divorced marriage counselor doesn't inspire confidence, which is the reason Elise dons a wedding ring. Her fake marriage status results in her slipping to the other side of town to date. The man she sees the most is Jackson the bartender at the local seafood restaurant.

Her clients think he's her husband. Unfortunately, someone else has her eye on the handsome bartender.

Author Notes

- If you enjoyed this book, please lend it to a friend.

- Write a review.

- Do you have an idea for a story or a character name? Love to hear it. I can be reached through my website at www.morgankwyatt.com

- Want to get free books, read excerpts before everyone else, receive special members only swag and giveaways? You need to be on the mailing list. Go over to my website and sign up. (I don't sell my mailing list and guard it as well as I do my chocolate.)

- Do you like humor with your mystery? Check out my new cozy mystery series that I wrote with my husband. Book one of *The Painted Lady Inn Mysteries* is **Murder Mansion**. We write under the combined name of M.K. Scott.

- Check out the Morgan K Wyatt books too. **He Loves Me Not,** romantic suspense, will be out on March 1, 2016.

- Love to meet you, check out my personal appearances on the website too.

- Can you do one more thing? Go out and have an amazing day.

Morgan Kay

www.ingramcontent.com/pod-product-compliance
Lightning Source LLC
Chambersburg PA
CBHW020311200626
46814CB00006BA/2185